THE ROMARA CONFRONTATION

COLONIAL EXPLORER CORPS
BOOK 5

JULIA HUNI

The Romara Confrontation © 2025 by Julia Huni
All rights reserved. No part of this book may be reproduced in any form or by any electronic or mechanical means including information storage and retrieval systems, without permission in writing from the author. The only exception is by a reviewer, who may quote short excerpts in a review. This book may not be used to train AI systems of any kind.

This book is a work of fiction. Names, characters, places, and incidents either are products of the author's imagination or are used fictitiously. Any resemblance to actual persons, living or dead, events, or locales is entirely coincidental.
Cover designed by JL WIlson Designs
Editing by Paula Lester at Polaris Editing

Julia Huni
Visit my website at juliahuni.com

IPH Media
20250419.2

For those who fight for freedom and justice

CHAPTER ONE
LIEUTENANT SERENITY "SITI" KASSIS

BERZA SYSTEM

JUMP COMPLETE, the crew went through the usual procedures, reporting in from each section of the CEC ship *Loyal Observer*. Maintenance, cargo, life support, and the others all checked in with an all clear. I leaned back in my corner, trying to stay out of the way of the organized, efficient crew. Captain Salu had invited me to be present for jump. Usually, the commander of the Phase 1 team witnessed arrival in the new system from the bridge, but my boss was "indisposed." I certainly didn't mind filling in.

My little sair-glider, Yasmi, chittered agreement in my ear. She didn't understand language the way Liam had, but she echoed my emotions uncannily well.

An ensign flicked a holo-file to the captain's chair. She glanced at it, then waved her hand through the approval icon, still focused on the reports coming up on the duty officer's station.

The alert klaxon blared.

"Captain! Multiple contacts!" The communications officer sprang from her seat as if it was electrified. "Many, many multiples!"

"Many, many multiples? Is that what they're teaching at the

academy now?" Captain Salu muttered as she swiped the flashing red holo-icon that appeared before her. "Ship, defstat two."

The ship's system acknowledged, flashing the lights blue in an assigned sequence. The alert tone sounded in the overhead speakers and my audio implant, followed by the ship's calm, flat voice. "Defense status is set to level two. All personnel, confirm."

I swiped the confirm icon that appeared, acknowledging receipt of the alert. As everyone else on the bridge did the same, the captain turned back to the communications officer. "Put 'em up."

Before comm could reply, the ship went on. "Captain, defstat set to two. Confirmation at sixty-seven percent and climbing."

"Acknowledged." Salu pointed at the communications officer. "Comm?"

"Working on it, sir." The comm officer—a newly commissioned ensign—hunched over her console, swiping through the display. The space at the front of the room filled with line after line of data, rolling upward at a rate too fast to allow us to read it.

"Pause!" the captain snapped out.

Ensign Warburton jumped a little, then hit the correct icon on her screen. The data stopped flowing.

"What am I looking at, Ensign?" Salu rose from her chair and stepped closer to the data.

"Standard comm data," Warburton said, her voice pitched high and wobbly. "First column is assigned ID numbers—our system doesn't recognize any of these sources, so it assigns a number. The rest is vectors, projected sources and destinations, and digitized packets."

Salu turned to stare at Warburton, her fists clenching against her hips. "Berza is an unexplored system. How can there be this much—any comm data?"

"I don't know, sir! If I didn't know we just jumped to Berza, I'd think we'd landed at Sally Ride. Or maybe Lewei since I can't translate any of this stuff. But even there, our system would recognize the identification packets. My computer is assigning IDs as if every signal was coming from an unregistered source."

"You're saying our newly discovered system is occupied?" Salu's face bore an uncommon expression: surprise.

Warburton jawed for a moment, then snapped her mouth shut and shook her head, hands raised in confusion.

Salu swung to face the other side of the bridge. "Intel! What's out there? Any hostiles?"

The intel officer, a Navy major with at least a decade of active service, stiffened. "No, sir. I'm getting nothing identified as hostile. No signals locked onto us, no obvious weapon frequencies. We'll keep scanning, of course. But we have no idea who these people are. Or if they're even… people."

"Theoretically, if an alien species—" She raised a hand, and the muttering broke off. "I'm not saying these are aliens, but we know it's a possibility." Her glare fell on the little green and white sair-glider shivering on my shoulder. Which wasn't really fair. Sure, gliders were aliens, but they weren't smart enough to build communications systems. Or use them.

At least not most of them. And the one "sair-glider" who was known to have used a comm system was under quarantine on Darenti Four, with the only known, sapient alien species in the galaxy.

Until now.

"Unless they have a form of weapon completely unknown to us—in which case, we're probably screwed—your system should recognize if anyone targets us, correct?" Salu's voice cut through my reverie.

"Yes, sir. After Darenti—" Andrade cast a glare at me, so fast I almost missed it. "We've done everything we can to ensure that's the case."

I almost missed the glare, but Salu hadn't. She made eye contact with me and jerked her head toward the conference room door. I nodded and turned on my heel to make my exit, one hand cradling Yasmi in comfort.

I'd barely taken a seat when Salu entered. As the acting commander of the Phase 1 team, I theoretically held an equivalent station to Salu—she commanded the ship, I was acting commander of the exploration team. But since she outranked me by many years and a lot of rungs, I jumped to my feet. "Sir."

"Take a seat, Lieutenant Kassis." She waved a hand at the conference table, then dropped into a chair next to me. "Before the others join us, what's your take on this?"

As I took my seat, I moved Yasmi from my shoulder to my specially constructed pocket. Gliders were allowed—welcome even—on Phase 1 teams, since the species had been deemed "planet neutral," but I'd noticed the captain didn't have one. Usually that meant they weren't a fan of the little creatures.

"I'm as baffled as you, sir. The automated beacon dispatch is supposed to scan for comms. It should have recorded and reported the same data Warburton found and sent it back to us in the initial burst." I flicked my holo-ring and pulled up the mission files.

Salu tapped her fingers on the table. "That's what I thought, too. Have you reviewed that burst?"

"Of course."

The Explorer Corps sends a drone to any newly discovered planet thought to be capable of supporting human life. They take decades to arrive at their targets, then do an automated scan. If all the results land within the safe range, a beacon is launched, and that data is sent back to headquarters in the first burst.

The Berza beacon was one of the earliest automated systems. It had flown for almost thirty years before sending the all-clear. Scientists in the Commonwealth had analyzed the data, and CEC leadership dispatched our ship, the *Loyal Observer*, to do a Phase 1 review. Because so many new planets were available to explore thanks to the many automated beacons launched over the intervening years, this Phase 1 exploration had been rated low priority. Which was why a mere lieutenant had been assigned as deputy commander of the exploration team.

I tossed the file to the projector above the table. "There's nothing here. This beacon was one of the first automated ones—they didn't scan for all the things we do now. It just confirmed the target planet's location in the Goldilocks zone and that the jump beacon was functional. You have to remember—they used to send a full Phase 1 team to do the recon *before* deploying the beacon. These first automated ones were rudimentary, at best. Plus, despite Darenti, they weren't really expecting aliens. But it should have recorded and transmitted comm signals."

"Lieutenant, I don't need to be lectured on—" She broke off, a tinge of shame flashing over her face. "Sorry. I forget you were one of the last deep-sleepers and actually experienced that mode of travel."

Before going to the academy, I had accompanied my father on one of the last Phase 1 beacon deployment teams. It took twenty years in deep-sleep to reach Earth, which meant technically I was older than the captain. "I forget it myself, most of the time, sir. And I was just a kid, not an officer. But that experience is relevant now." Under the old system, explorers knew almost nothing when the ship arrived and had to determine whether a permanent beacon should be installed or if they should activate the temporary beacon with delayed self-destruct, return to headquarters, and place a system on quarantine.

"Still, I can't believe those old, automated beacons didn't find comm signals. That seems really basic." Salu shoved her fingers through her short gray hair, making it stand on end.

"There's an errata section in the report." I pull up the data. "I noticed on my first review that some of the equipment was apparently damaged in transit. CEC decided the omissions were minor and that we could fill in the blanks when we got here." I swiped to a screen, then scrolled down. "See, we've got reports from the atmospheric probes—half of them were destroyed before they completed their missions."

"Destroyed?"

I shrugged. "At the time, we thought it was age-induced failure. The probes that reported back showed all environmental factors well within safe tolerances. In fact, that's why we're here—the third planet is almost perfect for human habitation." I choked back a laugh. "I guess someone else figured that out."

The door slid open and Major Andrade, the intel officer, joined us.

As he approached the table, Salu fired off her first question. "Who is it?"

Andrade flung some data onto the table, pushing my probe reports aside. "We don't know, sir. All signals are encrypted. Ensign Warburton is working on cracking them, but it'll take time." He pulled out a chair and sank into it, leaning his elbows on the table and steepling his fingers.

"Surely you can offer an educated guess." Salu sat up straighter, as if reprimanding Andrade for his poor posture. "Leweian? Gagarian?"

Andrade looked up, his head swinging slowly side to side. "No. Neither of them. If this is them, they've completely reworked their comm systems—and with this volume of traffic, that's not—" He broke off. "No. This is someone new."

CHAPTER TWO
SITI

CAPTAIN SALU STOOD SO QUICKLY, her chair shot away from the table and bounced into the padded wall. "What do you mean, 'someone new'? From where?"

"Earth?" Major Andrade leaned back, his slight paunch straining the buttons of his uniform.

I shook my head. "Earth doesn't have the tech to launch—well, anything. Completely planet-bound. And based on the volume of comms, this is a big settlement. Base? Infestation?" I chuckled, thinking of some of the ancient films in which humans battled bugs in space.

"Let's go with settlement. The idea of bugs gives me the creeps." Unsuccessfully suppressing a shiver, Andrade swiped his screen and new data appeared. "There's a lot of chatter happening, which makes me think it's a lot of… people."

Salu pulled one of the files toward herself. "These vectors indicate comms off the planet—they're talking to ships or stations, not just chatting among themselves. Whoever these…beings… are, they have space flight." She glanced at the door. "Enter."

The door slid open for Ensign Warburton, who must have pinged the captain via her audio implant. "Ma'am, this place isn't as crazy busy as we thought. I've been able to isolate most of these signals—they're carrier signals." She hurried forward, almost skidding to a halt at the foot of the table.

"Show me."

Warburton flicked her file to the table and stretched it wide. "See these small data packets? They're all the same size. I believe these—" She swung a finger through the hologram, and three quarters of the entries turned red. "These are carriers. They're basically the different transmitters saying hello to each other. In old-style comm systems, every comm node is constantly sending out a 'here I am' signal, and the other nodes say 'I see you.'" She waved her hands back and forth in demonstration.

Salu's lips twitched for a brief second. "So those aren't actual messages—they're part of the tech?"

Warburton nodded. "Exactly. It's a really old-fashioned way of communicating, and we don't use it anymore, so we didn't automatically filter those out. They can probably send short text messages on those frequencies, but mostly they're used to maintain the connection, not actually communicate." She flicked her hand, and the red coded entries disappeared, leaving a much shorter list.

"But these *are* messages—" Salu nodded at the display. "And they're between locations on the planet as well as others off-world."

"Yes." The list flickered and the entries changed to a rainbow spectrum. "The blue are surface-to-surface. Green are to what we believe are stations in orbit. Or possibly orbiting ships. The red ones are from the planet to moving locations—inbound or outbound ships. Yellow is between those ships. Lieutenant Forster plotted the ships' current locations." She pushed the data file aside, and a schematic appeared beside it, showing locations relative to the planet with lines running between. "The colors match."

"I would have been disappointed if they hadn't." Salu leaned forward, her lips twitching again. "Anything to add?"

The younger woman's cheeks went pink. "Not at this time, sir."

"Thank you. Dismissed." When the door swooshed shut, Salu turned to me. "You've got experience with… *unexpected* populations, Kassis. Did you find similar signals on Earth?"

I shook my head. "The communities on Earth didn't use radio signals when we arrived. And, as I said, they were not a space-faring civilization at that time."

"How did they communicate?" Andrade leaned forward. The man had been uncharacteristically quiet. In the past three days, I'd gotten tired of listening to him bloviate on the various topics on which he considered himself to be an expert.

I shrugged. "Pony express?" They had other means of communication, but I wasn't at liberty to discuss those.

His brows drew down, giving him a sinister look. "What?"

"Historical reference. Old Earth paper-and-equestrian-based mail carrying system." Salu mimed riding a horse.

I shot her a surprised glance. Most people wouldn't have caught my reference. She must be an old Earth history fan. "Exactly. They passed information personally. Written and oral."

"Primitive." Andrade slid his chair back, as if the people of Earth were beneath his notice. "And not relevant to this situation."

"The fact remains that Lieutenant Kassis is the only member of the crew who has any experience dealing with an unexpected indigenous culture. Not to mention her time on Darenti. We're fortunate to have her." Salu slid her chair back and stood. "Time to say hello to the natives."

"Sir." I stood with her. "If I may… Please don't fall into the trap of underestimating this civilization simply because they're 'natives.' We have no idea what they're capable of."

Andrade lounged in his chair, nodding. "Now *that* I agree with. At close quarters, a pointy spear can make you just as dead as a blaster."

Salu glared at Andrade. "I am aware, Major. And if they have space flight, they are unlikely to use pointy spears." She continued to stare him down until he finally lumbered to his feet. Then she turned her stern eyes on me. "Lieutenant." She pivoted sharply and left the room.

I followed her back to the bridge, squirming under the weight of her tone. Had she been offended by my gentle reminder? She had asked for my expertise. Maybe the difference in our ranks meant she didn't appreciate suggestions that hinted at ignorance on her part. I'd have to watch my step.

Andrade and I joined the captain at her chair. Ensign Warburton finished a quiet conversation with the navigation officer, Lieutenant Forster, and hurried back to her station. The graphic she'd shown us filled the front of the bridge, with our location flashing in a slow green strobe.

Forster stood and turned to face us. "None of the ships are nearby, Captain. Based on their speed, I estimate they are cargo haulers, but there's no real way to know for sure. They could be heavy armament platforms. But we aren't getting any weapons signatures from them. There are several large items in orbit around the habitable planet, however." As he spoke, some of the green dots indicating orbiting stations or ships gained a pulsing red circle. These newly flagged nodes moved around the planet, from west to east and south to north in a coordinated sine-wave pattern. "As you can see, they have a robust network encompassing the entire planet. I recommend we stay beyond their probable range."

"And what range would that be, Lieutenant?" The captain's fingers tapped against the arm of her command chair. Was she aware of her nervous tic?

Forster turned red. "I don't know, sir. That would be LeVoir's area of expertise." He jerked his chin at the weapons chief.

Senior Master Sergeant LeVoir peered over his archaic glasses at the young man. "Thank you, Lieutenant, *junior-grade*." He put a heavy emphasis on the part of the rank no one ever actually used, reminding the youngster of the difference in their levels of experience. As a senior enlisted man, he had years of expertise in needling junior officers without technically crossing the line into insubordination.

LeVoir stood to address the captain. "We can't give you a precise safety zone, of course, sir, since we don't know what weapons they have. I think it's wise to assume they *are* armed." His gaze flicked to Andrade—whose job included enemy force assessments—then back to Forster, clearly trying to show the younger man how to *not* throw his teammates under the shuttle. "When those numbers come in, we'll adjust. But based on the speed most of the ships are traveling, I think this perimeter is our minimum safe approach distance." A haze of red appeared in a sphere around the planet, fading out to almost invisible.

"Excellent work. Comm, do we have any idea where the seat of government—assuming they have one—might be?" Salu asked.

"I collaborated with Science." Warburton nodded to the civilian sitting at the station next to her. "Life-sign scans show this planet is lightly populated. The highest population centers are here and here." The hologram zoomed through the red safety line, bringing the largest of the continents into sharp relief. Two glowing shapes appeared, one long and narrow, the other smaller and star-shaped. "Most of the comms originate from these locations. They appear to be towns located in deep valleys or gorges. The orbital weapons systems seem to be controlled from here." She indicated the larger settlement.

"That's who we need to talk to, then." Salu sat up straighter. "Can you match their frequency and send a message?"

"Yes and no, sir. I've isolated the system control frequencies from the comm frequencies. But everything they're sending is encrypted, so I can't understand it. How do you want to do this?"

"There's no manual for first contact." Salu sighed. "On *Ancient TēVē*, they just use hailing frequencies. As if that's a universal constant, and someone is always watching for an incoming message." She shook her head in good-humored derision.

I cleared my throat—I was the official First Contact Specialist on the *Observer*. Which meant very little in reality. Achieving that status only required an explorer to read the reports from Darenti Four and take a multiple choice test. The truth was, even after encountering an alien species, the CEC had only the barest of outlines for how to handle the next one.

In reality, I was probably the best prepared First Contact Specialist in the Corps. That wasn't idle bragging. My father had been the first to encounter the Darenti, and I'd grown up on his stories. My later experience with the Earthers and the Darenti—again—cemented my lead in a field with only two contestants. Which left me feeling very much out of my depth.

"Actually, sir, there *is* a manual, but it was written on Darenti and assumes we'll encounter a new species on the ground. Which in hindsight is a huge oversight." Too late to worry about that now. I wrinkled my nose in thought. "We can record a message and have the ensign broadcast it on repeat using the frequencies she isolated. I'd recommend audio and video—although there's no guarantee they'll be able to decode either one."

She nodded. "It's a starting point. Warburton, set up recording and count me in."

Warburton swiped a few commands, then counted down. "Recording in three, two, one—" She pointed at the captain on the next beat.

"Greetings. I am Captain Dramira Salu of the Colonial Explorer Corps ship *Loyal Observer*. We came to this system to survey an uninhabited planet, but clearly our data was wrong. Please forward this message to your planetary government. We come in peace." Salu pointed at Warburton to end the recording, then grimaced. "We come in peace. That's about as corny as it gets, but I felt like I needed a reassuring ending. Let me know when you're ready to send, Warburton."

"Yes, ma'am. Prepping the recording."

Andrade leaned close and spoke in a low tone. "That might not have been the best way to conclude, sir. These people have a global defense system. That implies they have enemies. Showing weakness might get us shot."

"Peaceful negotiation is showing weakness, Major?" Salu frowned and shook her head. "I don't want them thinking we're with their enemies. Ensign, ready to go?"

"Yes, sir. The message is ready."

"Send it."

Warburton flicked a command, and a green "message sent" banner appeared above the maps and data in the holo-field.

A klaxon blared. The red-encircled icons on the screen flared brighter.

"Sir!" LeVoir swung to face his console. "The planetary defense system just came online. I believe they are attempting to acquire a target."

CHAPTER THREE
QUINN TEMPLETON

LUNESCO

Quinn leaned down to scratch behind the ears of Doug Parra's guard dog, Pasha. Now that the requisite snacks had been dispensed under Doug's watchful eye, the dog deigned to allow the caress. Not something she'd attempt if Doug weren't here, of course. His dogs were well trained, and she'd seen what they could do to an attacking *panza*. She didn't want to be on the wrong end of that.

At Doug's command, Enrique padded forward to receive his greeting. Quinn offered the little biscuit, which the big dog set between his front feet. Then she scratched his ears. When she stepped back, Doug barked out another soft command, and the dog snapped up the cookie and retreated to his post.

"That does not get less unnerving." Quinn dusted her hands on her pants, carefully keeping both dogs in view as she spoke to Doug.

"Then they're doing their job." Doug smiled in grim satisfaction. "What can I do for the republic?"

Quinn took a step back and lifted both hands. "I don't represent the republic! I'm here on Lou's behalf."

Doug snorted a harsh laugh. "Not sure that's any better. Lou's in Krimson Empire's pocket."

With a short laugh of her own, Quinn took a seat by the small table on the patio. "Lou might work *for* the N'Avon Commonwealth, but she's hardly representative of it." She leaned on the name to remind Doug that "Krimson Empire" was a derogatory nickname. Since the revolution, the Romaran Republic had made friends with the Commonwealth, unlike the Federation they'd grown up with.

Shading his eyes, Doug looked across the narrow valley. His home sat on a perch almost halfway up the steep side of the ravine, occupying a shelf on the inner corner of a ninety-degree turn. From here, they could see the entire fertile valley as well as the switchbacks leading through the town that clung to the far wall and up to the plains. To the right, the valley narrowed as it ran perpendicular, then turned away to the south again in a giant lightning bolt.

A wooden pergola stood over the wide patio, providing structure for the sugar vines that grew rampant, and offering shade for the small table and chairs. The wind gusted, shivering the leaves and dropping a cloud of pink petals across the stone, furniture, and occupants, then whisking them away along with their faint, sweet scent. Quinn laughed as she brushed the last remaining petal from her brown hair, then crossed her arms. Despite the sun, the spring air was cooler than she was used to aboard ship.

Doug's observant gaze took note. "Let's go inside. It's still a bit chilly for visiting with a friend." He snapped his fingers and uttered a command. The dogs leapt up and preceded them to the front door.

Inside, they climbed the steps to the bedroom. Quinn wrinkled her nose as she stepped over discarded clothing. She supposed it provided good camouflage—no one was going to leave dirty underwear on the floor of the lobby to their planetary defense center. No one except Doug Parra.

Leaving the dogs on guard on the landing outside the bedroom, Doug shuffled past Quinn and opened the closet door. "After you."

She pushed aside the clothing hanging from the rail and opened the secret door at the back of the closet. "Don't you think the secrecy is a bit… overdone at this point? Everyone in town knows where launch control is."

Doug followed her through the opening into the large, darkened room. Four desks filled a good part of the space, with a threadbare couch and small kitchenette at the back. Multiple screens stood on each desk, most of them dark, although their power lights glowed bright in the gloom. Long, narrow windows high in the exterior wall had been darkened to keep out the desert sun. A young man sat at the farthest desk, hunched over his keyboard as he played some kind of card game. He glanced at them, waved a negligent hand, and went back to his screen full of cards.

"Just because half the town—nowhere near everyone—knows we're here doesn't mean we should advertise our existence." Doug gestured to the couch. "You want a beer?"

Quinn dropped onto the sofa with a nod. "Sure. I'm not on duty."

He gave her a piercing look, then pulled two bottles from the fridge. Slouching in the opposite corner, he handed her one, and they tapped the bottoms together and drank.

"Yes!" the kid at the monitor hissed under his breath, then cast a quick look over his shoulder.

Doug raised his beer in response. "Good game?"

The kid made finger guns at them. "I won twenty-three pensos."

"Is that good?" Quinn asked softly.

"That and a credit chip will buy you—" Doug broke off, as if calculating. "Pretty much nothing, these days."

"A credit chip still buys a cup of coffee at Auntie B's," the kid said.

"True. She takes care of us old timers. Flip the scans on and you can go home, Vendi." Doug jerked his head toward the door.

"You got it, Chief." The kid stood and stretched his back, then leaned over to tap at the keyboard. The game disappeared, to be replaced by a scrolling column of data. Vendi flipped a switch on the second monitor, and a schematic of the planet and the space around it appeared. "See you tomorrow."

"Thursday." Doug corrected the kid. "I'll be at the Homestead tomorrow."

Vendi grunted as he opened the door to the closet exit. "Don't envy you the meetings, Chief. See you Thursday."

When the door clicked shut, Doug rose and ambled across the room to fiddle with the computer system. He turned up the brightness of the display and flicked through a couple of screens. "Vendi's a good kid but not as conscientious as I'd like. If this were the Space Force…"

"It's not." Quinn put her empty bottle on a side table and rose to join Doug at the computer system. "He's monitoring space on a backwater planet in the new republic. It should be an easy, no stress job. Romara and N'Avon are at peace. The threat of the Krimson Empire is long gone, and the Federation is just an ugly memory. Life is good. And it's okay for life to be good."

"That's what they always say right before the other shoe drops," Doug growled.

As if in response to his words, the computer blatted out a harsh sound. Doug smashed a finger on a key, and the blare cut out. "Sorry about that. Pizza delivery. You staying for dinner?" He crossed the room. "It's ham and pineapple."

Quinn shuddered dramatically. "Pineapple? On pizza?"

He mimed throwing something at her, and she ducked. With a chuckle, he opened the door. "Pizza is the one good thing N'Avon gave us. I'll be right back. Watch the store for me, will you?"

She rolled her eyes. "Only if I get hazard pay," she called after him. Under her breath she added, "For walking through your dirty laundry."

While she waited, she turned on a second computer system and pulled up Doug's surveillance feeds. She'd been here enough times to know the commands, and he hadn't locked her credentials out of the system—a miracle with someone as paranoid as Doug. Since his wife had been killed in the service—not in combat, but to cover up the Federation's corruption—he'd become reclusive and suspicious of everyone. Their long association, and the adventures they'd shared since, had cemented their friendship, but she was surprised he'd left her access to his system.

Although he'd definitely mellowed since the revolution. She figured safety and freedom could do that to a person. In fact, she knew that from personal experience.

Barking echoed through the speakers, followed by a sharp command. Quinn pulled up video, revealing Doug on the front patio receiving a flat box from a youngster in a green uniform. The dogs stood at attention on either side of the older man. Dappled sunlight filtering through the vines gave his bald head a patchy appearance. The grey fringe of hair around the sides was long, blowing in the breeze, giving him a crazy old man vibe. *Not far from the truth.*

Doug watched as the kid backed his little cart down the steep driveway and performed a neat turn at the corner, racing down the slope and away from the house. Casting a quick look at the camera, as if he knew Quinn was spying, he headed under the pergola for the front door.

A loud alert blared in the room again. Quinn yelped and jumped, then took a deep breath to slow her pounding heart. The pizza kid must have tripped another alarm on his way down. She frowned at the screen but couldn't find an off switch. Crossing to the other system, she glared at the display then dropped into the chair, eyes wide.

A red banner flashed bright words across the screen: "INCOMING ATTACK!!"

CHAPTER FOUR
SITI

"Warning. The ship is under threat of attack. Unknown adversaries are attempting to lock on. What are your orders, Captain?" The emotionless voice of the ship's system cut through the rattled chatter on the bridge, silencing the crew.

Blood rushed to my gut, leaving me lightheaded. I'd been in sticky situations before, but I'd never been in a ship under fire. Gripping the arm of the captain's chair, I tried to ignore the alarms blaring around us. I definitely preferred to meet my adversaries on the ground.

The captain seemed to have no such qualms. "Defensive positions! Weapons, set our systems hot but do *not* acquire targets. Navigation, plot an exit jump. Helm, bring us around and head for jump distance. Comm, cut the alarms and start another recording."

The klaxon cut out. "Go, Captain!" Warburton didn't bother counting down this time.

"Attention, planet. We are not attacking. But we will defend ourselves. Please stand down your weapons." She snapped up a hand in a halt signal. "Put that on repeat."

"Aye, sir." Warburton flipped a few icons. "Sir, should I send it on the other frequencies?"

"Send it on all frequencies! Wait, what do you mean—what *other* frequencies? Don't send it on their weapons control freq. That could be construed as an attack."

Warburton's face went white. "I wasn't supposed—you said send the message on the isolated frequency. I thought you meant the control one. That's the one I isolated."

"For the love of—what are they teaching at the academy these days?" Salu spun her chair, ripping the arm out of my loosened grip. "LeVoir, tell me we're out of range!"

"I would if I could, Captain." LeVoir swiped through his screens so fast his hands blurred, but his tone was blasé, as if he came under attack every day. "I believe we're safe, but that's an educated guess. If they have some kind of laser guided plasma torpedo or—"

"Those are fictional, LeVoir," the captain snapped.

The sergeant shook his head. "Fictional weapons are often in development. At least that's what my friend in R and D says. And who knows what these aliens can do." He raised both hands. "But we're out of range of any known weapons and getting farther." He glanced at Sergeant Stalz at the helm.

"Affirmative, Captain," Stalz said, reading off our vector. "1.2 AD and widening."

"Thank you, Sergeant." The captain turned back to Warburton. "Any response?"

Warburton, who had been feverishly scanning through screens, shook her head so hard her ponytail nearly took out LeVoir. "No, sir. No response. That I can see."

"Elaborate, Lieutenant."

"Sir, the data coming from the planet isn't static. It's conversations." Warburton quailed under Salu's narrow-eyed stare. I surreptitiously made a "go on" motion, and she continued. "They could be responding to us, but since we can't decrypt their transmissions, what looks like a signal directed at us could be a response to—" She broke off and swiped at the planetary schematic, zooming in. A point in the display lit up then a cone extended from it as she described the problem. "This station is almost directly between us and the planet. This packet might be a response to them, or it could be coming to us. There's no way to know."

Salu frowned. "Capture any data coming toward us. If they respond, it's going to be in the clear."

"Yes, sir. But we don't know what 'in the clear' looks like for them. They won't speak Standard, and even if they did, we don't know how they translate that to the ones and zeros of data."

I cleared my throat. "Did we send that video of the captain in analog?"

Warburton's eyes went big, and her voice trembled. "No, sir. I'm not sure how to do that."

Salu's face turned red, and she rose from her seat, suppressed anger oozing from every movement. Although Salu outranked me by a million degrees, I felt compelled to protect Warburton. "They don't teach that at the academy, sir," I whispered.

Salu froze for a microsecond, then continued smoothly to her feet. "Let's see if we can figure this out, Ensign. Call in Sgt Nestor—maybe he'll have some ideas."

Warburton blew out a breath that did nothing to dislodge the bangs plastered to her sweaty forehead and swiped through an icon at her station. "Sgt Nestor, report to the bridge immediately."

The captain gave me a quick nod and turned to LeVoir. "Status?"

"Nobody shooting at us yet, Captain." As the senior enlisted person —and someone with more years of service than anyone else—LeVoir could get away with a more casual attitude. And no doubt the captain appreciated his ability to diffuse the tension. "Not even targeted."

"At least we've got some good news." She spun toward me. "What's the protocol, Kassis? Do we hightail it out of here so we don't impact the local civilization?"

I bit back my nervous giggle at her reference to the "Prime Directive" from the old stories. "That's not in the book, sir. My recommendation is we stay out of range and keep trying to make contact. If they wanted to blow us out of the sky—and had the capability—we'd be stardust by now."

"Agreed." She pointed at Andrade who'd been uncharacteristically quiet. "Intel? What's your assessment."

Andrade stood slowly. "I don't have enough information to make an assessment, let alone a recommendation." He raised a superior eyebrow at me.

"So your recommendation is to stay and continue gathering data?" the captain pressed.

"If you believe the ship is not in danger, sir. But I can't make that assessment." His tone grew smug. The rest of the crew tried—and failed—to pretend they weren't listening. Andrade had been added to the complement at the last minute and had made no effort to make friends with the rest of the team.

He was Navy, not CEC. Phase I missions didn't usually include an intelligence officer. Intel's job was to know what the enemy was up to. But the CEC explored *uninhabited* planets, so we didn't need them.

Since Andrade's arrival, rumors had swirled. Some said he'd angered a superior officer back home, and this mission was punishment. Others claimed he'd been assigned to investigate someone on the ship. Still others mentioned an inappropriate relationship with a junior officer. But none of those rumors made sense to me.

Until now. Did CEC HQ suspect we'd encounter aliens on this trip? How had they come to that conclusion? I whipped open my copy of the initial report and checked the sections I'd marked earlier. The gaps in the data suddenly took on a more suspicious cast.

The captain's finger tapped on the arm of her chair, recapturing my attention. "Major, if you can't make an assessment, I'm wondering why you're taking up space on my bridge."

Every eye turned to stare at the major, no one even pretending to ignore the discussion anymore.

Andrade cleared his throat. "I made an assessment. That we don't have enough information. I recommend we return to Grissom and leave these people in peace—and ignorance." Under his breath, he muttered something about space marines. So much for peace.

"Thank you for your input, but we're pretty sure they aren't really ignorant of our existence. Please continue to refine your assessment."

She scanned the bridge, pausing to meet the gaze of every member of the crew. "Forward all data to my ready room. Warburton, capture any signals that come within a standard delta of our position. Get Nestor to help you translate the video to analog and send it. And you let me know the instant you decode anything. The rest of you—watch for incoming. Kassis, you're with me. Forster, you have the conn." Ignoring Andrade's outraged gasp—as the next highest in rank, he should be in charge, even if he was Navy—she swung around and headed out of the room.

CHAPTER FIVE
QUINN

Before Quinn could silence the alarm, Doug burst back into the room. He flung the pizza box on the couch and lunged across a chair to reach the keyboard. "Who is it?"

"I don't know." Quinn hit the klaxon mute. "Unidentified ship. It's not projecting any recognizable identifiers. The defense system is trying to lock on, but something is defeating our targeting. Maybe a new hull treatment? N'Avon has that camouflage stuff."

"We aren't at war with the Krimson Empire anymore." Doug habitually used the old nickname for the N'Avon Commonwealth. He swiped through files, sweat springing up on his forehead. "And that's definitely not one of their ships. They are sticklers for proper identification."

"Unless they're testing some new tech?" Quinn tapped her lips in thought.

"They've never targeted us before. And they'd warn the planetary government before a test, wouldn't they? To prevent exactly this kind of scenario?"

"You'd think. But maybe it's a stealth tech and they wanted to see if we noticed them?"

Doug snorted. "It doesn't work very well, then, does it?" He poked another button and relaxed. "Looks like they're retreating. They were never really within range—that's why we couldn't lock on. Get Harim on the horn, will you?"

"Aye, sir." Quinn flipped a snappy salute at him and returned to the other console. Her call to the planetary governor went to messaging. "Hey, Harim, it's Quinn. Something... unusual going on over here at Doug's. Call back asap. It's important." She looked up this week's codes and added the "really super urgent" tag to her message.

After a decade in the Federation Space Force, another decade as a civilian spouse, and a short but exciting stint as one of the catalysts of the revolution, Quinn tended to follow protocol. But on this fringe world, the Lunescans operated in their own extremely casual way. Nowhere else in the republic had Quinn encountered a planetary defense system owned and run by a volunteer civilian. Nor had she come across a government as haphazard as the one here. Harim had probably turned off his comtab or left it in his office while he worked on his farm. Using the "really super urgent" tag ensured he would get back to her as soon as he realized she'd left a message. Theoretically.

Or perhaps not. She'd quit trying to guess how things would work out here and preferred to hedge her bets. "I'm going to call Tony."

Doug looked up, brightening. "Is he here with you?"

She nodded as she pulled out her comtab. "Yup. Stopped to get the news from Auntie B." She tapped his image, and the system connected.

Unlike the planetary governor, Tony Bergen answered immediately. "Yes, m'love?" His smile lit up his face, as if seeing her was the highlight of his day. As if they hadn't been together a little over an hour ago.

A little thrill of happiness fluttered through her in response. Even at the beginning of her relationship with her first husband, she'd never felt as happy as a simple greeting from Tony made her. Mindful that their comms were not encrypted, she went for vague. "We have an interesting situation over here. Any chance you can cut your visit short?"

Tony's brows drew down—he clearly got the message. "Yes, I can do that. Do you want some coffee?"

She never drank coffee this late in the day, so that was code. "Something extra would be lovely." She blew him a kiss and signed off.

"You two are repulsively happy," Doug grumbled.

"Not sorry." Quinn pulled a chair closer to Doug's console. "What are you doing?"

"I've got a scan directed at the ship. At this distance, and without a transponder code, we can't collect much data. But we can watch where it's going, and we'll know if it's targeting us. Their weapons are hot, but they haven't locked onto anything. And since they're now pulling farther away, it would appear they are not currently a threat."

"Can we talk to them?"

"They aren't responding to direct hails." He flipped a few switches. "Or let me rephrase that. They're sending a signal back, but my system says it's gibberish. Maybe some kind of comm malfunction."

Quinn's brows drew down. "If their comm system is sending garbage, we'll have no way of knowing if they've received ours. Just because their outgoing is messed up doesn't mean incoming is broken, too."

"You know more about that stuff than I do." Doug poked at a button. "I say the words and expect the computers to do their thing. Do you have any contacts in N'Avon? Maybe we should reach out to them."

"Only Lou. Tony probably knows someone." Rising, Quinn stretched, then crossed the room. She'd picked up her husband's habit of pacing. "Do you have something to write on—that we can all see?"

"I think the white board Auntie B used during the battle of Lunesco is in the closet." He started to rise, but Quinn cut him off.

"You keep an eye on our friends. I'll get it." She opened the door at the back of the room. This facility was built into the side of the cliff, behind Doug's house. The only access—through Doug's bedroom—kept most people out. In town, she'd heard rumors about the existence of the hidden base, but despite her claims to the contrary, most people didn't believe it existed. Only because most of them didn't realize they'd used the hidden base to blast attackers from the sky during the revolution.

She rolled a large, freestanding board from the closet and positioned it in the front of the room. "Let's catalog what we know." She picked up a pen and started writing. "Crap, Doug, when's the last time anyone used these?" She tried again to make a mark, but the pen was dry. Tossing it into the trash, she tried two more and they followed the first.

"Couple years. Since the war." Doug tossed a pen at her.

She caught it and pulled the cap off. The pungent odor reassured her as she tested the pen. "Good. First: the ship is not broadcasting an ID." She scrawled "no ID" on the board.

"That's not one hundred percent correct." Doug swiped his screen then spun it so she could see. "They're transmitting something that could be an ID. We just can't read it."

"Right." She added "readable" above the two words on the board. "They aren't responding to our hails. They have weapons ready but haven't targeted us." She paused as she wrote the last bit. "Are we sure about that?"

Doug's eyes widened. "Uh…" He scrabbled at the console then sat back and swiped a hand across his brow. "Why do you have to scare me like that? The system says nothing locked on."

Quinn held up both hands, the pen still clenched in one. "I'm not trying to scare you, but since we don't know who they are, we don't know what 'locking on' would really look like. I mean, we're a stationary location. They could program our coordinates into their system, and we won't know they're targeting us until the missile is headed our way. Assuming it's a missile. If it's a pulse cannon, we won't know until they fire—and they'll hit us before we can respond. Another reason to keep this location secret. We should set up a comm relay."

"I did not sign up for this." Doug clenched his shaggy fringe of hair with one hand while the other reached for the beer he'd abandoned earlier.

"You kind of did, by purchasing this defensive system." Quinn moved closer and patted his shoulder. "But there's no point in stressing over something we can't control. We watch the ship, and if we see something that looks like an active threat, we respond. But since we aren't at war, I think we're safe to sit back and observe." She spun the pen in her fingers. "I wish Harim was here—this should be his decision, not ours."

Doug opened his mouth, but whatever he was going to say died as the door opened. Tony appeared in the opening, followed by Auntie B. The elderly woman ran a local bakery, but before she had retired to Lunesco, she'd been a highly decorated member of the Space Force, General Beatrix La Gama. And more recently, the architect of the Lunescan defense in the revolution.

"Tony." Quinn met her husband in the center of the room, and they exchanged a quick kiss before she turned to extend a hand to the general. "Thanks for coming, Auntie B."

The older woman shook hands then turned to scan the white board. "What have we got?"

Doug gave her a quick rundown on their limited intel. Auntie B reviewed the data, then drummed her fingers against her chin. "Unknown potential adversary. Have you notified Harim?"

Quinn coughed. "We left a message for the planetary governor."

Auntie B rolled her eyes. "He's probably up in the mountains. It's hunting season."

"Isn't it always hunting season on Lunesco?" Tony asked.

The older woman nodded. "Convenient if you don't like your job. Call Ro'Sheen. She can get through to him."

While Doug contacted the governor's assistant, Auntie B pointed at the white board. "Looks to me like we're dealing with an outsider."

"Outsider?" Tony stroked his chin. "You mean someone from the Commonwealth?"

"We used to consider you all outsiders, but since the revolution, we've changed the definition. You're a known ally now. These people are not."

"You're saying they're from somewhere outside both the republic and the commonwealth?" Quinn sat down, hard. "That's not possible."

Auntie B shrugged. "It's very possible. Lunesco itself was 'outside' both nations for a time. Until the Federation took us over sixty years ago."

"Yeah, but you didn't have a ship like that." Quinn's finger stabbed at the data scrolling down the computer screen. "Lunescan ships were all purchased from the Federation or the Commonwealth. You didn't build anything unique to you."

"True. Mostly." She waggled a hand back and forth. "I mean, Severin McTomsh tried to build his own, but it barely got out of orbit." She rolled her eyes again. "Talk about a waste of public funds. Rescuing him was— Never mind. You're right. No fringe world could support development of a brand-new technology."

"That leaves aliens." Tony's eyes sparkled as he said it.

"That does not leave aliens." Auntie B threw a repressive frown at him, then cocked her head in thought. "Although I suppose it could be aliens. But we all know mankind traveled here from Terra."

Quinn's jaw dropped. "You think that's an Earth ship?"

Doug's head came up in surprise. "What? I thought Earth was dead. Lost."

Auntie B patted the air with both hands in a placating gesture. "It is. I don't think it's an Earth ship. And I don't think it's aliens. The most likely explanation is the one you came up with first—a N'Avon experimental ship."

"Except they aren't responding on N'Avon frequencies." Quinn leaned over Doug's shoulder to double check the comm system. "They're sending unintelligible data bursts as they move away from us. Out of range of our defenses. They've made no move to jump away. We have no way to communicate with them."

With a regal nod, Auntie B turned away from the board to face them. "Then I suggest we send an envoy."

CHAPTER SIX
SITI

Captain Salu stood behind her chair in her conference room, shifting her weight from foot to foot. I'd never seen her so agitated—generally she stood ramrod straight and completely still rather than rocking as if she held a restive baby. She frowned at the data hovering over the table. When our eyes met, her body stilled, as if she'd suddenly realized she was being observed. "I assume Commander d'Souza is still… indisposed?"

I grimaced. "I pinged him, sir. His response was… less than genial."

She barked out a laugh. "It's just us, Kassis. We both know the man is drunk."

"Then why did you ask, sir?" I bit my lip. That sharp response strayed close to insubordination, but I was tired of skirting around my boss's poor decisions.

Her eyes glinted. "Alcoholism is a disease, not a choice."

"He chose not to take the BuzzKill I ordered from the med bay." I stiffened my spine. The CEC tended to protect its own. Captain Salu had given me no reason to think she wouldn't do the same.

The exploration team didn't technically work for the ship's captain. She provided transportation for us, both into and out of the system. Commander d'Souza worked for Admiral Hortense at headquarters back on Grissom. Salu reported to a different flag officer in the same headquarters. While the service heads technically held equal positions, everyone knew explorers were more important than mere transports. That unwritten rule—and the fact that I was currently filling in for the commander—gave my opinion more weight than that of any other lieutenant. But it didn't mean I could get snippy with the captain.

Having worked for d'Souza for months, I'd grown tired of the way the system protected him. I'd been doing his work the whole time: analyzing the scanty data from the original drones, building the exploration plans and personnel requisitions, filing the supply requirements. That and my natural cockiness meant I tended to be more direct than most senior officers appreciated. It had paid off. In the past.

"I've been waiting for you to come to me, Kassis." Captain Salu dropped into her chair and flicked her holo-ring. "You know he doesn't work for me. But if I have a legitimate complaint—" She gave me a significant glare. "You shouldn't have to cover for him."

I stared at her, my mouth open. *I* protected *him*? "No. I'm not trying to—" I broke off. It's exactly what I'd done. Swept his addiction and refusal of treatment under the proverbial rug—but only because I expected my concerns to be written off. He'd managed to stay on active duty despite his condition. "I didn't think you'd—" I swallowed the end of that statement, too. Suggesting she'd refuse to do her duty wasn't exactly the way to ingratiate myself, even if it was the status quo.

She waved a hand, both reassuring me and sending a holo-ring command in one efficient move. "I've ordered him to report here. If he complies and is ready to assume his duties, you're off the hook. If he isn't, I'll file a report and officially replace him pending review." She pointed at a chair. "Sit. And before he gets here, tell me your opinion on this… situation. You have more experience with anything that remotely correlates to this than any other officer I know."

I pulled out the chair and sat on the edge, still unnerved by the captain's willingness to tackle d'Souza's dereliction. "I've had some unusual experiences."

She snorted and began ticking my duty history off on her fingers. "First contact at Earth. With multiple cultures. That entanglement at Saha with the Gagarians. Your association with the Darenti."

"You've read my file."

"Of course." Her brow wrinkled. "And you aren't exactly unknown. Your father's notoriety increases your own. When your team was assigned to my ship, I jumped at the chance to read your file. The d'Souza situation made me grateful I had done my homework. Although I had some advance intel on that, too. I suspect it's one of the reasons your transport was dropped on the *Observer*. I'm known for my willingness to stick my neck out. Maybe whoever's protecting him is losing interest. Or influence." She checked her chrono, then pulled up a staff tracking program that showed everyone's location on a schematic of the ship. Zooming in to d'Souza's cabin, she frowned. "He hasn't replied. And he doesn't appear to be moving."

"He's alive, though, right?" I crushed the little spurt of satisfaction at the idea he might have drunk himself into an early grave. Metaphorical grave, that is. I didn't really wish him dead. Besides, now that I knew Salu was willing to do the right thing, I should take the high road.

"His medical records haven't flagged anything life threatening." She flicked the files away. Privacy laws meant she could only access data that indicated a current emergency.

"Good." I rubbed my cold hands on my pants. "As to the current situation… Gagarin has been placing bases on every planet they beat us to for decades. But none of their settlements are this big or well established. Even at Saha, they were using recognizable communication systems." My only personal experience with Gagarian expansion was five years old, but since the Saha mission, I'd read every report on their activities.

"Agreed."

"I'm not as familiar with Lewei, but it's my understanding their expansion is slower than Gagarin's. And again, I'd expect to encounter recognizable communications." I bit my lip then glanced at the captain. "Warburton knows what she's doing, right?"

Salu chuckled dryly. "As much as any other ensign. Why do you think I had her bring Nestor into this? He's got the experience to back her up—if she's smart enough to listen to him."

I nodded. In the Academy, they trod a fine line between teaching officer candidates to take charge and encouraging them to listen to their more experienced enlisted team. "Then, assuming she's correct that these signals are unrecognizable, we have to entertain the idea this is an alien culture. Although, technically, we're the aliens."

That prompted an outright laugh. "Good point." She checked on d'Souza's status again then swiped up a file. A red "recording" icon flashed over her palm. "Effective immediately, Lieutenant Serenity Kassis is the Phase 1 exploration team commander pending review of the attached documentation. Commander Tensil d'Souza will be escorted to the med bay for treatment. Once completed, he will be reevaluated for return to duty." She flicked the recording off. "That gives us a minimum of five days before he comes up for review. Longer if medical is busy. Which, given our current situation, could happen quickly." She pushed back her chair and stood. "How do you feel about a planetary recon mission?"

I gaped at the captain. "There are potentially hostile aliens—I mean natives. They tried to lock weapons on us. And you want me to take a team to the surface?"

"When you put it like that…" She leaned across the table to swipe through a few screens. "We'll launch a few probes and see what happens. But eventually we'll either have to retreat or go visit. The only question is whether you're up for the challenge if the latter occurs."

"Of course!" I replied without hesitation. For my entire life, I'd been the daughter of the Hero of Darenti Four. My father had been the first person to encounter a sapient race, and nothing I could do would ever top that. But being the first to communicate with an advanced alien—or native—race would come close.

"Well, then, since Andrade won't even weigh in, we'll stay and continue to attempt communications with the planet. I'll send a full briefing back to HQ, of course, as soon as we have sufficient information. And if—when—they issue further orders, we will comply. But until then, I see no reason for us to turn tail and run." She stalked toward the door, which opened at her approach.

Striding onto the bridge, she fixed her gaze on Andrade, then looked away as if he was beneath her notice. "Warburton. Anything new?"

"No, sir." The young woman gestured to the grizzled enlisted man hunched into her chair. "We've created an analog recording device, but you'll need to redo the message. We don't have the equipment to convert digital to analog."

"Captain." The ship's operating system flashed red, and the calm voice spoke. "A craft has launched from the planet. Extrapolating current vector indicates an intercept course with us in twenty-six point three hours."

Salu's gaze snapped to me. "Someone coming to say hello?"

"Potentially, Captain," the ship said. "There is a seventy-six point nine percent chance that craft contains a diplomatic envoy. Thirty-three percent chance it is a suicide attack."

I did the math. "Are you saying there's a nine percent chance it's both?" The ship didn't reply.

The captain's lips twitched. "I'll take those odds."

Why not? She wouldn't be the one meeting with the potential kamikaze. "Did the ship use human behavior to make these predictions?"

"Respond, please," the captain said. Generally, the ship responded only to the person in command.

"That is the only data available."

I stifled a laugh at the ship's flat tone. Assigning humorous intent was silly, of course, but I couldn't help hearing it that way. "You have nothing on the Darenti?"

Salu pointed at me. "Good catch. Ship, include any data from Darenti in your analysis."

"Done." The ship's icon flashed green again. "Inclusion of data from Darenti *decreases* the chance of ill intent to twenty-nine percent."

"The Darenti have no weapons." Andrade spun his chair around to face us, his hands behind his head. "These aliens clearly do."

LeVoir nodded reluctantly, as if agreeing with the major pained him.

"True, but they're the only non-human data we have. And based on that very small sample size, humans currently hold the prize for most hostile." Salu's nose wrinkled, then she turned to me. "Any volunteers for a peace envoy?"

"Hell, yes." It wasn't the traditional CEC call and response, but the answer felt appropriate anyway. "Sir."

Salu's lips quirked again. She flicked a control on her holo-ring. "Flight control, I need a shuttle immediately."

"Roger, sir. We have one on standby," the disembodied voice replied.

"Navigation, send the data to the flight bay. Kassis, get armed and head down there."

"Armed?" I hesitated by the door to the float tubes. "Is that advisable for a peace envoy?"

"I'm not sending you unarmed." She frowned at me. "The shuttle will be armed, too."

"Aye, sir." I stepped into the float tube and plummeted toward the flight deck.

"You also aren't going alone." Salu's voice came through my audio implant. "Take your glider. And someone from your team. Someone useful. But not someone irreplaceable."

"No one on my team is replaceable, sir."

"You know what I mean. I probably shouldn't send you—if you don't come back, I'm stuck with d'Souza."

"I'll come back, sir."

CHAPTER SEVEN
QUINN

Quinn dropped into the jump seat on the left, with Tony on the right. Tony's cousin, Liz Marconi, worked through the *Swan of the Night*'s launch checklist. She tossed a quick glance over her shoulder at the couple. "Who are we meeting?"

Tony and Quinn exchanged a quick look before focusing on fastening their seat restraints. "We aren't sure," Quinn mumbled.

Liz nodded as if this was normal. The Marconi family's penchant for trade that frequently skirted the bounds of "legal" meant they often met with unknown or unconfirmed contacts.

"We do know they're potentially but not actively hostile." Tony clicked his buckle shut and tightened the straps.

Liz froze. "How hostile? I just paid off the new engines. Don't make me regret agreeing to this."

Tony spread his fingers. "If it looks like they're going to get cranky, we'll back off."

"And you know I wouldn't be here if I thought it was dangerous." Quinn put a hand on the back of Liz's seat. "I'm not going to leave my kids parentless."

"They wouldn't technically be parentless." Liz pursed her lips and went back to her checklist.

"Exactly. Leaving them with Reggie would be worse than parentless." Quinn's children were on Romara, visiting their father in prison under the protection of the president of the republic. Not that the president was personally supervising, but the government had arranged for guardians so Quinn wouldn't have to face her ex. "Actually, I changed my will. They're your responsibility if anything happens to me."

Liz rolled her eyes. "Worse than parentless. Thanks very much. I did just fine raising End and Dareen. Your kids would be lucky to live with us."

"They would." Quinn put as much gratitude into the short phrase as she could manage without sounding sappy. Having Liz and Maerk in her life had given her a sense of family she'd never felt with the LaRaines. She pushed the surge of emotion down to focus on the mission.

Tony cleared his throat. "The ship is truly unidentified. They're emitting a signal that could be a transponder, but our systems aren't able to decode it. They have weapons which they activated when Doug's defenses locked on, but they haven't obviously targeted anything."

"And they moved away from the planet initially. They've halted now—well beyond the reach of Doug's system." Quinn tapped her comtab to look up her notes. "It seems like they're watching."

Liz finished her preflight and shoved her stylus into her messy bun, then activated the comm system. "Maerk, you about done?"

"Sealing up the back ramp right now." A clanging came through at the end of her ex-husband's comment, confirming his statement. On the dash, the cargo lock light flicked to green. "We're cleared for launch."

Liz pressed her fingers against her forehead. "You don't get to say that. You're supposed to say, 'Cargo is secure.' How many times—"

"Cargo is secure." A hint of laughter came through the comm system. Maerk and Liz would argue until the sun went nova. It was one of the reasons they divorced years ago. Liz claimed arguing with her business partner was less stressful than arguing with her husband.

Whenever she said that, Maerk disagreed, as a matter of course. Their non-marriage seemed to work for them.

The door to the cockpit opened, and Maerk slid between the seats to take the co-pilot spot. He was tall and lanky, with curly hair that showed more gray than black these days. A stained coverall hung loosely from his shoulders, secured around his hips by a worn tool belt. He sighed as he settled into the creaking chair and ran a hand over the ship's worn dash. "You ready, sweetheart?"

Liz raised her eyes to the sky, shaking her head slowly, a tiny smirk quirking the corners of her mouth. "I finished the checklist. It's ready."

"She. She is ready." Maerk leaned closer to the dash and lowered his voice to a whisper. "Ignore Liz. She's jealous of our loving relationship."

"Nope, you are one hundred percent welcome to his love, *Swan*." She toggled the external comm system. "But if she ignores me, you're toast, Maerk."

"Come again?" The voice from the tower cracked in the middle.

Quinn cringed a little. Lunesco tended to hire on the young side. Older adults either migrated off world or were too busy with farming to bother working for the rudimentary—and notoriously underfunded—space port. Fortunately, the few ships landing at Lunesco were used to unmanned fields. Quinn wasn't sure why Harim insisted on keeping a human on the payroll—probably some kind of tax break in the new Federation.

"I wasn't talking to you, Lunesco Tower," Liz replied, her crisp tone all business. "*Swan of the Night* requests launch vectors."

"Roger, *Swan*." The kid's voice cracked again. "You are cleared for launch. Vector transmitted to your system. Transfer to Lunesco One at ten. Safe flight."

"Thank you, tower. *Swan* out." Liz flicked the switch and released the brakes. The ship rolled down the apron to the far end of the short strip. Liz turned onto the deserted runway and stopped. A few more flicks to her controls sent the ship rocketing down the rough runway, in a tooth-rattling launch. Then they lifted off, and the flight smoothed.

While Liz checked in with the orbiting station, Lunesco One, Maerk unfastened his seat belt and headed for the main cabin. Tony and Quinn followed to the more comfortable seating in the small living area. The *Swan*'s crew quarters consisted of this living room/kitchen combination, with bunks and sanitation modules above. Cargo took up the bulk of the ship, although Liz and Maerk had done a lot more ferrying of passengers than things since the revolution.

"Coffee?" Maerk pulled the pot from the machine, tapping his fingers against the glass. "Oops, need to run a fresh batch."

Quinn looked at her watch and shook her head. "Too late for me, thanks."

"Tony?" Maerk filled the pitcher and dumped water into the machine. "Liz is going to want some."

"I'll take a cup." Tony pulled Quinn to the small sofa beyond the dining table and flicked his comtab. "Auntie B says Harim approved the mission. Finally."

Quinn snorted a laugh. "Like he'd say no to Auntie B."

"He did once." Tony slid the device into his pocket. "It did not go well for him." While Harim was the elected governor of Lunesco, everyone knew Auntie B ran the place—which was fine with Harim. It gave him more time for hunting.

The coffee had just finished brewing when the door to the cockpit opened and Liz appeared, her mug in hand. Maerk filled it without comment, and they each took one of the armchairs at either end of the couch.

Liz sipped her drink and sighed, raising her cup at Maerk. "This makes all of the aggravation worthwhile."

Maerk dunked his tea bag in his mug, ducking his head in a failed attempt to hide his self-satisfied smirk. "I'm sure there are other reasons you keep me around."

"Nope, pretty much just the coffee." She set her mug on the low table. "It's going to take about twenty hours to reach the target's current position. They're out near the jump points."

Tony pulled his comtab out again and connected it to the ship's display system. The large screen on the wall lit up, displaying a schematic of the system with the *Swan* at the center, pulling away from the planet. He manipulated the display, bringing the unidentified ship into view. "Auntie B will send any communications from the ship directly to us."

Quinn opened her mouth, but Tony held up a finger. "Let me rephrase that. We'll get the comm directly from the ship, but it's indecipherable so far. If they manage to get anything translated, they'll forward it to us." He switched the display, and instead of showing flight vectors of all traffic, it displayed comm signals. Red dashed lines emanated from the unidentified ship, and a stream of green signals went back to it from the planet.

"So, now we wait." Quinn took a deep breath and let it out again, but the tension in her shoulders didn't ease. "I don't suppose you have any Sergeant Sinister aboard?"

Maerk laughed and went back to the kitchen. "Are you kidding? We always carry Tony's jump buffer." He pulled the familiar bottle and a shot glass from an upper cupboard. Returning to the seating area, he poured a shot into Tony's coffee and his own tea, then offered the glass to Quinn. "Liz?"

She shook her head. "I'm flying."

Quinn took the shot of spiced rum and clicked it against Tony's mug. "One shot is all I'm having. Here's to... I'm not sure what we should be toasting."

"Let's drink to positive outcomes." Liz raised her mug.

"And no bug aliens." Maerk tapped his mug against Tony's.

"Aliens?" Quinn paused with the shot glass at her lips, untasted. "No one said anything about aliens."

Maerk frowned. "It's an unidentified ship putting out indecipherable communication signals. I never considered it could be anything *but* aliens."

Quinn closed her eyes and tried to slow her breathing. "I—it has to be humans, right? Didn't we decide it was super-secret N'Avon tech? Advanced R and D stuff?"

Tony slid a warm arm around her shoulders. "That's what we decided, but that doesn't make it true. Drink your rum."

Quinn knocked back the shot and let it burn down her throat. She really hated the taste of spiced rum without a mixer, but it had kind of become a thing for them. Tony couldn't endure hyper jump without getting sick as a dog unless he was drunk first. After a chance comment about parties involving "the sergeant" in her junior officer days, he'd bought a bottle of the stuff for their next interplanetary trip. And it had become a tradition.

As the liquor warmed her, she held the glass out to Maerk. "I think I need a second one if we're going to meet aliens."

CHAPTER EIGHT
SITI

When I arrived in the shuttle bay, the explorer on duty nodded at the second craft in the row. "Your pilot's running the preflight, sir. And Explorer Rodriguez is aboard."

"Thank you." I slung my emergency bag over my shoulder and followed the yellow path to the shuttle. The engines hummed softly, gently warming the air around them. Stepping into the airlock, I pulled it shut behind me, waiting for the lights to turn red before opening the interior hatch. Here on the ship, both could be open at once, but standard procedure dictated we cycle through even in "safe" locations.

Stowing my backpack in the rack beside the airlock, I moved to the forward compartment. This shuttle could carry four in the front and twenty in the back. Since they were sending only one pilot, I'd act as co-pilot. While I was qualified to fly, it wasn't my favorite pastime. But the ability to get off planet on my own was a skill I'd wished for early in my career, so I'd learned and kept my training and certifications up to date.

I stepped into the cockpit and paused by the jump seats. Rodriguez wasn't there, so I toggled my audio implant. "Rodriguez? Where are you?"

"I'm in the passenger section, sir. I don't like launches." He sounded embarrassed. Air sickness—in those predisposed to it—was still untreatable. Luckily, in most people it disappeared once a ship was in motion. If it didn't, those people didn't stay on exploratory teams.

"Roger. Come on up after we get underway. Kassis out." I didn't wait for him to respond, because I'd glanced at the pilot as he leaned around his front seat to look at me. "Joss?"

He jumped out of his seat to wrap me in a strong bear hug. "Siti! I was wondering when you'd show up."

"I didn't know you were on this mission! I thought you were on Partlow?" I squeezed my friend hard, then released him. "In fact, I know you were. And they aren't scheduled to come back for months." My sair-glider, Yasmi, leapt from my shoulder to Joss's, rubbing her body against his check.

Joss chuckled and stroked the glider. "I was on the Phase I team, but—" His grin faded. "My mom got sick. They sent me home with the transport."

"Is she okay?" I'd met his mother on our original trip to Earth, back before I joined the corps. After that, Joss and I had gone through the Academy together. Under the terms of the Earth treaty, he and the few other Earthers to join the corps received special dispensations allowing them to communicate with and travel to Earth more frequently than standard leave allowed. Plus, his dad was the Earth ambassador, so he could call in favors.

"She is now. Dad took her to Sally Ride, and they fixed her up. Apparently Earth has not gotten the newest med pods available. Or they hadn't. Dad fixed that." Joss smiled smugly. "And rather than sending me back to Partlow, they added me to the Berza crew last minute. I'm shocked you didn't see my name on the roster."

I flushed. I hadn't reviewed any roster updates, except those to my immediate team. Usually, I tried to stay on top of who would be doing what, even when they didn't directly impact my chain of command. You never knew when you might need to schmooze a pilot to take you somewhere the authorities hadn't preapproved.

Trying to hide my embarrassment, I shooed him toward the front seats. "Let's finish the preflight and get going."

"Already done. Just waiting for our passenger." He pointed at me, then at the glider still snuggling up to his cheek. "Who's our new friend?"

"This is Yasmi. She seems to like you. Strangely, I found her almost the same way I found Liam."

His eyes went wide and he plucked the glider from his shoulder. "Really? Random gliders don't just show up on CEC ships. You don't think she's—"

"No. We ran tests." I didn't specify which tests we'd run, but he'd know. He'd been there on Darenti. "She's definitely a normal glider."

"Sit." He thrust a finger at me, then deposited Yasmi on the chair back and slid into the left seat. Swiping a finger through an icon, he put on a fakey announcer voice. "This is your captain. Welcome to Air Torres. Our flight time will be approximately two hours. Please fasten your seat belt and put your tray table in the upright and locked position." Flicking the comm off, he smirked at me. "Any idea why those little tables had to be closed?"

We'd watched enough *Ancient TēVē* together to have a shared store of quotes and jokes. I shook my head as I fastened my five-point harness. "So you don't spill your drink? Hey, I'm sorry I didn't realize you were here. The last couple of days have been… stressful."

"Yeah, I'm sure alien contact can do that to you." He held up a finger as he requested departure vectors. We taxied to the launch position. The lights in the bay flashed three times, and a force shield lit up blue, separating us from the parked shuttles. When Joss flicked another icon, the shield between us and deep space parted, and we lifted off the deck, easing through the narrow opening. Once we were clear, he hit the preplanned route, and the shuttle blasted away from the *Loyal Observer*.

"It wasn't just the alien contact. My boss is—" I broke off. With Commander d'Souza in sickbay, my boss was now Admiral Hortense, back at HQ. "The whole mission has been—not great. But it's better now."

"Now that we're meeting aliens!" Joss laughed as he rotated his seat to face me. He'd been with me on Saha and Darenti, although his experience with the Darenti was less intense than my own. Now that I thought about it, the fact that both of us had been assigned to this mission, combined with the presence of Major Andrade, felt even more suspicious.

"Do you think HQ knew?" I grabbed Joss's hand.

He frowned, squeezing my fingers then releasing them. "Knew about the aliens? How could they?"

"How could they not?" I pointed at him. "I looked at the drone data. Half of it was missing." I poked my finger at him again to keep him from interrupting. "Drones don't malfunction like that. What if HQ stripped that data?"

"Why would they do that? They want explorers to be well-informed, not blindsided."

I pointed at him again. "You and me. That's an odd coincidence. We were on Darenti. And Saha. We've done this before—at least as much as anyone has done it before."

He leaned back in his chair, putting his feet up on my arm rest and his hands behind his head. "While it's true you and I have more experience with aliens than most explorers, we're hardly the only people who understand the Darenti. If anyone does. And there are buildings full of people who know more about Gagarin than us, even if we did tangle with them on Saha." His hands dropped to his arm rests with a slap. "No, if they thought we'd meet aliens—or Gagarians—they'd have sent eggheads from HQ or a university. We're small potatoes."

I blinked. "That's some pretty humble talk coming from Joss Torres."

He grinned his vid-star smile. "My humility is legendary."

I sputtered a laugh. "That sounds about right."

The cockpit door chimed, and Joss flicked the unlock icon. I turned in my seat to give Rodriguez a quick once-over. He glanced quickly at the forward screen—currently showing an apparently static image of the stars ahead of us with the system's primary dimmed in the distance—then focused on me. "What's the plan, sir?"

I unlocked my seat and rotated it to face the center aisle. They wouldn't go all the way around to face the jump seats— in a cockpit this size, that would have meant our knees knocking against each other. Joss's feet thudded into my lap, and I shoved them off, then flicked my holo-ring.

Data from the initial contact scrolled up my screen, but nothing readable. "Looks like comm still hasn't cracked the code." I glanced at each man in turn. "The planet launched a ship that is headed directly for us. It's slow, so we're going out to meet it. We probably shouldn't assume it's moving at top speed, but even if it's at fifty percent, they're still well below our regular cruising speeds."

"So, we're more advanced than they are." Joss nodded as if this confirmed his personal superiority. Joss liked to pretend arrogance, but anyone who knew him could see through the charade. Although since he was much smarter than he let on, the joke was on anyone who dismissed him as a pretty fluff-head.

"Apparently. We can't be complacent though. We're technically more advanced than the Darenti, but they had us fooled for decades." Very few people knew what the Darenti could do, but Joss and I had both seen their abilities firsthand.

"You know what happened on Darenti?" Rodriguez pinned a hopeful gaze on Joss. "The LT won't tell me."

Joss gave him a close-lipped smile and a shrug. Rodriguez sagged in disappointment.

"You know it's classified," I reminded the enlisted man. "And it's not relevant to this mission, so you have no need to know. The point is, we shouldn't make assumptions about these beings' abilities. They could have weapons we don't understand. Or they could be harmless."

"Not completely harmless." Joss flicked his holo-ring and brought up the planetary defense schematic our computer had generated. "Just mostly harmless."

I muffled a laugh at the reference. Joss had grown up on Earth with access to original books and videos. His knowledge of ancient entertainment came directly from the source material rather than the centuries of remakes and reboots I'd loved. "We could still end up mostly dead. Or completely."

Rodriguez's gaze darted from my face to Joss's in confusion. We didn't enlighten him.

I slapped my hands on my thighs. "The important thing is to stay alert, try to establish a common means of communication, and do our best not to start an interstellar war. If anyone gets agitated, we take a break and withdraw. Back to the ship, if it seems prudent." I stroked Yasmi, who'd returned to my shoulder. She was good at reading human emotions—it would be interesting to see what she made of these beings.

"When we rendezvous, we'll invite the… natives?" I gnawed on my lip. "We need a better identifier than 'aliens' or 'natives.' Let's call them Berzans."

"They probably have a different name for themselves," Rodriguez said.

"Definitely." Joss leaned forward and reached under his seat to pull out some water pacs. "Berza was the guy who led the Phase I team to Kaku hundreds of years ago."

"Look at you remembering your Academy history lessons." I accepted the beverages and passed one to Rodriguez. "Doesn't matter what we call them—we still call the Darenti by the name the CEC assigned. But maybe we can do better, once we know what their name is. What was I talking about?"

"Where we'll hold the meet and greet." Joss leaned back in his chair again, but at my glare kept his feet on the deck.

"Right." I pointed at Joss. "You have a universal docking sleeve on this thing." It wasn't really a question—the *Loyal Observer* had one shuttle with the non-standard system, and I'd noticed the markings when I came aboard. At Joss's nod, I went on. "We'll connect to their ship and invite them to come over."

Rodriguez raised a hand as if he were in school. "How do we know they breathe the same type of atmosphere?"

Joss and I exchanged a look. I'd chosen Rodriguez for this mission because he was steady and dependable, not for his intellectual brilliance. But I would have expected anyone who'd passed basic training to have an understanding of the CEC's planetary vetting system. Of course, this unexpected shift in business as usual could throw a person.

As I opened my mouth to answer, Rodriguez slapped his forehead. "Never mind! I withdraw the question. Clearly the atmosphere is human standard or we wouldn't be here. I was so focused on 'alien'…"

"No worries." Joss slapped the arm of his chair. "I had the same brain fart when they assigned me to this jaunt."

I made a mental note so I could throw that back in Joss's face later. "What do we know about their ship?"

"Looks like a small cargo vessel." Joss pulled up the visuals our long-range scanners had synthesized. "It's bigger than this shuttle, but not a lot. The computer estimates there's room for twenty-five to forty personnel in the rear compartment—if they're not going very far and not carrying anything else. And roughly the same size as us—" He held up a hand to forestall our excited comments. "The size of the hatch indicates they're within human-standard dimensions."

I blinked in surprise. "Good use of the scans, Lieutenant."

"I'm not just a pretty face." He fluttered his eyelashes at me.

Rolling my eyes, I nodded at Rodriguez. "We'll dock with their ship and invite them aboard. I'll take them to the cargo area—which we should reconfigure into a more usable space. You can switch those seats to rear-facing, right?"

Joss nodded.

"Rodriguez, you'll be with me, providing obvious security. Fully armed and stay by the hatch. Lieutenant Torres, you'll stay in the cockpit." I ignored Joss's faint attempt to argue. I had been placed in command of this mission, and he knew it. "Lock the airlock as soon as they're inside the shuttle, so we can pull the link and leave on a moment's notice. You'll secure us inside the cargo hold. If the Berzans are hostile, you can keep them contained. If anything happens to us, you hightail it back to the *Observer*."

"Aye, sir." The pause before he agreed told me we'd be discussing the details in private.

"Rodriguez, you know how to reconfigure the cargo hold? I want two pairs of seats facing each other, but far enough apart that we're out of physical range." I grimaced. "Assuming they use chairs. And their arm—er, appendages are similar length to ours."

"And they don't have extendable tentacles." Joss waved his arms in a wavelike motion.

"On it, sir." Rodriguez jumped to his feet, his gaze darting between me and Joss. He knew we wanted him out of the way so we could talk. But he also knew I'd clue him in on anything relevant. Before the cockpit door slid shut behind him, he turned back. "I'm going to grab a meal bar. Do you two want anything?"

"Toss me one of the cookies and cream ones, will you?" Joss raised his hands in a catching position.

"And I'll take a chocolate." I caught the bar the enlisted man threw and ripped open the wrapper. "Thanks. I didn't realize how hungry I was."

As soon as the door shut behind Rodriguez, Joss swung back to pin me with a glare. "You want me to stay up here? I thought you wanted someone else with first contact experience to help."

"I do. But I need you here, ready to cut our losses if necessary. Rodriguez can't fly the ship—you're the only one who can pull the plug if things get dicey. You'll be watching and listening. You're good at reading people, and I trust you to make the right decision if I'm not able to." I fiddled with the meal bar wrapper. "Remember what the Darenti can do. These Berzans might have the ability to influence my decision making. Rodriguez isn't going to argue with me. And if he's back there, he's equally susceptible to influence."

"You're assuming they can't use their freaky mind control through the ship?" Joss wiggled his fingers at the bulkhead and widened his eyes comically.

"We aren't assuming anything, remember?" I tried to frown and tamp down his enthusiasm, but Joss's cheerful attitude was contagious. "If they can control you from inside the cargo hold, we're in deep trouble, but there's nothing we can do about that if we want to make contact."

"Besides, if they could do that, they could have convinced us to land on their planet by now, right?" Joss made his eyes even bigger. "Or crash the *Observer* into the sun."

The overhead light flickered briefly to red, and the shuttle's auto pilot pinged. "Target velocity increasing. Intercept in fifty-six point three minutes."

"Interesting." Joss sat upright and swung his chair to the front in one fluid motion. "They really picked up speed." His hands flew through the interface. "You want me to slow us down?"

I thought about it for a second then shook my head. "They know we're capable of this speed, and we don't want to give them a reason to wonder what we're up to. We can be ready. I'll go help Rodriguez."

Leaving Joss, I let myself out of the cockpit. The tiny galley behind the cockpit was open. I filled a couple of pitchers of water and stacked them on a tray with a few glasses. Balancing my burden, I made my way aft.

This shuttle's hold held up to twenty passenger seats or several pallets of cargo. Rodriguez had stowed half the seats and was working on the rest, leaving a cleared area in the center. I set the tray on a fold-out shelf by the door and went to the storage area at the rear. "There's a table back here, isn't there?"

Rodriguez looked up from the chair he was folding. "No. In this model, it's behind the galley. This work for you, sir?"

I looked around the little space. "If the table will fit in this center area, it's fine. You don't need to stow the rest of the seats. We aren't trying to make this look like a fancy conference center. But grab the table, and I'll get some food."

Following him back to the galley, I stepped into the tiny cubicle while he pulled a flat panel from a slot between the kitchen module and the cockpit bulkhead. Like the cargo hold, the rest of the small ship was built for maximum flexibility. The galley and latrine modules could be removed and replaced easily. The only permanent fixtures in the ship were the cockpit and the reinforced bulkhead protecting it.

We set up the meeting area as best we could, with water and an assortment of prepackaged food bricks on the table in the center.

Hopefully one of them contained compounds the Berzans could safely ingest.

Visions of tentacled monsters from hundreds of fictional vids paraded through my brain, but I banished them with a less than comforting reminder. We'd already met the most terrifying aliens—shapeshifters—and survived. Surely these Berzans couldn't be much worse.

CHAPTER NINE
QUINN

Quinn surveyed the living area of the *Swan*. "Are you sure you want to invite them into your home?"

Liz looked up, a handful of steak knives in her hand. "I'm not going aboard their ship. They could kidnap—"

"*You* aren't going anywhere near them." Tony took the knives from his cousin and laid them in the box on the counter. "You and Maerk will be in the cockpit, with the door locked. Is this the last of the knives?"

"How should I know? I don't do the cooking." Liz grabbed the box and stalked across the room to the ladder leading up into the ceiling. "Got any more?"

Maerk climbed halfway down from the open trap door and leaned over to grab the box. He perused its contents then lifted the box to set it on the floor above. "Nope, that's the lot. I'll secure them up here." He climbed back into the overhead crew quarters.

"What about forks?" Quinn brandished one and made a stabbing motion. "They can be weapons.

"Anything can be a weapon in the right hands." Tony took the fork and put it back into the drawer. "I think as long as we eliminate the obvious problems, we're good. Do we want to offer them refreshments?"

"I have some lovely Sumaerian mushrooms." Maerk reappeared from the crew compartment, hesitating halfway down the ladder. "I was going to make soup, but I'll need my knives…"

"Don't bother." Quinn waved to catch his attention. "You saw the speed they're moving—they can easily get home in time for dinner. If we've got water and maybe some snacks, that's good enough. When—if—they come down to the Homestead, we can lay on the hospitality. This is just a… what did they call it in that pirate movie? A *parley?*"

"Technically, a parley would be held on neutral ground." Tony leaned against the back of the couch. "But since we don't have a handy abandoned station or asteroid with atmosphere, we'll have to do it here. Assuming they can breathe our air."

Quinn swallowed hard. Her subconscious had been dancing around the possibility that these visitors might be non-human, but now Tony had dumped the idea square in the middle of the room.

"What else would they breathe?" Maerk asked, his voice sounding higher than usual.

Tony shrugged. "Dunno. Methane? Water—"

Liz froze in front of the picture she'd swung away from the wall to reveal a safe. Then she shook herself like a dog and went back to the old-fashioned combination lock. Spinning the dial back and forth, she worked through a long string of settings until the door clicked. The spacious interior held a small arsenal of weapons. "Your usual, Maerk?"

Her ex-husband made grabby hands at Liz's back. "Come to papa, Evelinda."

With a roll of her eyes, Liz pulled the long-barreled blast rifle from the safe and handed it over. "Take a couple of power packs, too." She put a small pile of the batteries on the coffee table. After stowing a small stunner in her thigh pocket, she took out another blaster, smaller than "Evelinda" and hung it from a holster on her belt. "Do you need environmental suits?"

Tony and Quinn exchanged a quick look, and both spoke at once.

"I hadn't—" Quinn began.

"I can't believe—" Tony broke off and gestured for Quinn to go on.

"If they're coming here, we shouldn't need them…" Quinn's voice trailed off uncertainly.

"It won't hurt to have them in case we need to—" Tony wiggled his fingers at the hatch.

Quinn gulped. Meeting with an delegation inside her own—or Liz's—ship was one thing. She didn't want to investigate an alien spacecraft. On the other hand, being prepared for the unexpected appealed to her. "I vote we have them to hand, just in case."

"I say you wear them when you open the airlock," Liz said in a no-nonsense tone.

"Good call." Maerk put Evelinda on the couch and disappeared into the hallway that led to the airlock. He returned a few minutes later with two pressure suits which he tossed at Tony and Quinn. "Suit up."

"Aye, sir." Quinn snapped a salute at her ex-cousin-in-law. She frowned at the thought. That probably should have been cousin-in-law's ex, since Liz and Maerk were divorced long before Quinn and Tony married. Clearly, stress was making her loopy. Or maybe it was the two shots of the Sergeant, which now felt like a mistake. She'd originally thought it would take longer to meet their visitors.

"What's our projected arrival time?" Dropping the suit on the couch, she went to the kitchen to look for a snack that would calm her tense stomach while muting the buzz without killing it entirely. She needed to be relaxed but focused.

"We've got about ten minutes," Liz called over her shoulder as she headed for the cockpit. "Make that twelve point three." The second statement came through the overhead speakers.

"Maerk, get up front and seal the cockpit. We'll see you when we're done." Tony gripped Maerk's shoulder, then turned the taller man toward the interior hatch.

"You got it." Maerk hefted Evelinda, winked at Quinn, and disappeared forward.

Tony turned to Quinn. "You okay?"

She pulled out a chocolate chip marshmallow treat and ripped it open. "I will be." Sinking her teeth into the crunchy, sticky bar, she sighed. "Much better."

They spent the remaining time getting into their pressure suits and checking each other's gear. "We've got ten minutes of oxygen in these cannisters." Tony indicated the small cylinder hanging from his waist. "And there are larger ones in the airlock, if we need them."

"But we're staying here." The statement came out sounding like a question. Quinn straightened her spine and tried again. "I like being prepared, but we aren't leaving the ship."

Tony flashed his cocky grin—the one that still made her stomach flutter. "We gotta be prepared for anything. This is uncharted territory. I say we trust our guts."

"You know I like to have a plan. And stick to it."

"That's why we're such a great team. Follow my lead." Tony slid his helmet over his head and engaged the latch. "Check my seal."

"The alien ship is slowing to match our vector." Liz's voice sounded tinny in the helmet speakers as Quinn donned her own.

"Stop calling them aliens," Maerk said in the background.

"What should I call them?" Liz snapped back. "Unidentified visitors is too long."

"UVs is perfect."

Quinn tuned out the bickering as she checked Tony's helmet seal. "Seals are green." She patted the top of his helmet in confirmation, then turned her back so he could check hers.

"Seals are green." Tony's pat was more of a caress.

Something thudded against the side of the ship.

"They've got some kind of tube or bridge," Liz reported. "Looks like it sealed against the side of the *Swan*, so they can pressurize it."

Quinn swallowed hard and sucked in a deep breath to calm her thundering heart. "Go time." She gave Tony a tiny smile.

"Go time." He turned and led the way to the air lock. They stepped inside, and he cycled the internal hatch. "Liz, can you—"

His cousin interrupted. "The UV's connector is pressurized. My sensors indicate the atmo is pretty close to human standard. The probe in the hatch says it's breathable. If you trust these things."

"That's why we have these." Tony tapped his helmet. "Good thinking Maerk. Who knew first contact with al—UVs would be so complicated."

"Based on popular media, these events happen on planets, so…" Quinn took another deep breath, trying to settle the marshmallow bar now sitting like a brick in her stomach. It had helped clear her mind a bit—or maybe that was the terror seeping in.

They waited, taking turns peering through the tiny window in the external hatch. For what felt like a very long time, nothing happened.

"We have movement," Liz said, a tremor running through her voice. "Their hatch is opening. I see two beings in the opening, but they don't appear to be exiting the ship."

"That's our cue." Tony entered the commands, and the ship's hatch popped open. He stepped back as he pulled it inward, treading on Quinn's toes.

"Careful." She shifted to the side, then peered down the long, transparent tube connecting the two ships. The beings on the far side looked humanoid—two arms, two legs, heads protected by small helmets. Or maybe they had small heads. She stifled a laugh she feared might border on hysterical. "Do we—" She made a pushing motion.

"That's why we're here!" Tony's voice warbled the tiniest bit—just enough to reassure her he was nervous, too. "Liz, do they have gravity in the bridge?"

Quinn gripped Tony's arm through the thick suit. "It doesn't look like it." She sucked in another steadying breath as the two figures drifted toward them through the tunnel. About halfway across, the lead figure grabbed one of the ribs giving the connecting tunnel structure and stopped. The second one bumped into the first and bounced back, as if he—they? It?—weren't expecting the halt. The following one flailed for a moment, then grabbed another of the ribs. The leader's head turned to look back, then rotated back to the *Swan* again.

"Let's go." Tony gave Quinn's fingers a quick squeeze, then he pushed away from the hatch, floating toward the UVs.

Quinn took another deep breath and followed.

CHAPTER TEN
SITI

"They're human!" The words burst out of me before I could censor them. Remembering the Darenti, I added, "Or human shaped."

Yasmi's agitated chittering came through the comms until Joss shushed her. I'd left her in the cockpit for the initial meeting.

"I can see that." Joss's dry tone reminded me he could see the footage from the camera on my collar—as could Captain Salu and who knew how many explorers back on the Observer.

And this video would be preserved for posterity, so I should try to be professional. "They aren't coming out of their ship, so I'm going to the mid-point."

"I'm coming with you, sir." Rodriguez's bulky presence at my shoulder—with his obvious weapon held at the ready—provided little comfort. For all we knew, these beings could snap us like twigs or rip open the transfer tunnel with their minds, or— I clamped down on my imagination and pushed away from the shuttle.

Catching one of the tunnel's ribs near the mid-point, I set my magnetic boots to the floor with an inaudible snap.

Rodriguez bumped into me. "Sorry, sir. Didn't realize—" He sounded nervous.

I glanced back. "Take a second. Breathe."

While Rodriguez got himself sorted, I turned to watch the Berzans. "They appear humanoid." I'd already said that, but a little repetition wouldn't hurt anyone. And maybe they could edit my wild exclamation before sending this feed to the media. I'm sure the ship would be running data analysis on our vid, but CEC protocol demanded I narrate my findings. "About standard human size, too. They're coming toward me."

The two beings pushed away from the Berzan ship and drifted forward. As they approached, I gave myself a mental head slap and engaged my helmet's optical zoom. "They *are* human!" The lead Berzan's face appeared large in my optical display. He looked a little like the supply sergeant at the Academy.

"Is that Newsome?" Joss's voice shook in my audio implant. We'd set up a private call before I left the ship.

"Looks like him, doesn't it? They're either really good at imitating us, or…" Or what? How could they be human? "Did Earth send ships to other systems in the Exodus?"

"My dad has only ever mentioned the original five: Armstrong, Grissom, Gagarin, Sally Ride, Lewei." Joss's father had been alive on Earth when the Exodus ended, then gone into deep sleep for most of the intervening five hundred years.

As the Berzans set their feet against the deck—they didn't appear to have magnetic boots because they both drifted up—I inventoried them for the record, using my enhanced optics to zoom in on features and analyze their build. "The first subject appears to be male, perhaps one point seven meters tall, estimated seventy-five kilos. Brown hair, tan skin, brown eyes. If they're human, I'd estimate his age in the early forties, unrejuvenated." I scrutinized the other. "The second looks female, dark hair, eyes hazel, skin is more olive toned. Height, one point eight meters, mass, sixty-five kilos. I'm making assumptions, of course, based on our cultural standards and physiology."

"Understood, Lieutenant." Captain Salu's voice came through my helmet, surprising me. I knew she was watching but didn't realize she'd chime in. "And entered into the record. Please continue."

I lifted a hand, palm out, and activated my external speakers. "Hello. We come in peace."

The Berzan's eyes widened in surprise. "You speak Standard."

I choked. We were dozens of lightyears from home, but this Berzan spoke my language. With a heavy accent, but understandable. "I—yes. How is that possible?"

"You tell me. You're the alien."

I toggled my speakers off. "Captain, are you getting this? These are people. People! And they speak Standard. What—"

"I am monitoring the situation, Lieutenant. And I have no answers. But I will be asking a lot of questions when we get home. Please, continue."

"Are you sure, sir? Maybe *you* should be down here…"

"You can be assured I will meet with their leadership as soon as you set it up." Her clipped tones snapped me out of my confusion.

I flicked the speakers back on. "I'm Lieutenant Serenity Kassis of the Colonial Explorer Corps. We didn't realize this system was inhabited when we arrived—" I broke off. Maybe I shouldn't have admitted that. Too late now. "Captain Dramira Salu of the *Loyal Observer* would like to meet with—"

"My leader?" The Berzan bit his lip.

"Take me to your leader." Joss snickered in my ear.

I toggled my audio. "How can they know the same jokes?"

"Tony, cut it out." The woman pushed past the man and extended a flat hand, fingers pointed toward me. Her thick glove made her fingers look puffy. "Hi, I'm Quinn Templeton. This is Tony Bergan. We're from… well, I'm from Romara. He's from N'Avon."

I stuck out my hand, mimicking her positioning. She reached over and grasped my hand and pumped it up and down once then released me. "I'm from Grissom," I said. "Nice to meet you. My captain would like to meet the heads of your planetary government."

"Grissom?" Tony's brows came down, a crease forming between them. "Like Gus Grissom?"

"How does he know who Gus Grissom is?" Joss demanded.

I pointed a finger at the man. "You're from Earth!"

"Not personally." Tony turned to look at Quinn, then rotated back to me, catching himself on the curved metal rib before he turned all the way around. "But our people were originally from there. Centuries ago."

"Kassis," Captain Salu snapped. "Set up a meeting with their leadership."

"Yes, sir." I cleared my throat. "Can we arrange a diplomatic discussion with your government?"

Tony and Quinn exchanged another awkward look, then the woman pressed a hand to the side of her giant helmet and spoke. "Liz, tell Doug he needs to call Romara. We need someone in charge." Her hand dropped. "Would you like to come aboard while we wait?"

Rodriguez tapped my shoulder, and my audio pinged with his identifier. "Don't recommend, sir. We would be at their mercy."

"Overruled." Salu's tone brooked no argument. "Go with them, Kassis. Gain their trust and learn as much as you can. Rodriguez, you, too."

I made sure my external speakers were on but turned my head to face my companion before replying out loud. "We're well within the *Observer*'s weapons range, so I'm sure they won't try anything." I considered feigning surprise over my already activated audio, but when I turned back to the Berzans, Tony's lips quirked, and Quinn's eyes twinkled. Obviously, they knew that comment was for their benefit. With a shrug, I accepted. "Thank you, that would be lovely."

"Way to sell it," Joss whispered through my audio as I flipped my magnetic boots to neutral.

Drifting up from the floor, I toggled everything off except the internal audio. "I'm getting déjà vu."

"From Darenti?"

"No, Earth."

"How so?"

"Well, we arrived in system not expecting anyone to be here." I ticked the items off on mental fingers as I pushed away from the rib I'd been holding. "When we made contact, you all spoke our language."

"Don't forget accusing said natives of being Gagarians," Joss said dryly.

"No one's done that."

"Yet."

"I suppose they could be…" I followed Quinn and Tony into their air lock, Rodriguez close behind.

Tony stepped around me and pushed the hatch closed. "We can't open the internal with this unlocked."

Quinn's gaze darted to Tony, then back to me.

"Did you see that?" Joss asked. "That wasn't true."

"I'm aware."

"Aware of what, Lieutenant?" Captain Salu joined the conversation again.

"Tony lied about the airlock. They can pop both ends in this configuration."

Salu grunted. "They're protecting their ship—I would do the same. I don't think the danger to you or Rodriguez is significant at this point. Continue."

"Yes, sir." I fought to keep my tone even. Not that I disagreed with her assessment, but I suspected my safety was not her highest priority at this time.

The exterior hatch engaged, and my audio went dark. I toggled it on again. "Captain Salu?"

Nothing.

Tony opened the interior hatch.

"Joss, can you hear me?" As Tony and Quinn pulled off their bulky helmets, I held up a finger to stop Rodriguez from doing the same. I flipped through my settings and engaged my amplifier. "Joss?"

"I got you. Increased the gain on the system. Their hull appears to mute most of your signal." Joss hummed for a second. "I think we're good now."

"Roger." I nodded at Rodriguez and unsnapped my helmet latches, folding the flexible covering back into its casing. I sniffed the pleasant lemony air. "What is that?"

Rodriguez froze, his hand on his still-latched helmet. "Maybe I should stay buttoned up, sir." His question through my implant didn't really sound like a question.

"Affirmative," Salu said. "Verify before you trust."

"We did verify, sir," Joss put in. "Siti's suit is running a constant air quality check. And I think the saying goes the other way around. Sir."

Tony hung his helmet on a peg and unzipped the front of his suit. "Liz keeps a diffuser running. She hates canned air." He and Quinn stripped off their bulky pressure suits, revealing startlingly normal looking clothing beneath. Quinn wore a red top and black leggings, while Tony sported heavy-looking dark blue pants and a gray shirt with the phrase "I'm not like most teens, I'm 47," in difficult to decipher but legible text.

Joss whistled softly. "They use the same alphabet we do. Probably not Gagarians."

"Spelling is off," Salu muttered.

"Languages change over time." Joss's comment sounded like a quote but might have been personal experience. Joss had been born centuries before the CEC rediscovered Earth. As a pre-teen, he and his family had gone into suspended animation and woken only a few years before we arrived.

"Welcome to the *Swan of the Night*." Tony swung the interior hatch wide and stepped inside. "It's my cousin's ship."

Quinn frowned at Tony, clearly suggesting he keep personal business private.

"What's your working theory, Torres?" Salu asked.

"Lieutenant, my scan is lighting up," Rodriguez said at the same time.

"I'm sorry, sir, but can you take this discussion to another channel? I need to focus on the mission." Despite my words, I probably didn't sound sorry. But trying to keep track of multiple conversations meant I wasn't really present for any of them. I flicked that connection to mute. "Rodriguez, report."

"Multiple small arms present in the ship. Several more in the cockpit. Possible shielded weapons storage over there." As we stepped into a brightly lit room, he nodded at a painting on the far wall.

"Makes sense. Both Bergen and Templeton are wearing weapons." I jerked my head at our hosts. "As are we. That hideous picture probably hides a small armament cache."

"What did you say?" Quinn's bright eyes locked on my own.

Crap. Did I say that aloud? All CEC officers were trained to keep their internal audio at a subvocal level, but maybe I slipped. "That painting is interesting."

Quinn's frown twitched at the corners. "Interesting is a good word. I don't know where Liz found it. I wish she'd put it back."

"I heard that!" A woman's voice rang through the compartment, projected from obvious speakers in the corners of the space. "That's an original Karona. It's going to be worth a fortune someday."

Rolling her eyes, Quinn gestured to the table. "Please, have a seat. That was Liz Marconi, our pilot."

Liz heaved a loud, long-suffering sigh. "I'm the *captain* of this ship not just the pilot!"

"Hush, Liz, they aren't supposed to know we're here," a deep male voice said in soothing tones.

"Now they know about *both* of us."

Covering his laughter with a clearly fake cough, Tony stared at the ceiling. "Cool it, you two."

Quinn hurried to a small panel beside a door at the forward end of the compartment. She fiddled with something, and Liz's now indistinct muttering cut out. "Very professional, aren't we?"

"I take it you aren't an official delegation, then?" I pulled out a chair and sat, keeping both of our hosts and that door within sight. It was possible the cargo area held a platoon of soldiers, but watching them was Rodriguez's responsibility. Not that we could do much if they did bring troops.

Tony set a tray of glasses on the table and began filling them from a pitcher. "Water?"

Quinn pulled out a chair and sat. "Lunesco doesn't really do formal."

"Lunesco?" I asked.

"Our planet. Our... director of defense sent us, with the approval and oversight of the planetary governor." Quinn's gaze snapped to Tony and away again—her tell. That last part wasn't true.

"Perhaps your director of defense could meet with my captain, then?" I took the glass Tony handed me with a nod of thanks and set it on the table. My suit contained a small bladder of potable water, and I wasn't going to trust their offering without testing it first.

Tony sipped from his glass, as if to prove the water was safe. "You can test the water—and the glass—if you wish. I would." He shot a smirk at Quinn.

I dipped the tip of a gloved finger into the water and ran my analyzer. "Our primary mission is to explore new, usually uninhabited, systems, so we test everything before we consume it. I appreciate your forbearance." The water read clean. I lifted the glass and sipped a tiny amount for show.

"How did you happen to choose this system?" Quinn asked.

"There's a long vetting process involving unmanned probes, comm relays, and jump beacons. When we find one that's promising, we send a manned team." I gestured at myself. "The probe we sent this time didn't detect your communications, which is an unusual oversight. As soon as we jumped in, we realized this system was inhabited. You were telling me about your governmental structure."

"We were avoiding telling you about our governmental structure," Tony said with a laugh. "Lunesco is a fringe world. A well-protected fringe world, so don't get any ideas about conquest."

I lifted both hands, ignoring Templeton and Rodriguez's gasps of dismay. If Tony was going to be straight-forward, I would, too. "The CEC is an explorer corps, not military. We look for new planets for mankind to colonize and avoid those already in use. Of course, I don't speak for my government. I'm just a low-level explorer."

"How many inhabited planets do you have?" Quinn asked.

"Don't answer that," Salu snapped.

"More than one." I shrugged apologetically. "Sorry, I've been advised not to offer that kind of information. I can't tell you where we are in relation to this system, how far away, or anything about our people. I have been authorized to request a meeting with your leadership for someone farther up the chain in the Colonial Commonwealth government who can answer—probably answer—some of those questions."

"Colonial Commonwealth?" Tony raised a brow. "That implies colonization by someone. Can you tell us who colonized your planet —or planets?"

I frowned in surprise. Hadn't I already answered that question? "Earth, of course."

CHAPTER ELEVEN
QUINN

Biting her tongue to keep from exclaiming, Quinn turned to Tony and raised her brows. "Are you still—is Earth— We were taught Earth was evacuated hundreds of years ago."

"It was. Mostly. The original five planets were colonized, and—" Lt Kassis broke off, consternation sliding across her face before she blanked it. "I'm not authorized to discuss our history. Perhaps you can tell me about your government. You said Lunesco is a fringe world. That implies a more central area?"

Quinn sat back, crossing her arms. "If you won't tell us anything, why should we share?"

"Yeah, what she said!" Liz exclaimed through the speakers.

"Liz." Tony glared at the door leading to the cockpit. "Will you excuse me a moment?" He rose and walked to the door, activating the communications panel. After a low-voiced but heated discussion, he returned to the table. "Sorry about that. My cous—captain is over eager."

Pulling out a chair, he sat and pulled his chair close to the table. "Lunesco is a fringe world but part of the Romaran republic. Romara is the seat of the government. We are not official representatives of either. There's also another… political entity called the N'Avon Commonwealth. That's where I'm from."

"Tony." Quinn put a hand on his arm. "Should you—"

He raised a hand. "I'm still a Commonwealth citizen. And if we've made contact with the lost colonies from Earth, I need to let N'Avon know."

"Lost colonies?" Rodriguez, who had remained standing by the entrance, took a half-step forward. "If anyone is a lost colony, it's you. We know where Earth is."

"Rodriguez!" Kassis snapped.

Rodriguez flushed and stepped back against the wall again, his weapon still held across his body. "Sorry, sir."

The lieutenant turned to face us again. "It sounds to me like we need to set up a three-way—" Her face went red, and her lips pressed together. After a second, she took a deep breath. "I'm clearly not a politician. We need to set up a meeting between my people, Romara, and N'Avon. Any idea how we do that?"

"General La Gama has already sent a message to Romara." Quinn sipped her water, wishing it were something stronger.

"I sent one to N'Avon, too." Tony pulled his comtab from beneath the table and waved it at them.

Quinn blinked at him in surprise. "When did you do that?"

"I drafted it on the way out here, added the details—and a video of our meeting—when I spoke to Liz, and sent it just now." The comtab made a whooshing noise. "Well, now. It'll take a while to get from my handler to the appropriate levels, of course."

"Auntie B's message is probably going to take a while, too. You know what they think of Lunesco." Quinn eyed their guests. She probably shouldn't have admitted anything like that in front of the strangers, but as Kassis admitted, she wasn't a politician, either. "As we said, Lunesco is a fringe world. Romara may take their time responding to our messages."

"Well, that's easy to fix." Kassis slapped her hands on the table. "If you tell us where Romara is, we can go to them. I'm sure an armed vessel arriving in their system will—what? Hang on." She lifted a finger, and her gaze went to the ugly painting on the wall, but Quinn got the impression Kassis wasn't looking at Liz's beloved Karona.

They waited while Kassis seemed to zone out, Tony drumming his fingers lightly on the scuffed table. Quinn sipped her water again.

"Sorry about that." Kassis's brown face flushed a warmer pink. "I've been instructed to stop threatening sovereign governments with military actions. That wasn't my intention at all. As I said, we aren't a military ship. The *Loyal Observer* will wait in orbit here until your government issues an invitation to go elsewhere. If your government prefers we take a different, more distant orbit, we will comply. I have also been instructed to tell you that several smaller ships will be jumping into the system with official government envoys. They will take any aggressive actions toward the *Observer* or any other CEC ships as acts of war." She raised both hands. "I tried to tell her that last part was way more aggressive than anything I said, but—hang on." She went blank again.

"How is she communicating with them?" Quinn asked Tony in a low voice.

He shrugged. "N'Avon has experimented with integrated communications devices. And you know the Federation tested some that failed spectacularly."

Quinn shivered. She hadn't read the official reports on that technological blunder, but it was an open secret the volunteers had ended up in a facility for victims of brain injuries. "We should have brought Sashelle."

Tony nodded. "I thought about that, but she's off with Francine. Maybe I should send her a quick message, too."

Since the revolution, Doug had been employing Sashelle to vet personnel applying to work in Lunesco's defense station. The caat—a sapient, sentient species indigenous to Hadriana—had the ability to scan applicants and determine their intentions, aspirations, and potential personality flaws. But Sashelle had no desire to spend the rest of her long life on Lunesco and had rejoined Francine as soon as Doug's organization reached a stable level. Her expertise would be valuable now.

"Sorry." Kassis smiled grimly. "I've been instructed to reiterate my request for a meeting with the governments of Romara and N'Avon and to tell you we will withdraw to an orbit at the outer reaches of your system to ensure safety for all of us." She pushed back her chair. "I've also been ordered to return to my ship. They want to send someone with stronger diplomatic skills."

Quinn's comtab buzzed. She glanced at the screen and frowned. Why was Auntie B calling her? "Please don't leave yet. I have to take this. General La Gama." She rose and hurried past Rodriguez. Pulling the airlock closed behind her, she answered the call. "What's up?"

"I like that girl. We want to keep dealing with her."

"I don't have any control over who they send." Quinn pushed the hair that had fallen free from her bun away from her face.

"No, but we can request her next time they want to chat. Make her our liaison."

"Why?"

"She's honest. Not too polished. Willing to say what she means, not just what she's been told."

Quinn frowned and stopped pacing long enough to straighten Tony's helmet in his locker. "You can tell all of that by listening to our conversation?" They'd tried to rig up a video, but the distance from Lunesco made that difficult.

"Sashelle says she's the one."

"Sashelle is with Francine." Quinn dropped to the bench beneath the suit lockers.

"Yes, and they're both listening to the audio, too."

"You put us on an interstellar call with Francine?"

"Hi, Quinn," Francine said.

"They take a lot of power, but with our new solar array, power is cheap." Auntie B cackled a little.

"Hi, Francine. Hello, Sashelle. Can she really *read* people this far away?" Quinn asked.

Francine hummed for a few seconds, then spoke. "Not as well as she can in person. But based on what she's heard, she thinks Lieutenant Kassis is honest. More importantly, she's impulsive enough to let things slip out—like the bit about just flying to Romara. We'll meet you there. Sashelle feels she needs to be there." She sighed. "Not my choice, but apparently my primary role in life is now caat transportation. See you soon." She disconnected.

"Do what you can to keep Kassis on the team, Quinn. La Gama out."

Quinn chuckled as she looked down at her now dark comtab. Auntie B reverted to General La Gama like switching a light. She slid the device in her pocket and opened the airlock to find Kassis and Rodriguez standing outside with Tony right behind them.

"Oh, you startled me." Quinn clutched a hand to her chest. "Auntie —I mean General La Gama, has requested Lieutenant Kassis be retained as our liaison with the CEC ship."

Kassis frowned. "I'm not sure how that's going to—" She broke off, then shook her head. "Never mind. The captain approves. Do you need me to stay here, or go to Lunesco, or—" She lifted both hands in question.

Quinn blinked. "The general didn't say. How long will it take for your governmental types to get here?"

Kassis pursed her lips, brows raised. "About a week, the captain says."

The comtab buzzed with a message, and Quinn waved it at the lieutenant. "General La Gama invites you to join us at the Homestead until that time."

"Do you mind if I pop back to the ship and pack a bag? I wasn't intending to stay long…" She looked down at her body then back at Quinn. "I don't have a toothbrush. Or a change of clothes."

Tony slid past Quinn and looked out the little window in the airlock hatch. "Can that thing fly to the planet?"

"Of course," Kassis answered. "We use those shuttles to drop teams dirtside all the time. It's what we do."

"And is it armed?"

"Yes—in case we need to fend off wild animals." Kassis rubbed below her ear. "I can have Joss bring me down. Do you mind if he stays, too?" She rubbed her neck again and wrinkled her nose.

"Joss?" Tony asked.

"My pilot, Lieutenant Joss Torres. My friend. He's from Earth."

Quinn and Tony exchanged a quick look as Quinn's comtab rattled again. She read the message and nodded at Kassis. "Yes. Please bring the Earthling."

CHAPTER TWELVE
SITI

As Joss piloted the shuttle toward the Lunescan landing field, I reviewed my conversation with Captain Salu when we returned to the ship. She'd called HQ as soon as they got the beacons launched, of course. The Colonial government had decided on an official delegation to meet with the Romara Republic instead of leaving it up to Salu. Even the fastest Naval vessel required three days to reach the jump rings. And while the pilots and ship were ready and waiting in orbit above Grissom, the politics involved in selecting the envoy was expected to take several additional days.

Meanwhile, Salu had been instructed to stay on the ship. Officially, the government didn't want additional personnel muddying the waters. I—and my pilot—were to be the only interface with the Lunescans until our delegation arrived. *After* the meeting, Salu told me to watch my step. The government would be quick to sacrifice my career should I say or do anything to which the Lunescans took offense.

"I'm not thrilled with being the scapegoat again," Joss said, as if reading my mind. He flicked through his navigation screens. In the rear view, the *Loyal Observer* grew visibly smaller as it withdrew to a more distant orbit around Lunesco's star.

I glanced at my holo-ring to ensure the audio jammer our friend Diz had invented was still running. Officially, every moment of this visit was supposed to be recorded, but I wasn't above bending the rules a little to protect my privacy. The admirals up the chain of command didn't need to listen to my private conversation with my friend. "At least you have Earth to protect you."

Since Joss wasn't a Colonial Commonwealth citizen, being thrown under the shuttle for any perceived slip-ups would land him back on Earth rather than in prison for treason. Not that I had any intention of doing anything treasonous, but based on past experience, I wasn't one hundred percent sure my intentions would save me if the government chose to blame me for something later.

"Don't worry. If you go to jail, Dad will take care of you." Joss made a note in his flight log and leaned back in his chair.

"Because you have a lot of CC spies in custody on Earth that you can exchange me for?" I chuckled. When we first met on Earth, Joss and his friends had watched a lot of original Earth spy movies. "Or are you going to stage an illegal prison break?"

"Whatever it takes. But it would be easier if you stayed out of trouble." He kicked his feet onto my armrest and laced his fingers behind his head.

I shoved his boots off my chair. "You think I don't know that? I don't go looking for it."

"It always finds you."

"You're almost always with me—I think you're the trouble magnet." I shook a finger at his face. "But seriously, we need to be careful. Did Salu talk to you?"

"Of course." He made a face, his eyes darting to the flashing red icon of Diz's jammer floating above my side of the little cockpit. "She told me to keep my mouth shut—which she knows is not my strong suit. I think the only reason she let me take this mission instead of Hillard or Drenton is because of that Earth protection you mentioned. She's uneasy about us being alone on Lunesco, and not because she's worried about the locals."

I narrowed my eyes at him. "A minute ago, you said you didn't want to be the scapegoat, so why'd you volunteer for this gig?"

He grinned, his white teeth bright in his dark face. "How could I pass it up? I mean, first—aliens. That's why I joined the CEC. And once you mentioned my Earth heritage to the Lunescans, it was kind of a done deal." He leaned across the narrow aisle to shove my shoulder. "You know I wouldn't leave you on your own. Plus—aliens."

"They aren't really aliens, though. They're originally from Earth, too. They're some kind of long-lost cousins." I jutted my chin at his holo screens. "The *Swan* is changing trajectories."

Joss snapped to attention, his body swiveling to face his controls faster than seemed possible. His hands flicked through the screens, zooming in on the ship. "They're taking a landing vector. Did you know they require a runway to take off and land? No VTOL."

"Yeah, I got that." I smirked. "I may not be a full-time pilot like you, but I'm good enough to understand the lingo." My smile faded as my mind turned back to the upcoming visit. "I'm supposed to be under constant surveillance—gotta record it all for posterity. I'm betting Salu knows we're cheating right now, but no one is going to care what a couple of lieutenants say in the ship. But if you have anything private to say while we're on the dirt, call me." I tapped below my ear to indicate my implant.

"I figured. Time to buckle in." He nodded at the screens and reached for his harness. "Should be a smooth ride, but this is an alien planet." A huge grin spread across his face. "Isn't it weird to think we're the first people to—"

"We're CEC. We're the first people all the time." I pulled the straps over my shoulders and clicked the buckles.

"Yeah, but those are regular planets. Empty. This is a whole new civilization. And we're first, first. You and me—no one but us has ever met these people." He frowned. "I'm kind of surprised we don't have a squad of explorers providing security for us."

"Yeah, me too." The captain had insisted Rodriguez stay on the *Observer*. "Salu said she wanted to project trust."

"I got the briefing, too. We trust them enough to only send a couple of idiot junior officers, but they'll be armed." Joss patted the stunner in his holster. "Not with anything lethal, of course. We haven't been in touch with these people for hundreds of years. Why are we in such a rush right now?"

That thought had occurred to me, too. Once we'd established these were humans who would welcome a diplomatic delegation, why hadn't the government mogs insisted we retreat to the ship and wait for them?

The comm blipped. As Joss accepted the incoming message, I remembered to turn off Diz's jammer. I wasn't sure how it would interact with the shuttle's systems.

"Kassis, Torres." Captain Salu's face appeared in a holo centered in front of the cockpit. "Any last comments or questions before we begin the recording?"

I exchanged a look with Joss. I'd been under the impression the recording had started the moment we left the ship. He rolled his eyes toward the bottom corner of the display where a tiny red triangle flashed. Recording in progress.

I smiled brightly at the captain. "No, sir. We have our orders. We're ready."

Her left eyelid dropped a fraction in what could have been an involuntary twitch but might have been a wink. "Excellent. We're eager to see how this plays out. Anyone want to chicken out?"

We automatically responded to the ritual question. "Hell, no!"

"Excellent. I am available at *any time* if you need advice or a sounding board. Or an excuse." She nodded and the holo flicked off.

Joss swiped the comm holo away and double checked the landing coordinates the Lunescans had given us. My internal audio pinged with his ID. "An excuse?"

"She told me if the Lunescans asked something I shouldn't answer or wanted me to do something I wasn't comfortable with, I could use her as an excuse. 'My captain won't like it.' Kind of like blaming your parent."

"She didn't offer *me* that."

"That's because as far as the Lunescans know, you work for me. She's my excuse, and I'm *yours*."

"I'd like to remind you that you and I are exactly the same rank. Down to the date of commissioning."

I rolled my eyes. "Yes, but on this mission, I'm in charge. And you know it."

"Yes, sir." He tapped his index finger to his brow and then flipped it at me in a gesture I recognized from my time on Earth as a sarcastic salute.

The comm flashed again. "Colonial shuttle, this is Lunesco field. The *Swan* has taxied off the runway. You are cleared to land."

"Thank you, Lunesco field." Joss's voice was calm and official. "Please indicate our parking spot."

"I'll direct you to a parking place after you land."

"We land in the parking spot, Lunesco. My ship doesn't require a horizontal runway or taxi. Please advise."

Surprised muttering and a muted conversation issued from the speaker. Then the voice returned. "My mistake, Colonial. Transmitting parking coordinates now."

A small map of the field appeared above the console, with a blue outline flashing. Joss swiped the map and pushed the coordinates to the navigation system. "Roger, Lunesco. Landing now. Thanks for your help."

"It's amazing how quickly the tech guys were able to interface our comm systems with the Lunescans'." I leaned back in my seat and tightened the straps. Not that I didn't trust Joss's flying—he really was one of the best pilots in the CEC—but this shuttle was old, and the artificial gravity might not compensate fully for turbulence as we came through the atmosphere. Joss grunted in agreement, his attention fully focused on the landing.

I patted my pocket to make sure Yasmi was safe. I'd debated whether taking her to the dirt was a wise idea. The captain hadn't forbidden it, and gliders often accompanied Phase 1 teams. They had proven effective early warning systems for ravenous local creatures as well as having a sixth sense when it came to geological dangers.

They'd even been known to bring rescuers to explorers who'd been injured. But those were alien planets with no civilized occupants.

My cheeks grew warm as I remembered my first planet-fall, on Earth. I'd casually brought my sair-glider, Liam, without checking with the mission commander. And been properly reprimanded for it. Older and wiser, I'd learned from my errors. But now *I* was the mission commander and had to make the decision myself. And since the captain hadn't forbidden it—despite her apparent dislike of the creatures—I decided to ask forgiveness instead of permission, should it become necessary. Under my hand, Yasmi snuggled deeper into the padded pocket.

The ship performed flawlessly, and Joss landed us neatly in the center of the indicated rectangle. He ran a quick shutdown checklist, leaving the ship in fast-launch mode. If we needed to get away, we'd want it to be quick. I unlatched my harness and headed to the back where I unstrapped our luggage. We'd each packed a small bag with essentials and a larger one we'd leave in the shuttle with extra uniforms and equipment. As explorers, we'd learned to pack light for fast and easy travel.

I slid my grav belt around my waist and latched it. "You about done up there?" I called.

"Gotta do it right." Joss appeared in the doorway to the cargo hold. "You got my stuff?"

Using the straps, I swung the duffle at him. He caught it and slung it over his shoulders like a backpack, then accepted the grav belt. As he latched it on, he chuckled. "Remember how impressed we were with these things back on Earth? And now I wear one all the time."

I patted Joss's cheek as I passed him. "You Earthers were so cute. Ready?"

"Ready." He followed me into the airlock. "Engaging personal shield." According to the Lunescans, fierce winds blew almost continuously on their planet, filling the air with dust and grit.

Activating my shield, I flicked the airlock's cycle command. The system whirred, and lights flicked from red to green. Then the external hatch clicked. "Here we go." I opened the door to a new world.

CHAPTER THIRTEEN
QUINN

THE COLONIAL SHIP settled neatly in place, as if set there by a careful hand. Quinn and Tony listened to the landing field controller welcoming them to Lunesco, then pulled their goggles over their eyes and headed out onto the field. At Quinn's request, Pender had given the Colonials the closest parking spot, forcing the *Swan* to take a farther one.

Maerk waved as he and Liz approached. He said something, inaudible over the howling wind.

Quinn pointed at her ear and shook her head, wondering what it would be like to have an internal comm system like Lieutenant Kassis clearly had. She'd been at the Federation's Defense Research Program —DRiP in common parlance—when they'd pioneered integrated audio tech. Initial human tests hadn't gone well, but that never stopped the Federation. Rumor had it the N'Avon Commonwealth— also known as the Krimson Empire, thanks to their red flag—had perfected the gear, but even Tony didn't have one.

Maerk moved closer, crowding her into Tony. "I said, they're right behind us."

"They landed before you got to your parking spot." Quinn pointed at the Colonial ship. "Just plunk, right there, on the spot."

Maerk turned to look at the newcomers' ship and whistled. "Sweet. I gotta get us some VTOL engines."

"I dunno what they use—they didn't even lift any dust when they dropped." Liz shook her head in admiration.

"You saw them? I thought you were watching me taxi." Maerk looked both disappointed in his ex's lack of interest and impressed that she trusted him to taxi without supervision.

"I watched both. You were moving so slow I didn't need to watch continuously."

"You told me to drive slow!"

"Because I wanted to watch the Colonials." Liz flung an arm at the ship.

As if in response to her gesture, the exterior hatch folded down into a ramp, and two black-clad figures appeared in the opening. One lifted an arm in greeting, and they trotted down the ramp.

"They don't have goggles on," Maerk said.

Quinn winced as a particularly forceful gust stung the tiny, exposed slice of her face. She adjusted her scarf, squinting at the visitors. "Maybe they have some kind of invisible protection. It's becoming very clear they are ahead of us in tech development."

On her other side, Tony grunted in agreement. "Even by N'Avon standards, they appear to be advanced. I hope that isn't a bad omen."

"What do you mean?" Maerk asked.

"Getting invaded by a technologically superior force never works out well for the indigenous people. Even if the invaders are human."

"Especially if the invaders are human," Quinn said. "Look at Hadriana."

The two visitors stopped in front of the Marconis. Lieutenant Kassis looked much the same as she had before—tan skin, dark wavy hair pulled back in a braid. Her companion was taller with darker skin, short, tightly curled black hair, and the broad shoulders of a weightlifter. Both wore black uniforms with a stylized patch on the left chest and a name tag on the right. The letters were mostly legible but more angular than she was accustomed to. Two little silver circles on their collars might indicate rank. They each wore two belts—one with a holster containing an unmistakable weapon, and one that didn't appear to have any function—nothing hanging from it, no belt loops to hold up their pants.

Kassis reached out to shake hands. "Thank you for inviting us to visit. This is my pilot and friend, Lieutenant Joshua Torres."

Torres smiled, showing off straight white teeth. "You can call me Joss. Or Viking."

Kassis rolled her eyes. "Don't call him Viking. No one calls him that. His callsign is Caveman."

"Hey, this is a new world. A chance to reinvent myself. Thanks for nothing, Siti."

Failing to hide his smile, Tony gestured toward the little building at the edge of the airfield. "We have transport waiting. Lieutenant Kassis said you are from Earth?"

Torres glanced at the other lieutenant, then nodded slowly. "That isn't supposed to be common knowledge."

Kassis made a face at him. "Cat's out of the bag."

"Cat?" Quinn asked. "Bag?"

The other woman lifted both hands, palms up. "It's a figure of speech. It means you already know about him being from Earth. Funny how some idioms persist, and others don't."

Quinn cocked her head. "What do you mean? I don't think we've used any idioms in our conversations with you."

"No, but Joss, born and raised on Earth—he knew that phrase. I grew up on Grissom—five hundred years away from Earth."

"Five hundred years?" Tony gestured again toward the building, urging the visitors to move out of the wind. "You mean light-years?"

Although their heads were completely uncovered, the visitors didn't seem to care about the sand-laden gusts biting into every exposed bit of skin. Quinn noticed a sheen around their heads—some kind of shield protecting them from the elements? They'd said they belonged to an *explorer* corps. She supposed they'd need protection from alien environments.

Torres laughed again, sounding relaxed and friendly. "The Exodus happened five hundred years ago, but we have people on Earth who were alive at the time. Like my parents. They were in deep sleep for the intervening centuries. A lot of our customs and habits were impacted by their… ancient knowledge, if you will. So, we refer to some differences—and similarities—between Earth and the Colonies by time instead of distance."

Tony's jaw dropped, and Quinn felt her own mirror it. Luckily the scarf across her lower face kept her from swallowing more sand. "Five hundred year old people?"

"I'm two hundred and seventy." Torres laughed again at their expressions. "When I was a kid, my family went into the basement—the suspended animation chamber inside the Dome—and we came out a few years before Siti and her dad showed up on our doorstep. It's a long story. And usually requires something to drink."

Kassis slapped Torres's arm. "Joss."

Watching the interplay, Quinn realized the friendship between the two Colonials was real, not just comradery between military teammates. She hurried the last few steps around the building and opened the door to Jessian's van. "Please, come in out of the wind."

Kassis did a little double-take, then climbed inside. "I'm so sorry. We have our personal shields to protect us from the elements. It didn't occur to me…"

"Is that the shimmer around your head?" Quinn indicated seats in the back row, then slid in next to the other woman and demonstrated how to fasten the lap belt. The road to the Homestead was straight and flat, so the shoulder straps weren't necessary—even with Jessian's wild driving.

As if in response to her thought, the woman in the driver's seat swiveled to peer at them over the seat back. "Hi! I'm Jessian. I'm pretty much the only driver around here, so if you need transport, you'll have to call me." She extended a little cardboard rectangle to Quinn.

Tony casually pulled the card from Jessian's fingers as he climbed in and tucked it into his pocket. "No need, Jess. We'll be escorting the visitors. This is Lieutenant Kassis and Lieutenant Torres from the—" He broke off, catching Quinn's eyes.

"From a visiting ship." Quinn pressed her lips together.

"I get it. You don't want me to know they're from an undiscovered planet." Jessian grinned at their obvious dismay. "You didn't think I'd miss that, did you? Please. But don't worry, I won't say a word to anyone. Auntie B would slay me."

Tony laughed. "Of course Jessian knows." He reached across Torres to pull the door closed. "We're in."

"Okay. I'm hitting the vacuum. Folks, shake that dust off yourselves." Jessian flicked a switch on her dashboard.

Quinn unlooped her scarf and shook the dust from it, demonstrating for the visitors. Torres and Kassis both followed her example, but nothing came off their shimmering shields. "That's handy." Quinn brushed the last of the dirt from her hair and sat back in her seat. "I'll be finding sand in my clothes for hours. The vacuum never gets it all."

"Good thing Liz isn't here—she'd be negotiating import deals for that tech," Tony said.

"We don't have that kind of authority." Kassis broke off and clamped a hand over her side.

"Are you—" Quinn broke off. The woman didn't appear to be in pain, and asking about the odd action felt intrusive.

"It's my sair-glider. Do you mind if she comes out?" The shimmer of her personal shield disappeared, and Kassis slid a finger into the folds of her jacket. A little rodent-like head poked out of a previously invisible pocket. Big brown eyes glinted in a furry, friendly-looking white face. It blinked, and its pink nose twitched as it made a chittering noise.

Quinn reached a finger toward the creature, then hesitated. "Is it a pet of some kind?" In the middle row of seats, Tony twisted around to look, too.

The little animal climbed onto Kassis's hand, revealing green spots in its white fur. It sat in her palm, its long tail wrapped around the woman's wrist. Something about the creature reminded Quinn of Sashelle—the confident attitude more than the physical appearance.

"They're called sair-gliders. They're originally from Kepler Three, but they've been kind of adopted by the Explorer Corps as unofficial mascots. They're technically planet neutral—they don't have any impact on the environment—well, no more than we humans do. They don't carry communicable diseases—at all. It's very unusual—something about their evolution. And their superior sense of hearing and smell means they make great watch animals. Her name is Yasmi. You can pet her—she won't bite." Kassis held the animal out to her.

Quinn slid the tip of her index finger over the animal's head. It leaned into the caress, not unlike a cat or dog. "It's really soft. And warm. Will it—she—come to me?"

"Sure."

Holding her hand next to Kassis's, Quinn squeaked in surprise when the little animal launched itself into the air, leaping to her shoulder.

"Yasmi!" Kassis grasped the creature around its middle and pulled her from Quinn's sleeve. "Manners! We just met these people." She deposited the glider in Quinn's still outstretched palm.

Quinn lifted her hand to look more closely at the animal. The pads of its feet tickled her palm as the creature shifted and dropped to all fours to maintain its balance. "Do they have retractable claws?"

Kassis nodded. "Yes. They climb really well. And the membrane between their front and rear legs acts as a kind of sail—they can't fly, but they glide for incredibly long distances. Hence the name."

"What do they eat?" Tony stroked Yasmi's soft fur.

"Pretty much anything we can. They instinctively avoid anything they can't digest, and we've never found a substance they can eat that is dangerous to humans. Another thing that makes them good exploring companions."

"Forget the shields. Liz is going to want to import these." Tony turned to face the other visitor. "You don't have one?"

"Nope. Siti says I'm not responsible enough to care for a pet," Torres joked. "Besides, except on rare occasions, I'm busy flying instead of wandering around strange planets. I ferry them to and fro." He reached a hand toward the window, then waved it at the seat.

"Like me," Jessian said as she lounged over the back of her bench seat.

"Speaking of which—" Tony cleared his throat. When the driver didn't move, he went on. "Do you suppose we could get to the ferrying?"

"Oh!" Jessian snickered, then she turned and started the vehicle. "Next stop, Homestead."

CHAPTER FOURTEEN
SITI

THE LARGE BLOCKY building called the Homestead stood in the middle of a vast flat plain. The winds blew a continuous wave of sand across the barren landscape, scouring the exterior of the building. I tucked Yasmi into my pocket, then activated my shield before Tony opened the door of the boxy vehicle. Jessian had stopped right in front of the double doors, and we hurried across a narrow strip of pavement, the wind nearly sweeping me off my feet.

The doors opened at our approach, folding inward. Once the four of us got inside, they closed again, cutting off the sound of the wind with a muffled whomp. A motor whirred, and Tony and Quinn did the shaking thing again. I flicked off my shield and followed suit in case I'd picked up anything on the ride over. Joss caught my eye with a smirk, then did a quick, dog-like shake of his own.

The vacuum died, and the inner doors opened. In style, the interior resembled the City Hall from Joss's village on Earth—a large central two-story lobby with a railed balcony running around the second floor. Dark, purple-streaked wood covered the floor, and thick foliage hung from the walls as if it grew out of them. Above, I could see a number of doors off the balcony all around. Beneath the overhang on the far side, water tinkled down a slab of stone behind a tall desk. I deactivated my shield, and humid, warm air redolent of growing things hit me.

"Anyone here?" Tony called out.

No one answered.

"Pender's probably not back yet." Quinn crossed the room and looked at a screen barely visible above the top of the desk. "The system says—" She broke off at the sound of a door opening.

A dark man in colorful robes swept around the waterfall and smiled, revealing small crystals embedded in his teeth. "Good afternoon, honored guests. I am Pender, hotel manager and concierge. Welcome to the Homestead. I'll show you to your rooms." He narrowed his bright green eyes at Quinn as if she'd usurped his position, then he hurried around the desk to peer at the empty floor around our feet. "May I take your bags?"

"We've got 'em." Joss pulled on the straps of his backpack. "Easier to carry them ourselves. Lead on."

"Pender," Tony said. "Once they're settled, will you show them to the meeting room?"

"Of course." He didn't quite roll his eyes as he turned away, backing toward the stairs with his arms outstretched. "Come, please." At the base of the steps, he swung around, robes swirling, and trotted up the steps.

With a smirk, Tony gestured for us to follow Pender. We climbed the wooden steps to the second-floor balcony where the concierge waited. He gestured to the right. "This way, please."

"We'll see you in a few." Quinn lifted her hand in a half-hearted wave, then turned the other direction.

When we reached the back of the building, I looked across the atrium as Tony and Quinn disappeared through one side of a heavy double door.

"That's the conference center." Pender emphasized the last two words. I bit back a smile and resolved not to call it a "meeting room." With a flourish, he swung another door open. "The ambassador's suite!"

"We aren't really ambassadors." I stepped through the doorway into a nicely appointed room. A colorful woven rug covered part of the shining purple floor. Heavy wooden furniture with plush upholstery was grouped around an old-fashioned fireplace that currently held a basket of brilliant red and pale-yellow flowers. Citrus and something spicy tinged the air. I leaned closer to the flowers—the yellow ones smelled divine.

Heavy drapes hung along the wall opposite the door, and a low counter took up the wall across from the fire. One door on either side led to bedrooms—I could see the corner of a quilt in dozens of shades of off-white hanging over a large wooden four-poster bed.

"Yes, please take this room, Ms. Kassis." Pender pushed past me into the room. It also featured a fireplace, this one filled with more of the yellow flowers mixed with larger blue blossoms. The wave of citrus almost choked me.

Beyond the bed, a full bathroom in glinting white tile sparkled. I shrugged off my duffle and deposited it on the wooden chest beside the bathroom door. Peering inside, I took in the double sinks, commode with some kind of electronic panel beside it, and a large walk-in shower.

When I returned to the bedroom, Pender whipped aside the heavy drapes with a flourish. "You can sit here and enjoy the view." He indicated a comfortable-looking armchair near the windows.

I crossed the room to look down into a walled garden, lush with greenery and more of the flowers. Vines stretched from the wall to the building above us, with colorful globes hanging at intervals. Through the screen of vines, the desert plain stretched away to mountains tiny in the distance. "This is lovely."

"I took the liberty of providing snacks and beverages in the cooler in the sitting room, but you're welcome to come down to the bar, of course. It's quiet here—you two are the only guests at this time." He twitched the drapes shut. "It's best to keep them closed when you aren't here—keeps the blistering sun out. If you'd like to freshen up before the meeting, please do. I'll wait in the sitting room." Then he swept out of the room.

I released Yasmi from my pocket. While she explored the

bedroom, I used the facilities, marveling at the options the commode offered on this seemingly primitive planet, then washed my hands and face. After a quick check of my hair, I whistled to Yasmi. She launched herself from the bed canopy as I crossed the room, gliding to my shoulder.

In the sitting room, Pender perched on the edge of the couch while Joss perused the cupboards on the opposite side of the room. He pulled out a packet and waved it at Pender. "What's this one?"

The concierge squinted across the room at the blue and white packaging. "That's armilo and verbery."

"Huh." Joss tossed the package at me. "Try this one."

I snatched it before it hit me in the face. "Thanks for the heads up. And I'm not really hungry."

Yasmi chittered on my shoulder. The two men snickered. With a shrug, I ripped the package open and offered it to the glider. The faint whiff of undefinable fruit combined with the pale pink coating on the little brick didn't appeal to me, but Yasmi squeaked again. With a shrug, I broke off a chunk and offered it. She grabbed the morsel and shoved it into her cheek, grasping for more. "Good choice."

"Will the... animal be joining you?" Pender stood and straightened his robes.

"This is a sair-glider. Her name is Yasmi." Tucking the remaining food into a belt pouch, I pulled Yasmi from my shoulder and held her out to the concierge. "She's friendly."

The man and the glider eyed each other for a moment, then Yasmi squirmed to be released. Pender put his hands behind his back. "I'm not really a pet person." He backed away, turning to open the door with another customary flourish. "Please, after you."

I put Yasmi back on my shoulder, and she stopped wiggling. Clearly, she'd taken a dislike to Pender, which was unusual. As I followed Joss out the door, I wondered about the concierge. Sure, he was flamboyant and officious, but he seemed harmless enough. I'd learned to trust Yasmi's instincts, though, and filed it away in the back of my mind.

"You can go either way around." Pender indicated the double doors

Quinn and Tony had exited through on the far side of the atrium. His voice took on a slight tinge of disapproval. "As I told Mr. Torres, we'll have refreshments in the conference center."

Joss tossed a grin over his shoulder as he headed back the way we'd come. "I can always eat. Gotta feed the machine."

At the far side, Pender opened both leaves of the door and bowed us through. "Ms. Kassis and Mr. Torres."

The conference center's décor matched the rest of the facility. Potted plants hung on the walls, allowing greenery to hide the bland, pale wood. The purple floors shone, and a large conference table made of the same wood took up most of the room. Comfortable chairs ringed the table, and Quinn and Tony waited at the far end with two older people. The woman's stern wrinkled face and short steel gray hair gave her a formidable appearance. Her clothing was plain and functional. The man was balding, with kinky salt and pepper hair hanging around the sides of his plump face and brushing his shoulders. He wore a faded and wrinkled tunic over baggy trousers with many pockets.

"Thank you, Pender." The woman nodded graciously. "That will be all. Lieutenant Torres, Lieutenant Kassis, welcome to Lunesco. I am General Beatrix La Gama, and this is our planetary governor, Harim."

CHAPTER FIFTEEN
QUINN

A FLASH of surprise and dismay crossed Kassis's face before it went blank, and she stepped forward to shake hands with the general and governor. Quinn suppressed a laugh and carefully didn't look at Tony. She knew Harim presented a less than polished image. Unfortunately, the intellect beneath the surface matched the outward appearance. But the people of Lunesco continued to elect him governor—mainly because no one else could be bothered to run. Doug Parra and Auntie B ran the shadow government and most of the population was just fine with that.

After greeting the visitors, Auntie B gestured to the table. They all hovered for a moment, apparently unwilling to cause an interstellar incident by sitting down first, until Harim pulled out his chair and dropped into it. The others breathed a sigh of relief and followed suit. Pender poured water for the guests, then finally gave in to Auntie B's glares and left the room. Quinn had no doubt he'd be listening from his office.

Apparently coming to the same conclusion, Tony pulled a device from his pocket and set it on the table. He pressed the button, and it glowed a soft orange. "This will keep anyone from eavesdropping on our conversation."

Kassis gestured to her collar. Or maybe to the glider crouched on her shoulder. "I am recording this meeting for my government. I can't allow you to cut the transmission."

Auntie B made a face. "That's unfortunate. There are... people who feel they need to butt their noses in where they don't belong. But as long as we're all aware the conversation is being monitored by your ship—and possibly other factions—I suppose going without the suppressor is acceptable."

Kassis cocked her head for a moment, then nodded. "As it happens, the ship confirms your suppressor is not affecting our communications, so feel free to leave it on."

Quinn exchanged a look with the rest of her team. If the visitors could monitor communications despite the suppressor, that was something to be remembered. And passed to the government agents preparing to meet with the Colonial delegation.

"Well, at least it will keep Pender from listening in." Trust Harim to point out the elephant in the room.

Quinn closed her eyes in embarrassment. Inviting Harim to this meeting was both necessary and insane. He was a political wild card. She raised a brow at Tony, and he shrugged. Nothing they could do.

Auntie B kept her face straight. "Excellent. I am authorized to speak on behalf of the people of Lunesco—" She darted a look at the governor. "Under Harim's authority, of course."

Harim waved a hand, interrupting her. "I trust ya."

This time she allowed her annoyance to show. "Thank you, Harim."

It bounced right off him. "'Course!"

Auntie B cleared her throat. "I do not, of course, have the authority to speak on behalf of the Romara Republic. We are a loosely joined association—for the most part, power is held by the individual planets. But we have a mutual aid and defense clause in our constitution which means negotiations with entities outside the republic require federal participation. The seat of government is on Romara—hence the name."

"The republic is fairly new." Quinn leaned across the table, her hands flat against the warm purple wood. Talking about the revolution agitated her, but they had agreed it was necessary. "We overturned the corrupt Federation a few years ago and instituted the republic as more of a confederation of planets than a single nation. Our freedoms are important to us. But for something this big, everyone needs to be in the loop, so we reached out to Romara."

"I've also reached out to the N'Avon Commonwealth, which is the other political entity in our systems." Tony took up the prepared speech. "They will send representatives to Romara, and we will escort your ship there for more formal discussion."

Kassis nodded and held up a finger. After a short pause, she nodded again. "The captain agrees that is in our best interests and instructs me to tell you about our Commonwealth. There are three major worlds within the Colonial Commonwealth—based on three of the original five colonies. Armstrong, Grissom, and Sally Ride. The Explorer Corps is headquartered on Grissom, but we belong to the Commonwealth as a whole, not just Grissom. It sounds like our Commonwealth works in a similar manner to your republic, but despite the name, it sounds like we have more federal oversight than you do."

Torres set his water glass down with a loud click. "There are also two other factions originating from the first settlers—Lewei and Gagarin. They are loosely allied and often at odds with the Commonwealth."

Kassis gave Torres a surprised look. He lifted both hands. "What? I'm not a Commonwealth citizen." He turned back to Auntie B. "I'm from Earth. We have a treaty with the Colonial Commonwealth, and we're in discussions with Lewei and Gagarin, but we maintain political neutrality. My people will also want to be included in any discussions with your delegation and may choose to initiate separate dialogue with you."

Auntie B watched the two younger people for a moment before speaking. "Thank you. Obviously, any formal discussions will wait until the meeting on Romara, but I appreciate you giving us this background information. We invite you to stay and explore Lunesco until your representatives arrive. Meet our people. Enjoy our hospitality. We welcome this opportunity for informal discussion and friendship." She pushed back her chair and stood.

Quinn scrambled to her feet as did the others around the table. Auntie B and Harim left, although Harim destroyed Auntie B's stately exit by stepping on her heels. Pushing down the twinge of mortification, Quinn turned to the visitors. "I'd be happy to escort you to the village tomorrow." They'd agreed previously that letting the Colonials wander around on their own was risky. She and Tony would take turns, then fly on the *Swan* to Romara as part of the entourage.

Kassis smiled. "I'd love to see your village. I didn't see any indication of it on the way here."

"You wouldn't," Tony said. "It's in the rift."

"The rift?" Torres's eyes twinkled. "Like from the Doctor?"

"You know the Doctor?"

While the men discussed their obsession with ancient Earth digital theater, Quinn turned to Kassis. "It's in the valley. You might have caught sight of it when you flew in, if you didn't have that cool vertical landing capability."

"You don't?" Kassis asked.

"Some ships do. Newer, more expensive models. But most private ships in the Fed—I mean the Republic—aren't that nice. And if they are, you might want to think twice about flying with them." She clamped her mouth shut. Although the revolution had made a hearty dent in the Russosken's sphere of influence, and Francine's sister Dusica had done her best to pull the organization away from illegal activities, Quinn still felt like she had a target between her shoulders any time they were around.

Luckily, Kassis took the comment to mean the tech was unreliable. "I'm sure some CC tech firms will be happy to add some competition to the market. Once the government types work out the details, of course."

If Quinn knew anything about commerce, they'd probably show up before their governments agreed to anything.

THE ROMARA CONFRONTATION

THE NEXT MORNING, Quinn arrived at the Homestead at a civilized hour. She, Tony, Doug, and Auntie B had stayed up late into the night dissecting the meeting but had come to no new conclusions. She and Tony would let the visitors explore Lunesco—what little there was to see—while Doug and Auntie B attempted to convince Harim that he wasn't needed on the visit to Romara. Auntie B usually acted as the planetary representative to the republic, but Harim had gotten a bee in his bonnet.

Whatever that means. Quinn had never understood what a bug in the engine compartment had to do with being stubborn, but those old Earther sayings were odd. Maybe Lieutenant Torres could explain it.

Unexpectedly, Pender greeted her from the front desk when she arrived. The hotelier was notorious for being absent when needed, but maybe even he understood the importance of this visit.

"I hope you slept well." The man's delivery made it clear he hadn't. "Those Colonials were up at sunrise!"

"They are military—or pseudo-military." Quinn frowned. "Did they demand breakfast or something?" They hadn't seemed rude. But maybe that wasn't considered impolite where they came from.

"No. They haven't asked for anything." Pender made it sound like a negative. "My security system woke me when they left the building. They ran to the airfield and back. Ran! In the outdoors!"

"Again, military. I wonder how they knew the winds died at dawn."

"I told them, of course. They had all kinds of weird questions after you left—about the weather, the people, the planet."

Quinn scowled. "You're a concierge. You're supposed to expect questions. You recorded them, right? And didn't say anything... untoward?"

Pender's gaze hardened, and he drew himself up. "Untoward? Like about the sugar globes? Do you think I would endanger my planet's prime export now that we're out from under the Russosken thumb?"

"No, of course not. But Auntie B will want to know what you told them."

He flung a hand at the computer. "It's all there. She can access the files herself. I have a business to run!" He flounced out of the room as if he had dozens of guests to care for instead of two self-sufficient military officers she was about to take off his hands.

"Good morning!" Kassis leaned over the railing by the stairwell, waving.

Had she overheard their conversation? Quinn hoped not, but a quick mental review told her they'd said nothing incriminating. And she'd bet all the potatoes in Hadriana the two Colonials had had similar conversations about what was safe to discuss.

Torres jumped the last couple of steps to the lobby while Kassis followed more slowly. They both wore their black uniforms again, their hair clean and shiny, their faces well-rested. Quinn wished Harim would learn from their example. This was how planetary envoys should look.

"Morning." Quinn met them halfway between the desk and the stairs. "Have you eaten?"

"The nutrition cubes in the fridge were interesting," Kassis said. "I'm not familiar with any of those flavors."

"They're a local product. Low sugar, high protein. Excellent fuel, but not what I'd call an inviting meal." Quinn cast a dark look toward Pender's office, but the man did not appear. Clearly her powers of telepathy were limited to conversations with Sashelle. "We'll stop at Auntie B's bakery."

"Bakery? Yes." Torres pumped a fist into the air. "I'm all for healthy food, but what's the point of traveling if you can't taste the local cuisine? I was afraid those bars were all you ate around here."

Kassis slapped Torres's arm. "Joss, we're supposed to be ambassadors for the CEC, not tourists."

"If they wanted someone who toed the party line, they shouldn't have sent me." He bowed toward Quinn. "Pray, lead on to this bakery, Ms. Templeton."

She laughed and turned toward the door. "Call me Quinn."

He fell into step beside her. "And I'm Joss. Her majesty back there is Siti." He jerked his head at the woman following them.

"I'm not the one whose daddy is an ambassador," Kassis said. "And yes, please call me Siti."

"Admiral, ambassador, we're both privileged brats." He waited for Quinn and Siti to enter the vestibule before following them through.

"You'll want to turn on your magic protective shields." Quinn paused to pull her goggles over her eyes. A faint hum rattled her back teeth before settling into obscurity, and the sheen appeared around both her companions' heads. "Perfect. Let's get breakfast."

CHAPTER SIXTEEN
SITI

We climbed into Jessian's van and headed into town. Although her driving on the steep switchbacks down the side of the valley left me wishing Joss had flown us instead, the view was spectacular. White buildings clung to the lowest reaches of the almost vertical canyon walls, with bright green vines providing shade between them and in some places over the road itself. Large, colorful globes hung from the vines, but whether they were decorative or natural, I didn't learn.

Crops covered the floor of the valley in neat but irregular polygons, and a river wandered through the middle. The valley ran east to west, so the closer side and the floor enjoyed sunshine most of the day. The high top of the rift shielded the lower levels from the vicious wind.

Quinn took us to the bakery, where we were surprised to learn General La Gama and Auntie B were one and the same. Apparently, she did the baking herself, and it was excellent. Grateful I'd let Joss talk me into running that morning, I enjoyed the cinnamon bun and coffee without guilt. Then we spent the morning and early afternoon exploring the little village. The shopkeepers obviously didn't expect many tourists, but I purchased a couple of trinkets to take home. Or rather, Quinn purchased them for me since I had no Romaran cash.

"We'll need to work something out," Quinn said after paying despite my protests. "You'll need credits on Romara, too. I'll ask Auntie B about that."

The next day, we flew to the mountains. Tony and Quinn both joined us, taking their jobs as escorts seriously. The forested hills were vastly different from the desert plains. We took a short hike with a local expert, climbing to a rocky outcropping over a spectacular waterfall. As we walked, Joss and I explained how the CEC would have divided the planet for exploration and our classification systems. "Honestly—" I paused wondering how blunt I should be.

"What?" Quinn prompted.

"I am—was—the Phase I team leader for this exploration. But if this planet were uninhabited, I'm not sure my team would have recommended it for Phase 2. Obviously, we would have surveyed the whole planet, not just two small parts, but— There are enough habitable worlds in the universe—" I broke off then tried again. "No offense, but between the desert plains and what you say about the ferocity of the local fauna in this more hospitable region—unless we found something particularly enticing, like rare minerals, or potentially medicinal plants, I would have written Lunesco off."

Tony chuckled as if he knew something we didn't. If there *was* something enticing on this planet, they weren't sharing with us. "Is that your way of saying your government isn't going to try to wrest this gem from the Republic?"

"We wouldn't do that anyway!" I tamped down my automatic defense. I didn't actually know what the Commonwealth Council might choose to do. "But, no, I'm pretty sure Lunesco will remain unmolested. You don't seem to be too offended by my assessment."

"We've been here long enough to make the same appraisal." Tony tugged his shirt sleeves over his wrists and stuck his hands in his coat pockets. Despite spraying themselves liberally with an insect repellent the guide recommended, the bugs had been using Tony and Quinn as mobile feeding stations.

Quinn slapped a bug that landed on her arm, then wiped her hand on her pants. "Yuck. I want to go back to Romara where the only danger is the fish smell. Unless you can give me one of your magic protection bubbles."

"That's how we can get some cash." Joss held up both hands at my glare. "Kidding! Even Earther status wouldn't keep me out of prison if I sold CEC equipment."

"Not to mention it's wrong." I knew Joss would never do anything illegal, but our hosts didn't.

"Duh."

"I know someone who'd love to talk to your distributor, though," Tony said.

As we returned to the Homestead tired and quiet, my internal audio pinged with Captain Salu's ID. She'd been strangely silent, but maybe she trusted us to sightsee without micromanagement.

"Yes, sir?"

"Did you enjoy your nature hike?"

I frowned out the window, hoping our hosts wouldn't notice me talking. They clearly knew we had comms to the ship, but I tried not to advertise when they were in use. "Yes, sir. Although I don't think I would have recommended this planet for Phase 2."

"That's not relevant anymore. And our ambassadorial delegation has arrived in system. They're sending a shuttle down as soon as they reach a reasonable launch distance. You and Torres are to wait until they arrive, hand your duties over to the envoy, then return to the *Observer*. We'll return to Grissom and debrief."

"Yes, sir." I tried to hide my disappointment. I'd been hoping to stay with the Lunesco delegation and visit Romara. I should have realized the government officials would never leave a junior-grade officer from the CEC on a diplomatic mission. In reality, Captain Salu could have sent one of her higher-ranking subordinates down to the planet. Only Quinn and Tony's personal invitation had allowed me to be included this long.

I toggled my internal audio to Joss and filled him in. He swore under his breath, earning a curious look from our hosts. He faked a cough that no one probably believed, but they let it pass.

I pulled a face and lifted my shoulders in a tiny shrug, but Joss knew as well as I did that explorers went where they were told. I cleared my throat. "Apparently our replacements have arrived."

"Replacements?" Quinn looked up from her boxy communication device. "You're leaving?"

"Yes. The Commonwealth government has sent a navy ship with an official delegation to the Romara Republic. They're sending an escort to join your Lunesco representatives—do you know who that will be?"

They exchanged a quick look and both nodded. Quinn bit her lip as Tony replied, "Auntie B—General La Gama is the official representative to Romara. And Harim has decided to join her."

I kept my face blank, trying not to respond to their obvious dismay. Harim was not what most people would consider planetary emissary material. Although based on our interactions with the people of Lunesco, he was quite representative of the majority.

"Auntie B can keep him in line," Quinn added in a soft voice.

"We can hope." Tony scrubbed a hand through his hair. "I'm sorry we'll be losing you. I've enjoyed spending time with the two of you." Quinn nodded in agreement.

I spread my hands. "I'm surprised we got this far. The Commonwealth Ministry of State doesn't usually employ CEC officers at all, but obviously this is a unique situation. Even if they did, they wouldn't send lieutenants as political envoys. We'd be entourage at best."

"Bag carriers," Joss agreed.

The big van pulled into a parking spot beside the Homestead, and we activated our personal shields. I tapped Tony's arm as he reached for the door handle, staying the action. "The captain said a navy shuttle will be arriving soon. We need to pack up and head back to the airfield to meet them. Their ETA is a little under two hours."

Tony slid his goggles onto his forehead. "That soon?"

"Two hours?" Joss's voice rose in surprise. "That's fast. I thought you said they just arrived in system."

I flicked my holo-ring and pulled up the data tag the captain had forwarded. A couple of swipes gave us a visual representation of the system. It showed a small navy ship approaching the planet.

Joss whistled in appreciation. "Nice. That's the *Intrepid*—brand new model of EFT." We all gave him blank stares. "Expeditionary Fast Transport. The standard model carries small assault teams to hot spots, but I read they commissioned a couple for the Ministry of State. Super plush—built to transport diplomatic people. Gotta leave Gagarin fast sometimes."

I gave him a hard stare—he shouldn't be painting our relations with the Gagarians in a bad light. He shrugged it off with a wink.

"I'm more interested in your wearable tech than the navy ships." Quinn gestured to the hologram. "I'd love a holo-ring."

I flicked the display off. No one had instructed us to keep our tech hidden, but it felt like bragging or sharing classified information to show it off. "They are very convenient. I suspect once diplomatic relations are established, the manufacturers will be thrilled to find a new market."

Tony pulled his goggles over his head and checked to make sure the others were ready. Then he opened the door, and we hurried across the wind-battered sidewalk to the building's entry.

"We'll meet you here in the lobby in an hour and a half." Quinn poked a finger toward the floor as we exited the foyer. "Tony and I will ride with you back to the airfield and bring the new arrivals to meet Auntie B."

"Excellent." I thanked them for the excursion, then hurried up to my room to clean up and repack.

Yasmi chittered loudly when I opened the door, scolding me for leaving her cooped up inside so long. Although all CEC gliders were "house trained" they preferred free run and reliably returned to their owners each night. Gliders routinely accompanied Phase 1 teams, but I'd been reluctant to take her with me into the wilderness here, especially after Pender's description of the local predators.

My previous glider, Liam, had turned out not to be a glider at all, but rather a shapeshifter from Darenti. Since real gliders weren't as smart as Liam, I'd subconsciously decided Yasmi couldn't be trusted the way I trusted him. Which was stupid—explorers had been taking gliders on missions for hundreds of year.

I put out a hand, but Yasmi clung to the tall bedpost, refusing to jump to me. "I'm really sorry." I pulled one of the pink nutrition blocks from my belt pouch and broke off a chunk. "I should have taken you with me. I'm not being a good friend."

She scolded me some more, then jumped to my arm. I stroked her fur and fed her the food. "I won't let it happen again. But now I have to pack." I broke off another chunk of the bar and set it on the bed. Yasmi leapt to the quilt and happily stuffed her cheeks while I pulled out some clean clothes.

After eating, Yasmi followed me into the bathroom, chattering happily while I showered and dressed. Then I carried her to the bedroom and packed my belongings into my duffle.

Joss knocked on my door. "You ready?"

"Just about. Come on in." I went into the bathroom and grabbed my toiletries. "Are you as bummed as I am about being cut out?"

He shrugged. "I'd like to see Romara, sure. And N'Avon, and the other planets in this system. But you didn't really think they'd let us go along, did you? Besides, aren't you anxious to get back to exploring?"

"I thought I would be, but..." I snagged a pair of socks from the chair and tucked them into the bag. "I like exploring new worlds. But exploring inhabited ones is fun, too. It's like getting paid to travel. I mean, we do get paid to travel, but—"

"No, I get it. I guess we'll have to take a vacation to Romara someday."

"Yeah..." I closed the bag and double-checked the room for any stragglers. "I just... Earth was my first mission, and there were people there. This feels more like that than any of the other places we've been. Although, when you think about it—a lot of my missions have involved indigenous people. Or beings. It feels like this should be the norm, not the exception. And I feel like my expertise in that area— interacting with new civilizations... Maybe I should transfer to State."

"You'd hate it there." Joss grabbed my bag and tossed it over his shoulder like it weighed nothing. Ignoring my protest, he headed into the living room of our suite. "My dad works with them all the time. Talk about stuffed shirts." He grabbed his own bag, tossing it over the other shoulder, then headed for the door. "Get that, will you?"

Suppressing a smile, I moved past him and opened the door. I whistled for Yasmi, then followed him out.

CHAPTER SEVENTEEN
QUINN

QUINN JOINED TONY, who huddled near the front door in a low-voiced discussion with Auntie B and Harim. The general wore a white robe with highly textured stripes in bright colors running down the front. Harim wore what looked like the same frayed clothing he'd worn for the meeting when the Colonials arrived.

"I don't like being fobbed off on new people." Auntie B's voice was unusually tight. "We have no control. No leverage. And we'll be among strangers."

"They said we could bring a security detail." Harim pulled out his toothpick. Ignoring Auntie B's glare, he stuck it in his mouth. "Pender could round up a few guys—"

"And make us look even more—I've worked hard over the last few years to reassure the others in the republic that we're a modern planet, with state-of-the-art defenses. That rural and agricultural doesn't mean uncultured. If you want to undermine all of that work in one stroke, having Pender put together a security detail is the answer." Auntie B folded her arms and pursed her lips.

"We could ask to keep the lieutenants as our liaisons," Quinn suggested. When the others turned to stare, she lifted both hands in disclaimer. "Auntie B suggested it."

"No, it's a good idea," Tony said. "We know them. I'm convinced they're good people—and Sashelle agreed. Is she coming here?"

"She and Francine will meet us at Romara. I'd hope they could get there fast—the Colonials move quickly." Quinn chewed on her lower lip.

"It's a good plan." Auntie B dusted her hands together. "That gives us people we're comfortable with—and potential hostages if necessary."

"Auntie B!" Quinn stared, horrified. Auntie B was a military genius, but Quinn didn't realize how cold-blooded she could be.

"I didn't say we'd *use* them as hostages." Auntie B bared her teeth in a feral grin. "But the implication that we might do that could help keep those people in line. I wonder if we should insist on traveling on our own ship? Are Liz and Maerk still in the system?"

"Liz checked in from Daravoo yesterday." Tony shoved a hand through his hair. "We could request a government transport, but that cruiser they sent as escort is at least a day out. They're so much slower they had to stay in the jump belt or the Colonial ship would beat them to Romara."

A thud brought their heads around. Quinn tried to keep her expression bland when she saw Siti and Joss at the base of the stairs. Tony waved them over. "You ready?"

Siti reached for her bag, but Joss grabbed it. He said something that made her snort a laugh, and they crossed the gleaming purple floor.

Siti stopped in front of Auntie B. "We're ready to go. Although we've enjoyed your hospitality."

The general nodded regally. "And we've enjoyed hosting you. But all good things…" She raised a brow, as if questioning whether they knew the saying.

"Must come to an end," the Colonials replied in unison.

"Remarkable." The general shook her head. "It's amazing how much we have in common. Language. Dress, to some extent." She waved a hand at Tony and Quinn who both wore close-fitting pants and jackets, very similar to the CEC uniforms. "And yet we're separated by who knows how many hundreds of years."

"And light years," Harim put in.

"True, but we're many light years from Romara, too. It's not the distance that is significant, but the time since our two civilizations diverged. And yet we're so much the same." Auntie B pulled goggles out of her pocket and held them up as evidence of the contrary. "In some ways. Shall we?"

They rode in silence to the airfield. The Colonials made as if to walk around to their craft, but Auntie B beckoned for them to follow her into the small building. It contained half a dozen chairs, an unoccupied desk with one computer, and a large window beside the double door leading to the flight line.

The door behind the desk burst open, and Pender stumbled in. His eyes were slightly red and his clothing disheveled. "Oh, it's just you. Your visitors are on final. They said they don't need the runway." He glared at the lieutenants as if vertical landings were an abomination to be laid at their door. "You're making me work too hard! I gotta get back up there."

"Thank you, Pender," Auntie B said, but the man was already gone.

"He does air traffic control, too?" Siti asked.

"We don't get a lot of visitors to the Homestead, so this is his primary job." Auntie B indicated the chairs, inviting everyone to sit. "He's been here all day, waiting for your friends."

Siti frowned, ignoring the uncomfortable looking chair. "I only found out this afternoon that they were on the way."

"They arrived in system this morning, and since we don't know your capabilities, we weren't sure how long planetfall would take." Auntie B lifted both hands, then smoothed her robe and sat. "This blasted thing is a pain in the bahookie."

"Then why did you wear it?" Quinn sat beside the older woman.

"Traditional Lunescan garb." Auntie B glared at Harim. "I always wear it to the republic senate. He should, too."

"I ain't got one." Harim leaned against the desk and stuck his pick into his teeth again.

Auntie B's jaw clenched. "I had one made for you."

"I know. Don't like it. It itches my bahookie." He cast a devilish glance at the general as he said the last word in an unmistakable impersonation.

"Harim!" Auntie B jerked her head at Siti and Joss standing by the window. "Behave."

"Don't worry about us," Joss said. "I'm as bad as Harim. Siti hates it when I go all bumpkin on her."

"But you have obviously learned when that kind of behavior is inappropriate." Auntie B glared at Harim who grinned back at her, the stick protruding from his teeth.

Static spewed from the speaker in the corner of the room, and Pender's voice assaulted their ears. "They're landing!"

The lieutenants turned to watch, and the others hurried to join them at the window. A sleek, white craft appeared overhead. It looked about the same size as the Colonial shuttle but with smoother lines and a sportier shape. Only a few scorched spots marked the nose, as if it hadn't entered a planet's atmosphere more than once or twice before. It descended slowly, rotating lazily until it paralleled to the front of the building. Then it settled to the ground.

"That's not where I told them to land!" Pender yelled.

Auntie B flapped a hand at the camera over the door. "Don't worry about it."

The hatch in the shuttle's side popped open, and a single step unfolded automatically.

"Too important to jump down?" Joss muttered in a low voice.

An officer in a dark blue uniform jumped over the step, as if, like Joss, he couldn't be bothered with it, then headed around the front of the ship, probably to begin his landing inspection.

Siti sucked in a breath and grabbed Joss's arm. "That was Derek Lee!"

Joss scowled. "Yeah, I saw. Cool."

Quinn looked a question at them, but they were too focused on the new arrival to notice.

A group of dark-suited men and women exited the ship to cross the wind-blown pavement, their personal shields leaving them comfortable and unruffled. A small security detail followed. How many people could that small ship carry?

"It's like a clown car," Joss whispered.

Tony choked, but it sounded like a smothered laugh. He leaned close to Quinn. "Maybe it's bigger on the inside."

Auntie B and Harim took their places in front of the double doors that led to the flight line foyer, and Tony and Quinn stepped in behind them. The lieutenants picked up their bags but stayed by the window, out of the way.

The inner doors swung wide, and the delegation walked into the room. Their eyes darted around as they tried to look at everything without looking away from their hosts. They stopped in formation, and one of the men took another step forward, extending an open hand.

As he did, a young woman stepped to the side of the formation. "May I present Sherief Wisnall de Mandoval Schworak, newly appointed Ambassador of the Colonial Commonwealth to the Romaran Republic." The first man shook Auntie B's hand, then Harim's, then a woman moved forward to do the same.

"Associate Ambassador Caitlin Maroney Brittsan y Sadek," the young announcer intoned. They moved aside, and another, taller man moved to the front. "And the Earth Ambassador to the Commonwealth, Zane Torres."

After greeting the local delegation, Zane's gaze slid around the room and settled on the CEC officers. His lips quirked up, and he winked. Joss jerked his chin in response, and Siti gave a little finger wave. Tony watched the exchange, then stepped closer to the general to whisper in her ear.

Auntie B listened, then cleared her throat. "This is the Lunesco governor, Harim. I am Beatrix La Gama, Lunescan representative to the Republic."

"And retired general," Harim piped up.

La Gama glared at him, which seemed to affect him not at all. "They don't need our full pedigrees, Harim. We sent a dossier ahead."

She turned back to the dignitaries. "If you would like to visit the Homestead, we can offer hospitality."

"We'd like to meet with the Romaran leadership," Wisnall said in a tight tone. He clearly felt a visit to Lunesco beneath his dignity and a waste of time. "We came down to escort you aboard the *Intrepid*." He turned and gestured back at their shuttle. "We have room for you and your… staff." His gaze slid over Tony and Quinn as if finding them lacking.

"Speaking of staff—" The general cleared her throat. "We have a favor to request."

CHAPTER EIGHTEEN
SITI

La Gama's tone made it clear the "favor" was a requirement. "We'd like Lieutenants Kassis and Torres to be assigned to our party as liaisons."

I tried to hide my surprise as Joss and I exchanged a glance. My audio implant pinged with his ID. "Nope, I didn't know," he said before I could ask.

"We have a team assigned to assist you." Wisnall gestured to the half dozen grim-faced people at his back. "They're familiar with the ship and with Ministry of State protocol."

La Gama straightened her back, and her hardened voice and steely gaze turned the bakery owner into the formidable military leader. "We are familiar with Kassis and Torres. They're smart young people —they'll be able to figure out the ship. And your team can liaise with them."

Wisnall glanced at us, then at Zane. The Grissom man's poker face revealed nothing, but I suspected he felt Earth had somehow unfairly snuck in between him and his prize. His eyes went distant for a moment—an obvious sign to those who knew that he was using his internal audio. With an occasion this historic, he could be getting a call directly from the Prime Minister of the Commonwealth. He cleared his throat. "I'll have my assistant see if we can arrange that. Different part of the government. You know how these things can go."

"I'm sure you have the authority to make it happen." La Gama lifted a finger and beckoned us closer. "Tony and Quinn will ride with you, Lieutenants. Harim and I will go with the ambassador. I hope Pender got our luggage loaded."

"I did!" Pender's voice echoed through the speakers. "That navy chap took your stuff."

La Gama bit her lip. I got the impression she was amused rather than embarrassed. "Perfect. We're ready to depart, then."

"I assume you'll need to return your shuttle to the *Loyal Observer*?" Zane asked Joss. When his son nodded, he went on. "I'll ask the captain of the *Intrepid* to send ours to pick you up." He cast a close-lipped smile at Wisnall. "See, easy, peasy."

Wisnall, his face still serene, nodded and turned toward the door. "Shall we? My team will extend their shields for your protection against the wind, General." The entourage and security detail at his back snapped to attention and split, leaving an aisle between the ambassadors and the doors.

La Gama reached for her goggles, then looked out the window and left them hanging around her neck. "Not necessary. We're used to this. Lead on." She jerked her head at us and muttered something to Quinn, then swept between the Colonials and into the foyer.

We waited until the ambassadors and their teams cycled through, then went through with Tony and Quinn. Outside, the wind had died as Tony had told us it always did in the late afternoon. We angled away from the group to our parked shuttle. While Joss did his exterior check, I took his bag and led the others into the shuttle. Once through the airlock, I pointed toward the cockpit. "You can go forward. I'm going to stow our gear, and I'll meet you up there." I opened the hatch between the main part of the shuttle and the cockpit, then took our bags to the cargo hold.

When I reached the front, Tony and Quinn had folded down the jump seats and strapped themselves in. "This looks remarkably like our ships," Tony said. "Same five-point harness, same fold-down jump seats." He leaned into the aisle to look at the controls. "That looks very different."

"Are you a pilot?" I paused and gestured at the right-hand seat. "Do you want to ride shotgun?"

Tony's eyes sparkled. "Definitely—if that's okay with you."

"It's up to Joss. I'm the co-pilot. If anything goes wrong, I'll have to boot you out of the seat, of course, but for a routine lift, it should be fine." No one had said they couldn't look at our tech, and nothing on this shuttle was classified anyway. "If you were in the Navy ship, they'd never let you near the cockpit, but we're kind of an open book."

"I'll wait until Joss gets here, though." Tony unfastened his straps but remained seated.

"Sure." I slid into the left seat and activated the system. After signing in, I initiated the checklist. When Joss showed up a few minutes later, I'd gotten through most of it.

"Thanks for starting that." He leaned over my shoulder to review my progress. "Walk around complete. All green for launch. You wanna fly?"

"I was going to let you do it, with Tony in the right seat."

Joss raised his brows at Tony then shrugged. "Sure, why not? Come on up."

Tony grinned, rubbing his hands together like a kid on Christmas. I slid out of the seat and to the rear of the cockpit so he could get past me.

The *Loyal Observer* had moved into a closer planetary orbit when the *Intrepid* arrived. We landed in the shuttle bay, and Joss popped the airlock. Another CEC pilot appeared before we could get unbuckled. He pointed at Joss, then at me. "The captain says I'm supposed to take over the shutdown so you two can get packed. Carlyson is waiting to take your guests to the ready room."

"Okay." I rose and headed to the back to retrieve my bag. Slinging it over my shoulder, I jumped to the deck and strode across the landing bay. When the door opened, Captain Salu waited for me. "Hello, sir."

She gestured for me to continue and fell in beside me. "Siti. Good work down there. An official request has come through with lightning speed, reassigning you temporarily to the *Intrepid*. I assume you were aware…?" At my nod, she went on. "We've had formal uniforms printed for you, along with a full drop kit. And for Torres, too, of course. You can gather your things from your cabin and return to the ready room. *Intrepid* will send their shuttle as soon as they deliver the delegates. I'm sorry to lose you, but we're returning to base."

We took the float tube up to officer country and walked to my door. The captain lounged against the jamb as I stuffed my few belongings into my duffle. Explorers didn't take many personal items on a Phase 1 mission, but everyone had a few mementos. I tossed my digital photo screen and reader into my larger duffle bag, along with my remaining clothes and Yasmi's bed and toys. Then I double checked the small sanitation cubicle for stray hair ties and toiletries. "That's it."

"Fast and neat—the way the Corps likes it." Salu stepped away from the door, then turned to accompany me. When we reached the float tube, she put out a hand to stop me from entering. "One more thing. Major Andrade has been moved to the *Intrepid* as well. I'm still not clear on the reasons for his assignment to this mission. I will do a little digging when I get back and see if I can unearth any details." She paused for a long second. "Watch your back, lieutenant. This is a big deal, and if things go wrong, they'll look for a scapegoat. One of the reasons I usually counsel young people to avoid a career in State. You didn't really have a choice, but rest assured I will watch out for you as much as I can. You'll always be welcome on my ship." She extended a fist.

Touched by the gesture, I bumped my knuckles against hers. "Thank you, sir. I have Ambassador Torres on my side, too, but I'll take all the help I can get. And thanks for the heads up on Andrade."

"I'll leave you now. Good luck, Kassis."

I saluted her. "Thank you, sir. Safe travels."

She returned the salute and headed for the bridge.

When I reached the ready room, Joss, Tony, and Quinn waited for me. Joss lounged in one of the plush recliners, while the other two sat on a couch watching operations in the shuttle bay on the holo-display.

Tony whistled. "N'Avon has some big ships, but this is huge." He swiped the controls and switched to the gym, then to the mess, and back to the shuttle bay. "Can you see the bridge on this thing?"

I flicked my holo-ring and threw a view at the display. "You have to have more than general permission to see the bridge. It's more of a privacy thing than anything." A hologram of the bridge appeared. "This is a recorded tour. We don't have access to current operations." Besides, Salu was preparing to jump back to Grissom, and I wasn't sure our new friends were cleared to know where we lived.

Releasing the controls back to Tony, I dropped into the recliner beside Joss. "These are the best part about being a pilot. We don't have such nice chairs in the regular officers' lounge."

He smirked. "We gotta be in top shape to fly. That means relaxed and rested." He tapped a panel on my chair's arm, activating the massage setting.

The seat back heated, and integrated equipment dug into my tight shoulders. "Ahhh! Maybe I need to rethink my career choices."

"Told you. Many times." His eyes closed as he enjoyed the massage.

"You talk to your dad?"

He nodded without opening his eyes. "Yup. Nothing to report."

"How's your mom?"

His eyes popped open, and he peered at me. "She's doing well. That medical treatment fixed her right up. I gotta admit, the Commonwealth has excellent health care."

"As opposed to poultices and teas?"

"Don't knock 'em until you try 'em. Those poultices and teas are very effective for some things. But I'll take a med pod if it's available. Besides, I don't know any Lunescan botany, so I'd be hard pressed to find the right plants."

"You wouldn't know the right plants on Earth. Except that one…" I mimed smoking.

He laughed. "You've confused me with someone else."

"Any idea how long the shuttle will be?" Quinn asked. "I'd love to get a tour of this ship. I don't know if I mentioned it, but I'm former military. Ships fascinate me."

I checked the chrono. "It depends on how long the delegates take to unload. Ours, not yours. I'm guessing Harim and the general won't be the ones holding up the show."

"Ops says they have registered an inbound ETA of ninety minutes." Joss flicked his chair off and sat up. "And now that you mention it, I'm hungry. How about we give you the quick tour, then have some dinner?"

"Let me check in with the captain." I flicked my implant and shot the request to Captain Salu. She replied almost immediately. "She says we're good for the friends and family tour."

I rose and led the way out of the ready room, taking them on a tour of the same locations they'd been able to see on the holo-display. "We can't visit operational areas, of course, or life support, but since they're headed back to HQ, I can take you to the team spaces which are normally closed to visitors." I showed them my abandoned cabin, the enlisted barracks, the team meeting rooms, ending in the supply section.

"We bring a lot of equipment, of course. Portable living modules, mobile power stations, weapons for defense, shield generators. We also have fabricators to create things we need but don't have. Including things as mundane as uniforms." I gestured at the textile printers. "In fact, there will be a small pallet loaded on the Navy shuttle with appropriate uniforms for me and Joss. They have our measurements in the system and printed what we need from underwear to shoes to service awards before we left Lunesco." I tapped my chest where we wore medals and ribbons.

Joss groaned and gripped his short, curly hair with both hands. "Please tell me we don't have to wear the monkey suits."

I snorted a laugh. "Of course we do. We've been attached to State. You know the ministry loves everything formal." We answered a few questions about the equipment, then took our visitors to the officers' mess for a meal.

The place was mostly deserted—it was late swing shift ship's time, so few people were eating. We ordered some favorites from the Auto-Kich'n and took a table near the bulkhead. "These aren't actually windows." I tapped the screen that covered the interior wall showing the stars outside and a glimpse of Lunesco above. "And they're designed for multiple uses. They can display maps, data, whatever you need. This room works as a mass briefing room if necessary."

We finished our meals and stacked our dishes. I showed our guests where to put them. "During day shift, they have human wait staff, but we're on our own the rest of the time." I laughed. "I think it's more about keeping the young enlisted people busy while en route than the need for service. We take care of ourselves on the planet, of course."

Joss led the way back to the float tubes, walking backward to continue the conversation. "I dunno. Some senior ship officers are kind of—"

I grabbed his arm before he backed into an unwelcome sight. "Commander d'Souza?"

The short man glared at me as he stormed past but didn't respond. I swallowed the irrational spurt of embarrassment. I hadn't done anything wrong, and if he was back on duty, that meant his treatment had been successful. As far as it went. Addiction recovery still required a daily decision to stay clean.

"He's fun," Tony quipped as we watched the man disappear into the officers' mess.

"You have no idea." As we headed for the float tubes, my audio pinged. "Shuttle's on approach." I grimaced at Joss. Time to face Derek Lee.

CHAPTER NINETEEN
QUINN

THE LIEUTENANTS TOOK Quinn and Tony back to the "ready room," which was much fancier than any of the Federation's. Of course, she'd never spent much time in the pilots' lounge when she was in the Federation military—they didn't invite communications officers into their private space. She'd heard the squadron rooms could be quite plush.

They retrieved their bags, then watched the incoming shuttle land via the big three dimensional "holo-screen." The sporty little ship settled to the deck exactly on a brilliantly lit outline. When the door opened, a female officer jumped out to do the walk-around.

"I guess Lee is too busy for old friends." Joss picked up Quinn's bag and gestured for her to precede him through the door that slid silently open.

Siti sighed. "Crew rest?" She and Tony grabbed the strap of his bag at the same time, and a little tug-of-war ensued. Siti released the strap and lifted both hands in surrender. "All yours."

"Thank you, ma'am." Tony shouldered the bag with a little clink. Probably his supply of Sergeant Sinister so he could get drunk before hyperjump.

Quinn grabbed his arm as they walked to the sleek shuttle,

lowering her voice so only he would hear. "You don't suppose they do jump differently? Maybe you don't need—" She mimed tossing back a shot.

"It's possible. But I'll test it on the way home, not on the way there." Tony squeezed her fingers. "I want to be fully alert on this trip. Which, ironically, means getting drunk first."

A young blonde stood by the shuttle's hatch, a few brightly colored ribbons gleaming on her chest. A silver circle and a slash on her collar must indicate rank, which appeared to be lower than Joss and Siti's two circles because she snapped to attention, and her hand swung up in a salute.

The two lieutenants exchanged a smirking glance, then returned a slightly different gesture.

"Welcome aboard," the young woman said. "Please take seats in the passenger area."

"Thank you." Quinn stepped up into the ship and walked through the open airlock. Another earnest young woman, this one with dark hair, stood at the interior hatch, gesturing toward the rear of the ship. Quinn nodded in thanks and moved into the plush passenger area. This ship was clearly made for transporting dignitaries. Unlike those in the CEC shuttle, these seats looked comfortable and only had lap belts rather than five-point harnesses. The interior bulkheads looked like wood paneling, although that had to be fake. A thick brown carpet covered the deck.

Quinn sat in a front row seat. One of the 3-D holo-displays at the front of the compartment showed a plot of the Lunesco system, with a green dotted line running from the *Loyal Observer* to the *Intrepid*, clearly labeled in the Commonwealth's strangely angled letters. Tony dropped into the seat beside her.

"Where's our luggage?"

"The flight attendant took it." He jerked his chin at the brunette woman who now entered the compartment.

"I thought she was the pilot?"

Tony shrugged. "Me, too. Maybe she's both?"

Siti walked through the holo-display, the lines and dots sliding across her head and body. She sat on Quinn's far side. "She's the crew chief. In charge of cargo, which in this case is us. The lieutenant at the exterior hatch is our pilot."

"Lieutenant? She saluted you, and she has a different rank." Tony tapped his collar where the circles would be if he were military.

Siti nodded. "She's a lieutenant junior grade—circle and slash. I'm a full lieutenant—two circles" She touched her rank. "I'm not sure where the naming convention came from—I thought it was a relic from Earth."

Quinn bumped Tony's side with her elbow. "Just like the Federation."

"I suspected as much." He rubbed his chin. "Auntie B was right—the similarities are remarkable."

The crew chief cleared her throat. She wore stripes on her sleeve and nothing on her collar—similar to Federation enlisted rank, except the Federation had used chevrons, not stripes. "Thank you for joining us today. My name is Spacer Berlain. If you need anything on our short flight, please simply ask. This flight is very short—only about twenty minutes to the *Intrepid*. I see you're all buckled in. Please keep your seat restraints engaged until we're in flight. I'll tell you when it's safe. For now, I will report our status to the pilot, Lieutenant Robinson. We'll depart shortly." She made eye contact with each of them, then took an aft-facing seat near the door and buckled a five-point harness.

"I'm not sure I like this." Tony darted his eyes at the crew chief. "She gets better equipment than we do."

Quinn nudged him with her elbow again, but harder this time. "Behave, Tony. We're representing the Republic."

"*You're* representing the Republic. I'm tagging along to carry the bags." He leaned forward to wink at Siti. "Where's Joss?"

Siti looked around the compartment with a little frown. "He must have convinced the pilot to let him sit up front. He's been itching to see the cockpit of this thing since it landed. The other pilot—the guy on the dirtside drop—was a… friend of ours. Kind of. He must be off shift now."

Tony dropped his jaw and made his eyes wide. "Ooh, that sounds like a story. Dish, girl." Quinn elbowed him again.

The crew chief, obviously trying and failing to ignore their banter, choked. She pinched her lips together for a moment, then her face went blank. Quinn suspected she was receiving one of those internal calls. When the woman announced their imminent departure, Quinn congratulated herself.

They sat in silence for a few minutes, then the crew chief unbuckled her restraints. "The pilot says it's safe to move around the cabin now."

Quinn stared at the woman, then at the holo-display which showed a green dot moving away from the *Loyal Observer* at startling speed. "We're moving. I didn't feel anything."

Siti whistled softly. "I'd heard the new auto grav was seamless, but that was crazy smooth."

"The *Intrepid* has top of the line equipment," the crew chief said. "Everything. I can't believe I was selected for the crew."

"How long has it been in service?" Siti asked.

Berlain opened her mouth, then glanced at Tony and Quinn and snapped it shut. "I'm not sure I can answer that, sir."

Siti raised a hand. "Fair enough. I certainly don't have a need to know." She leaned closer to Quinn and lowered her voice. "Or care that much."

Quinn swallowed a laugh then turned her attention back to the holo-display, watching the green dot speed along the dashed line. "Did you say twenty minutes?"

"Looks faster, doesn't it?" Tony gazed at the display, too.

"Vector matching takes a few minutes. Then we have to wait for them to approve our landing. We'll probably dock earlier than expected." The crew chief gestured toward the back of the compartment. "Can I get anyone a drink?"

When they all declined, she returned to her seat. "You folks are way easier than—" Her face colored a little as she broke off.

"Diplomats can be prickly," Tony suggested gently. When she made a disclaiming noise, he raised both hands. "Not saying you thought so. But hypothetically."

The woman smiled a little and smoothed her hair. "Hypothetically, you are correct."

Quinn always marveled at how easily Tony charmed people into telling him things they shouldn't. It's what made him such an effective spy. His spying days were over, but she was happy to have him on her side for this weird diplomatic exercise.

The ship landed as smoothly as it had departed. The crew chief asked them to buckle their seatbelts again, but none of them had bothered releasing their straps for the brief flight. The only indication they'd docked was the image on the holo-display. Then the crew chief announced they'd arrived.

"Thank you for flying with us today." She unlatched her restraints and let them spool back into their hidden compartments. As she stood, the seat folded up into the wall, and she turned to close a door over it. "Your luggage will be delivered to your staterooms."

They thanked the pilot who stood outside the open cockpit door by the internal hatch, then met Joss in the airlock. The outer hatch popped open, and he led the way to the deck. He paused for a second to look around the flight deck. Crew members wearing dark blue jumpsuits moved purposely toward the ship, while others wandered around the huge space, checking things on their glowing palm-size holograms. Probably preparing for their departure from the Lunesco system.

One crew member spoke with Joss, then waved at the deck. Bright yellow glowed suddenly in the dark decking, lighting a path leading toward a door in the far bulkhead.

"This way, folks." He shouldered his and Siti's bags, then strode off between the yellow lines.

Tony followed more slowly. "I thought they were delivering our luggage?"

Siti shrugged. "Joss likes to keep an eye on his stuff."

"I do, too. If I'd known that was an option."

"Your bags were wrapped to our pallet." Siti turned then pointed back at the shuttle. A young man pushed a hovering pile wrapped in dark fabric toward another door beyond theirs. "If you want your stuff, I can stop them." She raised a brow at Tony.

"No, it's fine."

Quinn put a hand on his arm—she knew how much he hated to have his belongings out of his control. "Don't worry, I've got you." She opened her large handbag to reveal a small bottle of Sergeant Sinister Spiced Rum.

He snorted a laugh. "I'm not worried about that. I'd bet a ship this size has alcohol on it. And if anyone can find it…"

Siti frowned. "I'm pretty sure there's an officers' club on this ship. It might be transporting State wonks, but it's still a Navy ship. Are you a nervous flyer?"

"He has a—" Quinn frowned as she tried to come up with a logical and scientific sounding explanation. "I guess you can call it a medical condition. He requires a chemical depressant before jump. Otherwise, he's incapacitated for days."

"And booze works?" Joss barked out a loud laugh. "That's genius!"

"Unfortunately, it's also true." Tony fell into step beside the younger man. "When I was your age, it was kind of fun, but it gets old when you travel as much as I do."

"We'll find the club." Joss clapped a hand on Tony's shoulder, nearly knocking the shorter man down. "A ship this fancy must have one."

"I have an adequate supply in my bag."

Joss waved a hand grandly. "We can do better than adequate, I'm sure."

They reached the door, which slid aside to reveal an attractive room with comfortable chairs around the walls. Another handsome young officer waited for them, two circles glowing on the collar of his very formal-looking uniform.

"Welcome to the *Intrepid*. I'm Lieutenant Derek Lee." His dark gaze flicked over Joss and settled on Siti.

CHAPTER TWENTY
SITI

A LITTLE PUDDLE of warmth formed in my stomach, then rushed up to my cheeks. I hadn't seen Derek Lee since a party at his apartment when I'd cried all over his shirt. We'd recently returned from Darenti, where I'd had to leave my sair-glider Liam behind. Of course, Liam wasn't really a sair-glider, but he'd been my companion for many years, and not seeing him daily—and knowing I'd likely never see him again—hurt. Like a death in the family.

Derek had been there for me when I needed someone, but after the party, he'd been deployed. And neither of us had reached out to bridge the distance.

"It's good to see you, Siti," he said. Then he turned to Joss. "Caveman."

Joss smirked. "Nibs."

Lee tried to hide his grin, but the corner of his lips twitched.

"This is Quinn Templeton and Tony Bergen." I indicated the two visitors. "They're from Lunes—no, that's not right. Quinn's from Romara, and Tony's from—did you say Nabon?"

"N'Avon." Tony nodded genially and put out a fist.

Derek looked at Tony's hand, his own extended flat. "I though you did the shaking thing."

"We do. But I learn new customs quickly. I'm cosmopolitan."

Derek chuckled and curled his fist to bump Tony's. "Excellent. I've been assigned as your escort while you're aboard. Let me show you to your quarters."

I let Tony and Quinn fall in beside Derek while Joss and I followed behind. "Time to renew your bromance."

"That was a short-term fling." Joss bumped my arm with his own. "What about yours?"

"I'm not a bro."

"You know what I mean." His gaze darted from my face to Derek's back. "What's your status?"

Was the back of Derek's neck turning red? I watched him, but he seemed impervious to our existence as he chatted with the visitors. "There's no status. We had a nice moment that one time, but—"

"*One* time. Right," he scoffed. "And I'm an *adequate* pilot."

I crowed a laugh. "You finally admit it!"

We took a float tube up, which ended the conversation. On larger ships and stations, float tubes often accommodated two or more at a time, but a small, fast vehicle like the *Intrepid* saved room by using singles. A ladder ran up the inside of the tube, providing an emergency option. When we arrived on a deck marked by a large G, Derek led us down the narrow corridor.

"This is officer country. The captain's quarters are near the bridge of course, but the rest of us are on this corridor. My stateroom is here." He patted a door as we trotted by. His name was on a small plate in the center. "Normally dignitaries are housed on level H—which is where your ambassador and governor are staying. We're pretty full on this trip, so you all will be with us. Caveman, you're with me, I'm afraid. Siti, you'll bunk with Lieutenant Robinson—she flew your shuttle. And Tony and Quinn—they did say you'd be willing to share?" He ended on a questioning upswing as he stopped beside a door with no nameplate.

Tony raised his left hand, showing off a plain gold band. "Part of the marriage contract."

Lee nodded and gestured at the door. "You can register your holo-ring—"

"They don't have those," I said. "They use a hand-held device. Dunno if it will work."

He lifted a hand. "Not a problem. Register a handprint." He tapped the panel beside the door which glowed red. A message popped up, but he tapped one of the buttons before I could read it. "If one of you will press your palm against the screen, please?"

Quinn and Tony took turns registering their handprints, then entered the room. Quinn turned in the doorway. "You said we're going to jump soon?"

Lee checked his chrono then nodded. "Now that you're aboard, it will take a couple of hours for us to reach a safe jump distance."

"That seems fast." I leaned back a bit and gave Lee a puzzled frown. "I know this ship is supposed to be fast, but jump belts are usually *days* outside a planet's orbit."

He spread both hands, trying to hide a smirk. "What can I say? The Navy is good at this kind of thing."

"We're well outside normal travel routes in this system—according to the Lunescans." Joss wobbled a hand side to side as if he didn't agree with this assessment. "And these new EFTs really are that fast."

Lee's eyes went wide in feigned shock. "Is the Caveman finally admitting the Navy is superior?" While Joss spluttered, he turned to Tony. "I'll leave you to get comfortable. And if you require additional sedatives, I can have the ship's doc look in on you. Joss, you can dump your stuff in my room." Lee flicked his holo-ring, and the panel beside a door down the hall lit green.

Joss gave me a knowing look and an obvious wink. "Got it. You want some alone time. I'll see you guys later."

I tried not to imitate Joss's spluttering as he sauntered away. Gritting my teeth, I gave Tony and Quinn a brief nod. "I'll see where they've got me quartered and send you the information. If you would like to meet later, contact me via the comm system." I raised a brow at Lee. "I assume they've arranged for some way for our guests to connect?"

His chin went up a little. "This ship was designed to transport VIPs. Of course we have communications for our guests." As I rolled my eyes, he explained to Tony and Quinn how to access the communications suite. "There are guest holo-rings on the desk. Once you've registered your handprint, it's seamless. You have free access to this deck and the one above through your ring, plus access to the ship's public system. There are written and audio prompts to walk you through it all, but it's quite intuitive."

"It will be interesting to see if 'intuitive' is universal." Quinn put out her hand as if to shake, then shifted to the fist bump and back to demonstrate. "But I'm sure we can figure it out."

"Quinn's really good at that stuff." Tony put his arm around his wife and tugged her back into the room. "But if we only have a few hours until jump, I'd like to get settled. We'll meet you in the morning."

I nodded and waited until they closed the door before pivoting toward Lee. "Lead on."

He gave me a long look, then jerked his head in the direction opposite his cabin. "Robinson's down here. She's a good kid, but a little nervous to be sharing with the famous Serenity Kassis."

"Nervous to live with *me*? But she's served with you for how long? Or is that the problem? You've given her the impression all of us O-3s are arrogant and unfriendly?"

His cheeks darkened, and I immediately felt bad. After knowing him for eight years, I still didn't understand a lot about Derek Lee. He'd had a rough time at the Academy—so rough he'd transferred to the Navy rather than being known as the son of a disgraced CEC admiral. I'd always suspected the switch hadn't been enough to outrun his past, but it wasn't something he'd ever offered to discuss.

During our time together on Darenti, I'd come to realize much of Derek's arrogance was a way to insulate himself from distrust. He didn't seem to realize the walls he'd built made others distrust him more. And since we'd spent most of our academy years competing against each other, my natural instinct was to verbally jab him every chance I got. "Sorry, that was uncalled for."

He stopped beside a closed door, rearing back a bit in surprise. "I—it's okay. I probably would have said worse to you. And you're right—I'm not exactly warm and cozy. She's terrified of me." A little smirk twitched the corners of his lips. "As she should be. I'm the chief of shuttle ops—her boss."

I whistled. "Sounds fancy! And you're only a lieutenant."

He straightened his impossibly erect posture even more. "I've been picked up for major."

This time I whistled for real. "Below the zone? Impressive." Especially considering his rocky start at the academy.

His cheeks went pink again, and a genuine smile slid across his face for an instant. "Thank you." He looked like he wanted to say something more but instead gestured at the access panel. "This should be set to your holo-ring."

I waved my hand at the panel, and it flashed green. The door slid aside to reveal a small cabin with two bunks tucked into the wall on the right. A few pictures sat on the desk near the head of the bunks, while the one near the foot was clean.

"Robinson said she'd leave the lower bunk for you, and you can use that desk." He pointed at the door in the other wall. "Officers have private sanitation modules—there's a sonic shower, and they should have dropped off a standard toiletries pack for you. Your luggage will be brought up as soon as they get the pallet unloaded. Main meals are at six, noon, six, and midnight, but you can order food any time. And there are AutoKich'ns in the VIP lounge."

I dropped my bag on the lower bunk. "Wow, the Navy really is fancy. I'm used to carrying my own gear." That wasn't one hundred percent true. On normal explorations, the standard uniform pallet would be dropped outside the living module, and we'd only have to carry it to our lockers inside

Like I said, I can't help baiting Derek.

This time, he let the crack slide by. "This is a VIP ship. We treat guests—even Explorer Corps guests—well."

I snorted a laugh. "I deserved that." A flick of my holo-ring brought up a connection screen, and I logged into the ship's guest services. In a couple of swipes, I located the ship's schematic, which showed in great detail the two decks to which we'd been given access. The rest of the ship was grayed out, including the shuttle decks. "I guess we're stuck here until you let us leave?"

"Something like that." Derek rubbed the back of his head as if he wanted to say something more, then turned to leave. At the door, he turned back. "If you want to grab a drink, I can show you the officers' mess."

I blinked in surprise. That almost sounded like a date. Despite our rocky history, Derek and I had shared some nice moments, and I wasn't opposed to exploring the possibility of more. "That would be nice. I need a few minutes to—" I broke off, waving at the interior door.

"Cool. I'll go grab Joss and meet you back here." He disappeared down the hall, and the door slid shut.

So, not a date. I gave myself a mental eye roll and went to use the facilities. As I finished rebraiding my hair, a ping sounded, and the names Torres, J and Lee, D appeared on the mirror in the sanitation module. I flicked a hand at the "enter" icon, and the door slid open. "I'll be out in a sec."

"This ship has a full bar, Siti!" Joss appeared in the open doorway behind me, his face reflected over my shoulder.

"Do you always wander into women's bathrooms?" I twisted the hair tie around the end of my braid one more time as I turned to face him. "What if I was flossing my teeth? Or—"

"I'd hope you'd have the door closed before you let us into the room." He stepped back and shut the door in my face.

I took a deep breath, then waved the door open again. "You're like the baby brother I never wanted."

Joss grinned. "My job here is done."

"Isn't he older than you?" Derek pushed away from the desk he'd been leaning against.

"Yes, but he acts younger."

"True." He opened the door. "You two haven't changed a bit."

Joss flung an arm around Derek's neck and rubbed the top of his head with his knuckles. "And you've missed us, haven't you, Nibs?"

Derek shoved Joss away, bouncing him into the corridor wall. "Not you."

"Oooh!" Joss sing-songed, his index finger swinging back and forth between me and Derek. "Something's cooking here."

"Keep your voice down, Caveman." Derek shook his head, lips pursed. "Some of these folks might be trying to sleep."

"Maybe this ship isn't so amazing if you can hear people through the bulkheads." I paused beside Tony and Quinn's room, but the panel was red. "I've completely lost track of the time. What shift are we on?"

Derek continued toward the float tube. "It's near twenty-three hundred, ship's time. No idea what it'll be when we get to Romara, though, so there's no way to sync your sleep cycle in advance."

"We should have asked them." Joss paused at the end of the hall. "Or the general."

"We'll have two days at least after we jump." Derek stepped into the float tube and zipped up.

I followed, stepping out on the next deck, with Joss on my heels. "Two days from jump to planet?" Joss scoffed. "I thought this ship was super-fast?"

"It is, but according to the Lunescans, Romaran has strict rules about transit speed in their system. Ambassador La Gama said it's a much busier place." He named the dignitaries as we passed their doors. Most of the names I didn't recognize until we got to the far end. "Ambassador La Gama. Ambassador Torres. Governor Harim. And this is the guest lounge." He waved open a door.

This room looked nothing like my tiny, efficient quarters below. Comfortable furniture—much like the massage chairs in the pilots' lounge on the *Loyal Observer* but new—sat atop thick carpet. Sleek cupboards with two high-end AutoKich'ns filled the far wall, and a massive wall of windows provided views of the stars outside.

I moved closer to tap the curved glass. "That's not real, is it?"

Derek shook his head. "Completely fake. We don't let the VIPs live that close to the exterior bulkhead. But it looks good, doesn't it? Come on, I'll show you the bar."

CHAPTER TWENTY-ONE
QUINN

Once they'd gotten their gear stowed—which in this case meant dropping their toiletries in the attached bath and sliding their bags under the lower bunk—Quinn pulled out the bottle of Sergeant Sinister Spiced Rum she'd smuggled aboard. Tony found a couple of glasses.

"We could have gone old style." She mimed drinking straight from the bottle.

Tony chuckled as he took the bottle. "Only if I have to." He slowly poured rum into a glass, watching Quinn's face as he did. When she shook her head, he handed her the glass, then poured his almost full. "Bottoms up."

They each chugged their drink, both grimacing at the taste. Quinn set her glass on the little desk and dropped into the chair beside it. "Tell me again why we drink this stuff?"

"Tradition!" Tony poured another full glass. "Good thing we've got two hours—these glasses are deceptively small. Don't want to miss my optimum window."

Quinn slid the smaller of the two plain, silver holo-rings on her middle finger—she'd noticed that's where the others wore them. It spun loosely, then tightened to a comfortable fit. "Cool." Holding her hand flat, palm up, she tapped the ring with a fingernail.

A hologram appeared in her palm with a single green icon showing a small rectangle and a larger one. She poked it, and the space between the desks and the door to the bathroom lit up, displaying more icons in bright colors and the Colonial Commonwealth's odd script. Squinting in concentration, she cautiously waved her hand through an image that might indicate time. A digital chronometer appeared. "Huh. Guessed right the first time."

Tony dropped onto the lower bunk, his liquor sloshing but not spilling. "Knew you could do it." He shoved the pillow to the head of the bed and slouched against it.

A digital readout appeared near the ceiling, the numbers counting down from 2:05:56.987. "That is precise." Quinn flicked the interface, and the decimals disappeared. "Nice. You might want to slow down, Tony. We have two hours."

After playing with the system, she figured out how to use it in her palm rather than via the two-meter projection. They found a video to watch on the ship's entertainment center, the story oddly familiar but the settings and actors unknown to them. Quinn unearthed some snacks to munch on while Tony continued his quest to hit the right degree of intoxication before the jump. As the countdown approached zero, they finished the video, and Tony polished off the last of his booze. "That'll do it."

Quinn caught the glass as it slid from his fingers and looked for restraints but found none. "They don't seem to worry about jump safety."

A faint snore was the only reply she got.

"Jump in thirty seconds," a pleasant voice announced. As usual, Tony's timing was impeccable. "Auto restraints deploying in ten. Nine. Eight…" When the voice reached zero, invisible hands gripped Quinn. Then the zinging sensation she always felt during jump hit her nervous system. The invisible restraints disappeared. "Jump complete. Arrival at Romara confirmed."

THE ROMARA CONFRONTATION

Tony sat up, running his tongue over his teeth. "Is my kit in the bathroom?"

Quinn nodded. His immediate transition from blind drunk to sober still boggled her mind. A single glass of the Sergeant gave her a nice buzz—if she drank as much as Tony did, she'd be out for the count. But jump sobered him faster and more comfortably than any of the anti-alcohol medications on the market.

AFTER A SOLID EIGHT hours of sleep, Quinn looked for a way to contact Siti or Joss. Their job, according to Auntie B, was to continue to befriend the young officers and learn whatever they could about the Commonwealth. No point in wasting time. She brought up the ship's interface again and looked for an icon that would indicate communications. She tried one with concentric arcs—that did nothing as far as she could tell—and another with little waves that turned on an ocean sound. Then she tried the green one with what looked like a squared letter C with fat ends. A list appeared.

"Ah ha!"

Tony wandered out of the bathroom, drying his face. "What did you find?"

Quinn waved a hand upward, and the list scrolled. "Looks like a directory. Names and duty stations or maybe titles. We're even listed here under 'guests'! And here's Siti." She pushed a hand through the name, and an image of Siti appeared, but nothing else happened. A swipe seemed to delete the list, and she gasped in dismay, but then another message popped up. "Calling."

"Kassis." Siti's disembodied voice startled them both.

"Hi, it's Quinn."

"And Tony."

Quinn rolled her eyes. "Are we allowed to wander the ship on our own, or do we need an escort?"

"You can look around. Lieutenant Lee says you won't be able to go anywhere you aren't supposed to, so wander at will. Do you want to join us for breakfast?" A schematic appeared, with a dotted line showing them how to reach a large compartment marked "Lounge."

"Thanks. Can we—" She broke off as an exploratory wave of her hand expanded the schematic in her hand. Another gesture sent it to hover in front of the bathroom door. Then she pulled it back to her palm. "This system is very cool. We'll be up—up? Up. We'll meet you in a few."

"Sounds good. Kassis out."

A bright ping noise seemed to indicate the communication had ended. Tony glanced around the room, looking at the upper corners as if seeking something. Quinn shrugged in reply. She had no doubt the ship's system was recording everything they said in any case. "You ready?"

He lifted the towel and gestured toward the bathroom. "Let me get rid of this." When he reappeared, he'd combed his hair and buttoned his shirt. "I'm good."

"Shoes?" Quinn nodded at his feet and tried not to smile. The bumbling Tony Marconi was back. It was a persona that had served him well over his years as a N'Avon spy. It would be fun to watch him work on a mutual… enemy wasn't the right word. At least she hoped it wasn't.

Tony activated the door, bringing her out of her reverie. She followed him out then lifted the hologram to indicate the corridor to the right. At the end, they took the drop chute up one level and stepped out.

This section of the ship had thicker, softer carpet, walls painted a soothing pale blue, and art hung between the doors. The cabins appeared to be larger as the doors were farther apart. The panel beside each door bore a name. She recognized the two members of the delegation they'd met on the planet and a few more she didn't. Then Ambassador Torres from Earth, and finally Harim and Auntie B. All of the doors were closed, and the panels showed red.

"I wonder if that means they're not in there, or if they don't want to be disturbed?" Tony flicked a finger at Harim's panel as he passed, and it lit up green. "Crap. What do I do now?" Words scrolled across it, too fast to decipher the odd Colonial script. Then it went dark.

"I'd say don't touch the door panels." Quinn pointed at a door at the end of the corridor. "Maybe they're all at breakfast."

The door slid aside as they approached, and muffled conversation emphasized by the clink of cutlery on plates surrounded them. A wave of sweet, yeasty air accompanied by the comforting edge of fresh coffee beckoned them inside.

An enormous window stood in place of the far wall, displaying a spread of stars. A point of light nearby moved with them—perhaps a Romaran escort? The wall curved overhead then met with the ceiling.

"That can't be real." Quinn indicated the schematic in her palm. "We're inside the ship. There are other compartments out there." She showed him the grayed-out areas of the image.

"It's pretty, though." Tony pressed a warm hand against her lower back and leaned in close, his voice low. "Our escorts are over there. Assume they're listening to everything." He tipped his head at a table where Kassis, Torres, and Lee sat.

She gave him a half smile. "Including that. You've seen their tech. It's… advanced."

People sat at round tables, enjoying their meals. Quinn spotted Auntie B and Harim but didn't pause to talk. They appeared to be in deep conversation with the ambassador and his assistant. Zane Torres sat with them, listening intently.

They continued to Siti's table. The three young officers stood when they approached, and Lee pulled a chair away from the table. "Sera Templeton."

She frowned as she sat. "It's Quinn, not Sarah."

Lee chuckled as he took his seat. "That's a title, not a name. Formal, polite address in the Commonwealth. Ser for men, sera for women. Usually reserved for people of high rank."

"You have rank in your society?" Quinn glanced over the place setting, but the dishes and silver looked completely normal, although there was a fabric crown in the middle of the plate.

"Every society has rank." Tony sat next to her. Picking up the crown, he shook it out and draped the napkin across his lap. "The Federation—where Quinn grew up—liked to pretend everyone was treated exactly equal. But some were more equal than others."

Siti nodded. "Most rank in the Commonwealth—our Commonwealth—is due to money. Except in the services, of course. There, rank is earned. But still, the rich are treated differently." She wrinkled her nose as if she'd experienced the wrong end of that difference.

"Don't get me started on rank and money." Joss picked up his cup and sipped. "Earth is pretty much the same, except we don't have a lot of wealthy people where I come from. I've heard some parts of the planet are different, though."

"You two are ones to talk." Lee chuckled sourly at them and turned to Quinn. "But let's order, shall we?" He tapped an icon on the table.

A young woman in a severely tailored uniform appeared like magic. She wore her hair slicked back and bright red lipstick. Smiling politely, she nodded to each of them in turn. "May I tell you about our specials?" Her smile widened when Joss winked.

They ordered food. Quinn wasn't sure what she'd requested, but something with eggs and sauce and bread sounded good. And the aromas filling the room reassured her. The group chatted about food while they sipped their coffee—some of the best Quinn had ever had. She'd sworn off caffeine a few months ago, but she wasn't going to let that stop her from experiencing the cuisine of a new civilization.

When the breakfast arrived, it was startlingly familiar. Two eggs sat atop two rounds of toasted bread, with a slice of cured meat. A thick yellow sauce covered it all, with a sprinkle of green flecks for garnish. A pile of tiny round balls turned out to be roasted potatoes, almost identical to many she'd eaten on Hadriana over the years. The rich butter and sprinkle of salt elevated them to a delicacy.

"These are even better than Mama La Raine's." Tony winked as he raised his fork with a tiny crispy sphere on the end.

"As if she ever cooked anything." Quinn scoffed. At the lieutenants' questioning look, she explained. "My former husband was from Hadriana, where his mother ruled with an iron fist. Their one claim to fame was potatoes."

"Are you saying she was important on Hadriana but small potatoes anywhere else?" Joss tried to look innocent, but the grin playing around the corners of his mouth betrayed him.

Siti and Lee groaned, while Tony chortled. "That is exactly correct."

"Not exactly." The words popped out of Quinn's mouth before she could censor them. "I mean, yes, Gretmar La Raine was only a big deal on Hadriana."

"But…" Siti invited her to expand.

Quinn exchanged a look with Tony. Should they tell these newcomers about the native species on that planet? The visitors had shared information about those sair-gliders, but Quinn didn't think they were on the same intelligence level as Hadriana caats. Hadriana was bound to come up at some point. She should probably check with Auntie B before she said anything—

"Hadriana is home to a sapient, sentient native species." Tony apparently had no qualms about broaching the subject. "They're reclusive, and humans settled much of the planet without considering their prior claim. We've been working with the human government there to rectify that situation, but no one wants to give up their potato farm to what they consider animals. And mythical animals at that."

"Mythical?" Siti leaned forward, her food forgotten.

"Hadriana caats—" Tony nodded in rueful acknowledgement. "Yeah, the original settlers weren't very creative in their naming conventions. It's spelled differently and pronounced in two syllables: cah-at. Humans can't say their real name—we don't have the vocal chords for it. And the species looks remarkably similar to large felines."

"You'll meet Sashelle at some point, I'm sure." Quinn wiped her mouth and set her napkin beside her plate. "She was instrumental in our recent revolution, and we agreed to help her with the 'dirt people' as she likes to call them. At any rate, as humans took over larger portions of Hadriana, the caats retreated, and people started to believe they were a myth."

Siti looked at the table where Harim and Auntie B sat. "Do they know?"

"Definitely." Tony glanced over his shoulder and turned back to their companions. "Sashelle played a pivotal role in a major battle on Lunesco. Will they tell your ambassadors? Perhaps. But I suspect Sashelle will insist on being included in any discussions, much as your Earth people did."

Joss's eyes narrowed. "Earth people?"

"I have gotten the impression the Colonial Commonwealth doesn't really think you all are on the same level—it kind of goes back to the rank thing we were talking about earlier. You said Earth doesn't have wealth. So, you're like the poor cousins. Much like the Hadriana caats."

"Or the Darenti," Siti muttered.

"Darenti?" Tony's eyes snapped to Siti.

She pressed her lips together.

CHAPTER TWENTY-TWO
SITI

"I don't know what you thought you were doing, but that's close to treason!" Major Andrade waved a meaty hand at the frozen holo-vid. The image of Joss, Derek, and me having breakfast with our new friends hovered above the center of the conference table. Spit flew from Andrade's lips as he shouted at me, passing through the image of the Romarans. "Darenti is interdicted, and details are classified!"

I clenched my teeth in an effort not to reply. Nothing I said could help me—the major had made that clear from the moment he summoned me to this meeting. While he ranted at my complete lack of discretion and total failure to maintain political *something*, I mentally reviewed the discussion again. Nothing I'd said was classified. Darenti was known to the entire Commonwealth—and to Gagarin and Lewei as well. Everyone knew the natives were intelligent. I hadn't mentioned shape shifting or mind control. And since the planet was on the opposite side of our inhabited space, there was little chance the Romarans or N'Avonians would ever visit there.

And if they did, they'd be stopped by the Commonwealth Naval blockade.

Andrade finally wound up to his climax. "I am removing you from the delegation, lieutenant. And if we hadn't already jumped, I'd send you home on the *Observer*!"

I was relatively certain he didn't have that authority, but he could certainly recommend the action to Ambassador Wisnall, who would have final say on who belonged in his entourage.

"I expect you to stay clear of the Romarans from here on out. I'll have the captain assign you to a duty aboard the ship. If you're qualified for anything, which I doubt. Explorer Corps." He said the last two words in a derisive tone.

"Aye, sir." I gave the only possible response in hopes he'd let me leave.

"And I'm watching you." He pointed two fingers at me, then at his own eyes. "One more slip-up, and you'll be in the brig."

I was relatively sure the *Intrepid* didn't have a brig, but I was also smart enough not to say it. I was *completely* certain nothing I'd done up to this point merited a trip to the brig.

"Get your gear. You can bunk in the enlisted dorm. Dismissed." He turned his back on me as he waved his office door open.

Bunk in the enlisted dorm? I didn't really care where I slept, but the enlisted folks would not be happy to have an officer in their midst during their off-duty hours. And while I couldn't claim to be up on Navy regulations, I was pretty sure putting officers in the enlisted dorm was not acceptable.

But Captain Salu had warned me Andrade had friends in high places. His inclusion on this mission confirmed that fact. Normally, Captain Salu's recommendation would have been sought before reassigning him, and she'd made it clear she hadn't been asked. Time to shut up and color.

I snapped a salute at his back, careful to stand where he'd see my reflection in the faux window behind his desk. Nothing like a sharp CEC salute to piss off a stuck up Navy officer.

When I returned to Robinson's room, she had her bunk shutters closed with the "do not disturb" light on. Although the shutters blocked most light and sound, I kept the room lights dim and moved as quietly as possible while repacking my bag. Fortunately, I hadn't yet opened the gear printed for this mission. The large cube sat under my desk, its shrink-wrap still tight.

With a sigh, I activated my comm and called Derek.

"Siti." His face appeared in my holo, with a surprisingly genuine smile which disappeared so fast I almost didn't catch it. "Where are you? The Romarans were asking." He tagged that last bit on as if he didn't want me getting the idea he cared about my whereabouts. Typical Derek.

"I've been… reassigned. Is there a way to have my gear moved to another bunk, or should I take it myself? It's surprisingly heavy, but I could rig up my grav belt—"

"Reassigned? Why?"

With a swift glance at Robinson's closed bunk, I lowered my voice even more. "Major Andrade took exception to me mentioning the Darenti."

His lips pressed together, and his gaze shifted away. "Stay where you are."

"But I'm supposed to—" The system pinged with a disconnect tone.

Perfect. Although his early selection to major indicated Derek was an up-and-coming officer, he still didn't outrank Andrade. And since Andrade's inclusion in this mission had been suspect from the beginning, I doubted Derek's intervention would help me.

Still, I hadn't received instructions on which dorm I should move my gear to, nor had a new duty assignment been posted to my profile. I considered going in search of my friends, but I had been given a direct order to avoid the Romaran contingent. With a sigh, I pulled out the chair and dropped into it.

As if alerted by my emotions, Yasmi popped her head out of the spherical pet bed on the desk. Liam had always curled up at the foot of my bed or on a spare pillow, but Yasmi preferred the bright, felted wool "glider cave" my friend Anya had made. The little glider jumped to my arm and scampered up to rub her fur against my face.

We sat in silence for a while, but Derek didn't call me back. I dug out a favorite old comedy video, but two hours later when it was finished, I still had no messages and no new assignment.

When Robinson pulled her bunk shutters open, I was halfway through my third video. I'd invaded her stash of snacks, eating only the ones I knew were stocked on board and leaving what must be a private haul of candy alone.

As she jumped down from the upper bunk, I decided to make my presence known. "Hi."

With a gasp, she stumbled across the tiny room, spinning with her hands up in a defensive position. Her gaze snapped to me, and her eyes widened, then she snapped to attention. "I'm sorry, I didn't know you'd be here, sir."

I sat up with a laugh, and Yasmi jumped to the desk, scampering across to sniff at Robinson's arm. "You're fine. And it's 'Siti' when we're here, not 'sir.' There's no need to be so formal in private. I barely outrank you."

She swallowed. "But you're the Star of Darenti."

"Ugh. That's not a real thing."

She nodded emphatically. "Yes, it is! You helped save us from an alien take-over."

"I thought that was classified." I frowned in dismay. My father had always hated being called the Hero of Darenti Four, and now I could see why. Who wanted to be worshiped—or ridiculed—for doing their job? "And couldn't they come up with something more original than 'the star'?"

She gave me a wide-eyed glider-in-the-spotlight look. Then squeaked in alarm when Yasmi's nose touched her hand. "Oh, your glider! That's not Liam, is it? I thought he was blue striped." Her fingers strayed toward the little green and white spotted creature.

"That's Yasmi. Liam is… no longer with us." I wasn't sure how much she knew about Darenti, and despite Andrade's claims to the contrary, I knew not to share classified information. Liam's true nature was definitely classified. "You can pet her."

"I'm sorry to hear about Liam." Robinson slid a finger down Yasmi's head and back. The little glider leaned in, closing her eyes, and Robinson sighed happily. "I've always wanted a glider, but the Navy's not keen on them."

Getting up from the bunk, I picked up Yasmi and handed her to Robinson. "Good reason to transfer services," I joked.

She cuddled the little glider. "I've considered it. Not really, but you know…"

I nodded as I dropped back to my bed. "There are times when transferring seems like a great idea. Sometimes for the silliest reasons." Not that I'd dream of joining Andrade's service. I pointed to the far end of my bunk, then patted the mattress in invitation. "What's your first name?"

"Zadie." She perched on the edge of the bunk, still petting Yasmi. "You aren't at all like I expected."

I gave her a quizzical frown. "What did you expect? More of a hardass like Lieutenant Lee?"

Her jaw dropped. "Uh, what time is it? I have to go on shift." She held Yasmi out to me. The glider rubbed her face against Zadie's wrist, then hopped to my lap.

"Sorry to distract you."

"No, it's fine. I just—" She made an abortive move toward the bathroom.

I shooed her toward the door. "Go. Do your thing. I'll stay out of the way. I won't be here much longer anyway."

She stopped in the doorway, turning back. "You're getting off the ship at Romara."

I shook my head. "It looks like I'm being reassigned. Immediately."

"But there's nowhere for you to go. That's why you're with me—the officer bunks are all full." She frowned. "It's that Major Andrade, isn't it? He's been throwing his weight around. Sharon—Major Holmes, that is—she had to get the captain involved when he tried to kick her out of her own office! If he's messing with you, you should talk to Captain Wortman."

Good to know the Navy didn't like him any better than the Explorer Corps. "I might do that." Although I hated to be sent home—it could be a big stain on my career—getting removed from the delegation might get me back into the field faster. As a cadet, I joined the corps because I preferred exploring to politics.

Of course, that was before we discovered the Romarans. Part of me was dying to see this mission through and find out everything I could about this new civilization.

Zadie looked at her chrono and yelped. "I gotta get moving!" She zipped into the sanitation mod and closed the door.

"Figures." I stroked Yasmi's head. "I make friends with my roommate just in time to be reassigned."

My comm pinged with Joss's identifier. When I opened the holo, he waved. "Yo, Siti, where are you? Tony, Quinn, and I are playing Bantel in the lounge. We're up to two credit bids."

I snorted. "How are you bidding credits with people who use a different money system?"

He poked a thumb over his shoulder. "It's all fake money anyway. None of us are real gamblers, so we're using the word 'credit' for score keeping. I'm ahead."

"Of course you are. It's your favorite game. You should go easy on our guests."

"Tony suggested it. He said since we're getting to see their civilization firsthand, he'd have to learn about ours through games. You seen Nibs?"

"Not in a few hours. Listen, I'm not—"

"Come on! You gotta play! The Romarans are requesting you specifically."

"That might have gotten us assigned to this mission, but I don't think it's going to work anymore. I've been removed from the team."

His eyes went wide and his chin sagged. Then he snapped his mouth closed. "No way. I got this."

"What are you going—" Before I could get the full question out, the connection went dead.

CHAPTER TWENTY-THREE
QUINN

IN THE FINAL hours aboard the Naval ship, Ambassador Wisnall held a cocktail party. He and his assistant, Sera Maroney, stood near the doorway of the VIP lounge, welcoming the visitors. Quinn and Tony followed Harim and Auntie B into the room. For the occasion, Harim had finally agreed to wear his ceremonial Lunescan robe, although he'd already managed to spill something on the front.

They bumped knuckles with Wisnall and Maroney, then moved into the room where a young military man offered a tray of glasses. Tony gave the guy a conspiratorial smile. "Are these strong or wimpy?"

The waiter tried to hide a grimace. "They're pretty weak. Ser Wisnall said he wants everyone to be clear headed when we arrive."

Tony took a glass and offered a silent toast to the young man.

Quinn took a glass, too, and followed Tony across the room to a place near the huge faux windows. "What's the point of this party? We've been eating meals in this room with these people for the last two days."

With a shrug, Tony sipped his drink. "Yeesh. I'd rather have the lemonade they served at lunch. This is terrible." He set the glass on a nearby table. "And I don't know the why. Tradition?"

Auntie B wandered up and deposited her drink beside Tony's. When Quinn asked her the same question, she frowned at Wisnall who stood beside a buffet speaking with Zane Torres. "Romara is the host for this momentous occasion. Holding a formal meet and greet before the event gives him the illusion he's calling the shots." She lifted one shoulder. "At least that's the kind of maneuvering I've seen in the past."

"Humans are so weird." Harim chugged his drink and wandered away to get another one.

"For once, I agree with our esteemed governor." Auntie B turned to look around the compartment. "I haven't seen Siti lately."

"We haven't either." Quinn checked to make sure no one was listening nearby—although of course these aliens could have all kinds of surveillance systems they knew nothing about. "They reassigned her. She rubbed someone the wrong way, and boom, off into the bowels of the ship."

Auntie B stopped short. She turned to look at the ambassadors, then back at Quinn. "Do they know about it?"

"Ambassador Torres knows. Joss told him. They're father and son, you know."

"Yes, I'd heard." Auntie B tapped a finger against her lips. "Did anyone complain about Siti's reassignment?"

Quinn exchanged a surprised look with Tony. "I didn't." He shook his head.

"Well, if you want something changed, you have to make your demands known." She strode across the room toward the other high-ranking visitors. When she reached Wisnall and Torres, she interrupted their low-voiced conversation without waiting for a break. "Where is Lieutenant Kassis? I specifically requested her assistance, and she's apparently been reassigned."

Wisnall glowered at the interruption, then his brows went up in surprise. "Reassigned? By whom?"

Auntie B spread her hands. "I have no idea. I was told she's no longer available to me."

Wisnall's gaze went blank—an expression Quinn was coming to

recognize as someone speaking through their internal comm system. The concept of private communications tied directly to the brain both repelled and intrigued her. After a moment, Wisnall's gaze snapped back to the general. "Caitlin will find out what happened."

"Thank you." Auntie B turned to nod at Quinn and Tony, then lowered her voice to converse with the other two men.

"Sounds like a pissing match." Tony lounged against the top rail of a chair back. "Someone trying to prove they're more important. I've gotten the impression Siti is well-connected, so that seems like a stupid move to me."

"Her father was the commandant of the academy before he retired." Derek Lee seemed to materialize at Quinn's side. "And a hero of the CEC."

"Where did you come from?" Quinn asked, her voice squeaking in surprise.

"My mother always said—" Derek broke off with a cheeky grin. "I snuck in the back, so I didn't have to run the political welcome gauntlet. And I wanted to let you know I tried to undo Siti's reassignment but was unsuccessful."

Quinn gave the young man a long look. He returned her gaze stoically for a moment, then red crept up his neck and into his cheeks.

Tony chuckled. "Quinn is known for her mom-glares."

She slapped his arm. "That wasn't a glare. Thank you for trying to help her, but it would have been better to let Auntie—General La Gama handle it, I think. Have you also been reassigned?"

Derek shook his head. "But not for lack of trying. Fortunately, the captain has not taken a liking to the officer who is throwing his weight around."

"And that officer is...?" Quinn waited, using the mom-glare this time.

Derek's lips twitched. "I'm too old for that to work on me. And my mother was an admiral, so I'm immune to mere civilian mom-glares." He glanced around and lowered his voice. "I would suggest you view any Navy personnel who follow you to the surface as... what's the word I want?"

"Suspect? Dangerous? Out for themselves?" Quinn suggested.

"I don't think I'd use any of those phrases." Derek crossed his arms. "And I shouldn't say anything. We're on... opposite sides of the table."

Tony put a hand on Quinn's arm. "We need to remember at this level of politics, everyone has an agenda. Military officers attached to civilian envoys are usually spies. Isn't that right, Lieutenant Lee?"

He spread his fingers wide. "I'm just a pilot. The only thing I'm attached to is this ship."

Tony gave him a long look, then a nod. "And a certain CEC lieutenant, if I don't miss my guess."

Derek's face went bright red this time as he stuttered to respond. "No—there's nothing— We've been friends a long time."

"Friends." Quinn nudged Tony with her elbow. "We know how that works. We were friends for ten years."

Joss entered the room and made a bee line for his father. The elder Torres excused himself, and the two men moved away to hold a low-voiced discussion. Joss threw several pointed looks at Wisnall who was doing his best to pretend Auntie B's conversation held him in thrall.

Quinn nodded at the two Earthmen. "What about them? Papa is from Earth, son is attached—" She smirked at Derek as she said the word. "He's with the CEC. Which belongs to Wisnall's government. And he's assigned to us. Who's *he* spying for?"

Derek laughed, a genuinely humorous expression. "The Caveman isn't spying for anyone. He doesn't have that kind of deviousness. What you see is what you get with Joss."

"I wouldn't be so sure about that," Tony muttered under his breath.

"Earth is aligned with the Colonial Commonwealth." Derek frowned at Joss as the other man crossed the room. "Mostly."

Joss stopped in front of Derek, arms folded, leaning in close. "I thought you were taking care of Siti?"

Derek mimicked Joss's stance. "I tried. Andrade—" He broke off with a swift glance at Quinn and Tony. "The person who reassigned her isn't exactly in the chain of command here."

"That's why I didn't want to bother with all of that. We aren't really in the chain, either." Joss waved a hand at himself. "We were assigned to them." He pointed an elbow at the general.

"It doesn't matter. Ambassador La Gama—"

"If you wouldn't let me ask my dad, why do you think asking her—"

Quinn put a hand between the two young men. "Look. It's too late to change how it happened. Having the request go through Auntie B makes more sense than having Ambassador Torres ask—Siti isn't assigned to him. And at this point, Wisnall is interested in keeping on our good side, so I'm sure if anyone can get Siti back, it's him."

"Yeah, all you did was paint a target on yourself." Joss smacked Derek's shoulder.

Derek opened his mouth, then glanced at Quinn and Tony and closed it again. "I'm not worried." He did that glazed look thing, then snapped back to the present. "We're approaching our parking orbit. I need to start my pre-launch. If you'll excuse me…" He gave a half bow to the others and slipped out through a back door.

Joss watched him, eyes narrowed, then turned back to the others with a smile. "I'm anxious to see this new planet. What's the best drink on Romara?"

They told Joss about their favorite restaurants and bars in Romara City, then joined the ambassadors at Auntie B's invitation. Conversation became general, focused on the cultural sites in the capital. Quinn smothered a snicker as she watched Tony bite his tongue—as a N'Avon native, he didn't think Romara had much in the way of "culture."

When a ship-wide announcement declared they'd arrived at Romara, the party broke up so the participants could retrieve their personal possessions from their cabins. Quinn hadn't brought much with her—she and Tony maintained an apartment in Romara City. Her shoulder bag held her must-have items, and now that the Sergeant Sinister had been consumed, it weighed considerably less. They grabbed their small travel duffels and followed Joss to the shuttle bay.

When they arrived, they found Siti in the ready room, slumped in one of the massage chairs.

"About time you showed up." Joss offered a hand and effortlessly pulled her from the big recliner.

"Sorry." Her smile didn't hide the dark circles under her eyes. "I was busy cleaning scrubbers."

Joss's face went dark. "Officers don't clean scrubbers. The Navy has robots for that."

"That's what Derek said." Siti smiled wanly and gestured toward the door. "He also said we're cleared to get aboard as soon as you want."

"Should we wait for the others?" Tony perched on the edge of one of the chairs. "We're glad to have you back."

"Not as happy as I am to be back." She waved the door open. "They'll catch up."

As they boarded the shuttle, Quinn took a last look around the Colonial Navy ship. This would likely be her last opportunity—she was under no illusion their status as the Lunescan escort would grant them entry to the high-flown world of interstellar politics. And frankly, she was okay with that. Her stint as catalyst for a revolution had given her enough political intrigue to last a lifetime.

"Nostalgia?" Tony jostled her shoulder with his own.

"For the bad old days in the Federation Space Force? Not really, although I had some good times in the early years. I'm happier as a civilian. But I doubt we'll fly on anything this flashy again."

"You think the Republic won't want a couple of former revolutionaries this close to the center of intrigue?"

"I think Lunesco is a fringe world, and the only reason we're included in this meeting is because the Colonials landed in our back yard. Romara will kick us to the side as fast as they can. The fact that we were involved in the revolution doesn't help at all." Once the Republic was firmly established, everyone who'd participated in the overthrow had been encouraged to retire from public life. Even Amanda, who had been elected the first president of the republic, hadn't survived for a second term.

"We served our purpose. I'm okay with being a nobody." Quinn settled into the comfortable seat and latched her seat belt. "And as a Marconi, you're used to flying under the radar anyway."

"So true. Speaking of—have you heard anything from Liz?" He dropped into the bucket seat beside her.

"She said they'll meet us here, in case we need a quick escape." She rubbed her fingers against the leather-like material of the fat armrest. "I could get used to the good life, though."

He waved a hand. "Totally not worth the trouble." He looked up as the next wave of passengers entered.

Quinn supposed Tony was right. They weren't political people. But she'd come to enjoy the company of the young officers. Maybe they could encourage some kind of an exchange program. As she mulled that idea over, the ambassadors came aboard. Auntie B and Harim took seats in the front next to the Colonial representative and Ambassador Torres.

Caitlin Maroney, the Colonial ambassador's assistant, moved to the back of the shuttle where they sat. "Lieutenant Kassis, please let me know if there are any other mix-ups with respect to your assignment." Without waiting for a reply, she returned to the front of the ship.

"The words sounded helpful, but the tone sure didn't." Quinn glanced at Siti. "Where'd Joss go?"

"He's riding up front again. They let him take a jump seat. He doesn't like riding back here where there are no windows." She lowered her voice. "And the message I got was 'make sure you don't screw up again.' She's definitely watching me. Whatever. I'm not worried."

"What exactly was the mix-up?" Tony tried to sound casual, but Quinn could tell he wanted confirmation of something.

Siti lifted both hands. "Your guess is as good as mine."

For some reason, Quinn didn't think that was true.

CHAPTER TWENTY-FOUR
SITI

THE SHUTTLE LANDED SMOOTHLY, and the intercom pinged. "Welcome to Romara." Robinson's voice carried through the shuttle. "Please remain seated until our captain parks the shuttle."

"I bet Derek loves being called 'our captain,'" I whispered to Yasmi. She didn't respond.

In the front of the cargo hold, the ambassadors had ignored the request and climbed to their feet. All except Zane—he waited until the final landing announcement to stand and stretch. Wisnall ribbed him about following the rules.

Zane smiled blandly. "When they're for my safety, of course I follow them."

"There's no danger. It's all about control." Wisnall strode impatiently toward the airlock. "Everyone wants control."

Clearly the ambassador craved control. From the corner of my eye, I caught a significant look passing between Quinn and Tony.

Zane gestured for General La Gama and Harim to precede him. "I want to speak with Lieutenant Kassis."

I let the other Romarans exit the craft, then gave Joss's dad a swift hug. "First chance for a Zane hug!"

Zane always gave the perfect hug. Warm and friendly without any weird friend's dad awkwardness. "It's good to finally grab a chance to chat." He released me and stepped back.

"How's my dad?" I asked

"He's really taken to Earth life since his retirement. He's growing a garden." His hand against my upper back urged me toward the hatch.

I stopped short. "My dad? Growing things?" With a shake of my head, I continued into the airlock. "Thanks for springing me from scrubber duty."

"Is that where they had you stashed? Who did you piss off?"

I frowned and shook my head. "It doesn't matter."

"It does. I want to know who is sabotaging these talks."

"You think punishing me for a perceived mistake is an attempt to sabotage the talks?" I turned a puzzled frown on Zane. "Why would a mid-level intel officer want to do that? And how does pulling me away sabotage anything?"

"The Romarans like you and Joss. You're building good will. As to why he'd do it—I'm betting someone at a much higher pay grade put him up to it. Joss filled me in on his assignment to this mission. Someone had a reason to include him before we knew about any of—" He pulled up at the exterior hatch to gaze out at the planet. "Wow."

We had landed on the roof of the tallest building in a crowded metropolis. Romara City looked at least as big as New Sydney on Sally Ride. A rotor winged craft hovered nearby, either waiting to land in our place or providing surveillance and security. Based on the gun protruding from the front of the vehicle, I bet on the latter.

Far off in the distance, a ship glided at a steep angle to land on the long runway barely visible through the haze. In the other direction, the sunlight glinted off smooth water in a vast bay, with choppier water beyond. Large, bulky ships steamed in and out of the port.

"This looks so much like Earth before the Exodus." Zane shaded his eyes and turned slowly to view the harbor and city. The sun hung low above the sea, and lights glowed from some of the buildings around us.

"When you're ready, Ambassador Torres." Wisnall waited impatiently with the others on a red carpet leading from the shuttle to double glass doors leading into the building. A delegation of locals stood outside the entrance.

"I like to take a look at every new planet I visit." Zane stepped down from the shuttle's airlock hatch and gestured at our surroundings. "You only get one first look. And they're all worth seeing. After you."

Wisnall harumphed and strode down the strip of red as our hosts came to meet us. La Gama and Harim fell in behind Wisnall, with Joss, Tony, Quinn, and the assistant ambassador trailing behind. Zane poked an elbow at me and winked. "Milady?"

I put my hand on his forearm. "I'm supposed to be support, not arm candy."

He squeezed my fingers then released them. "Good point. Look tough." We stretched our strides to catch up to the rest of the group.

"On behalf of President Fandagi, I welcome you to the Romaran Republic." The dignitary from Romara introduced himself and his entourage to Wisnall and Zane, ignoring the rest of us, even Harim and General La Gama. A multitude of flunkies surrounded us, cutting us away from the higher ranking visitors as efficiently as herd dogs.

A woman circulated, handing out little cards and trying to take our bags. I held onto mine. Most of my gear was on the pallet in the shuttle, but there was no way I was letting some random person take my personal items—including Yasmi who took that opportunity to poke her head out of the bag.

The woman squeaked in alarm, her eyes wide. "Vermin!"

I cupped a protective hand around Yasmi. "She's not vermin. She's a sair-glider. A working animal. Part of the Explorer Corps team."

"Explorer Corp?" she echoed faintly. A sneer curled her lip then disappeared. "What, exactly, are you exploring?"

I narrowed my eyes at her. I knew my place with the higher-ranking officials, but no way was I going to let some low-level bureaucrat disparage my service. "Your planet? This civilization? We're the ones who made the initial contact. Without the CEC, none of this would be happening." I waved a finger at the dignitaries disappearing through the glass doors. Zane cast one quick smile over his shoulder at us as he allowed them to lead him away.

Why did it feel like we were being categorized and divided? Maybe because we were. In moments, only Joss, Quinn, Tony, and I remained on the rooftop, with a pair of Romaran underlings. Robinson and Derek had flown away, leaving the landing pad empty. The gunship circled noisily for a few minutes longer, then departed toward the landing strip.

"This way, please." The woman pulled the glass door wide and held one for us to enter the small lobby.

A door slid open, revealing a small, mirror-lined room. Joss nudged me with his shoulder. "That's an elevator. We had 'em on Earth."

"Not when I was there. But I've seen them on videos." I moved to the side of the small cubicle and waited for our escort to join us. The woman pressed a button and the doors slid closed. The box shuddered gently, then began to descend.

The man held one of the palm-sized cards aloft. "This is your access card. It gives you entry to your room and the floor to which you're assigned. You can also access the meeting rooms—when meetings are in session."

"What about our delegates?" Quinn asked. "What if we need to meet with General La Gama or Governor Harim? Will they be quartered on the same floor?"

"They're on seventeen." The man indicated the button with a well-manicured fingertip. "If they wish to invite you to their room, they can give you access through the system."

We all raised brows at each other while our two escorts faced the front, ignoring us.

I activated my internal comm system and called Joss. "Did your dad ever get one of these?"

A tiny shake of his head told me what I'd feared. We were cut off from our superiors. I tried calling Derek but went to his message system. Probably because he was currently flying.

"Call me," I muttered then ended the call.

The elevator opened, and we moved into a long corridor with a bland brown carpet and smooth white walls. Colorful pictures in a blurry style hung between wood doors each adorned with a number. The woman beckoned for Joss and me to follow her. The man took Tony and Quinn the opposite direction. When I looked back, they'd disappeared—either into a room or around a corner at the end of the hall.

Tapping her card against a black rectangle below the handle caused a light to glow red, then flip to green. Something clicked, and she pulled the handle down. Pushing the door open, she swept into a room furnished with a couch and two functional chairs. "This is your suite. There are bedrooms on either side. Your luggage will be delivered later. Please enjoy your stay." With that, she headed for the door.

"Wait!" Slinging my bag to the table, I hurried after her. Yasmi jumped to my shoulder as I followed the woman into the hallway. "Do you have a communications system? How will we know when we're supposed to attend meetings?"

"And where?" Joss crowded up behind me. "Also, where is the rest of our delegation quartered?"

She kept walking quickly, as if she didn't want to answer our questions. We hurried along behind her, catching up in the lobby. She waved her card at the elevator panel and finally turned to address us as the door slid open. "We'll deliver a meal to your room tonight, and an agenda for the coming week. It will include locations. Enjoy your stay." She backed into the little car and let the door close between us.

"Do you feel like we're being sidelined?" Joss waved his card at the elevator, but nothing happened.

"Definitely. Where do you suppose Quinn and Tony ended up? Are they being banished, too?" I tried my card, but nothing happened. "Looks like we're stuck on this floor."

"I wonder if there's a stairway anywhere?" Joss headed down the corridor in the direction Quinn and Tony had gone. He raised his voice. "This planet is pretty cool, isn't it?"

As we walked, we talked loudly about the little we'd seen of

Romara. By the time we reached the corner, a door farther on had opened. Tony stuck his head out and waved. "Hey! Come on down."

At my nod of agreement, Joss broke into a jog. We thundered up to Tony's door and slipped past him into a room identical to the one we'd been given. I glowered at Quinn. "What's up with these people?"

She held up a finger, then turned on some music. "Come on in. I think there's something to drink in that little fridge." Making a "just do it face" at me, she increased the music's volume a little more. "Grab me something bubbly, if there is one."

I opened the little cupboard she indicated, and cold air flowed out. Rows of cans and small bottles filled the little space. A drawer below the beverages held fruit and some slim packages. I handed a couple of random cans to Joss, then put a bottle on the counter above and grabbed one of the packages.

Quinn set a small, black device on the table. Its textured coating looked rubberized, and a small light gleamed on one end. She held a finger to her lips as she turned the music back down, sliding a lever on the device as she did so. With a nod, she sat back. "That should do it."

I raised a brow. "Counter surveillance?"

Tony nodded and took one of the cans Joss still held. "These are non-alcoholic. Help yourself." He popped the top, drank deeply, then set the can on a side table and dropped into one of the chairs. "They're definitely listening and actively trying to keep us away from Auntie B and the negotiations. Not that it matters—she doesn't need us."

"Then why did she bring us?" I squinted at the spiky letters on the cans and randomly picked one to open. A quick sniff gave me fruity notes, so I tried a sip. "Nice."

"She paired us with you all so we can get to know each other." Quinn tried Tony's beverage and made a face. "Too sweet." She rose and returned to the little cooler. "We're supposed to learn more about each other and report back later. Develop a real relationship with real people. Can someone get the door?"

Throwing a puzzled look over my shoulder—I hadn't heard any

kind of alert—I grabbed the handle. The door swung inward, and a huge, furry animal stalked into the room.

CHAPTER TWENTY-FIVE
QUINN

SITI GASPED, taking a step back from the door and slamming into Joss. The little green and white glider squeaked and dove around her neck to hide in Siti's thick braid.

Are these the aliens? Sashelle stalked into the room, her thick hair puffed out to maximum size.

"I'm not sure they're really 'aliens.' More like long lost cousins." Setting her drink on the table, Quinn moved between the Colonials and the Hadriana caat. She let her hand rest on Sashelle's shoulder as she made the introductions. "This is Sashelle of Hadriana."

The caat's faint growl shook Quinn's hand, and she tried not to roll her eyes. "Excuse me. I mean, this is Sashelle, Mighty Huntress and Eliminator of Vermin."

And?

"There's more?" Quinn's brows drew down as she looked at Tony.

He shook his head, hands spread wide. "She doesn't talk to me."

The growl grew louder, and Siti's eyes widened in response.

"You're making our guests nervous, Sashelle." Quinn stepped between the caat and the people again.

Her mouse is making me nervous. Or hungry. And you need to finish the introduction. My full title is now Mighty Huntress, Eliminator of Vermin, and Savior of Lunesco.

"My mistake." Quinn repeated the full title to the others. "Apparently she was awarded an addition after the war."

A mental shrug reinforced the meaning of the strange shoulder roll Sashelle performed. *Your president insisted. Your old president. The good one. And my empress concurred. It is in the interest of the pride to remind humans of our participation in the events of the revolution. Although they appear to be unwilling to include me in the discussions here.*

"No offense, but they might take you more seriously if you spoke to them." Quinn shepherded the group back to the chairs.

Sashelle sat beside Tony and glared.

"Sassy." Tony didn't try to hide his grin at Sashelle's growl.

"That's why she won't talk to you." Quinn sat on Sashelle's other side and gestured for the two officers to take seats.

Siti perched on the edge of the chair farthest from Sashelle, her hand cupped to her neck. "Yasmi is terrified."

I won't eat her mouse. Sashelle's eyes closed halfway, and she ostentatiously turned away from Siti.

"She says your glider is safe." Quinn crooked her fingers. "Let her see Sashelle isn't dangerous."

Siti pulled the glider from her hair, carefully extracting its claws from her braid. "Ow. Yasmi, she says she won't hurt you."

I said I wouldn't eat her.

"Sashelle, you aren't helping." Quinn glared at the caat.

The big animal sighed and dropped flat to the ground, her mental eye roll obvious in her demeanor. *She can come closer.*

"I'm not sure she wants to get closer." Quinn turned to Siti. "You wanna try…?"

Siti held the quivering glider in both hands. As she moved nearer to the big caat, the tiny glider froze, even its fearful tremors stilled.

Don't worry, little friend. You are in no danger from me. Now or in the future. She rolled onto her back, exposing the thick white fur of her belly.

"I've never seen her do that before," Tony whispered.

With an uncertain glance at Tony, Siti extended her arms to hold the creature closer to Sashelle's head. The glider seemed to understand the significance of Sashelle's pose, and her little pink nose wiggled as she sniffed at the caat.

A deep rumble issued from the caat, and Yasmi wiggled free of Siti's grasp. The glider jumped, landing on Sashelle's furry chest. She crept closer to Sashelle's head, and the bigger animal's pink tongue flicked out to lick the little one. With a swift bunching of muscles, the caat twisted to her feet, the glider scrambling to her back. *We are ready.*

"Ready for what?" Quinn dropped back into her chair and sipped her beverage.

To free the caats.

Quinn choked on her drink.

"Free them from what?" Tony asked.

"Oh, you heard that?" Quinn blinked at him in surprise as she mopped seltzer from her shirt.

"She talks to me when *she* wants, not when I want." He turned to Siti and Joss, who stared at them, bemused. "Sashelle says she and Yasmi are ready to free the caats."

The Republic promised to return Hadriana to us. I am holding you to that promise. Sashelle paced to the door. *Now is the time.*

"I think you overestimate our ability to influence the government." Tony gestured at the four humans. "Quinn and I don't even know anyone in control anymore. And these two are low-level officers. No offense."

Siti shook her head. "None taken. It's true. Although, we do have a small ace up our sleeves." She looked at the caat but pointed at Joss. "His dad has been able to negotiate some unprecedented deals. He's probably the person you want helping you."

Why is he able to negotiate deals?

Joss's jaw dropped. "I heard that."

Siti sucked in a disappointed breath. "I didn't."

He thrust out his chest. "I am special. But you already knew that."

"Sashelle, please don't encourage him." Siti put a hand out to the caat.

Fine. I'll talk to everyone. For now.

Siti's eyes went wide. "You have a beautiful voice. It's like—this is how Yasmi must feel when I pet her."

A surprisingly apt comparison. Still by the door, the caat settled to her haunches. The glider launched herself from the feline's shoulders, flying across the room to land on Siti's shoulder. *Bring the Earthman to me.*

"I'm not sure we're going to be able to do that." Joss pulled his card key from a pocket and waved it at the caat. "They've got us locked up tight. And Dad never got an audio implant, so I can't—"

"We can still call him." Siti smacked her own forehead. "I'm so used to internal comms—" She flicked her holo-ring and poked at the colorful interface that appeared in her palm. "He definitely has one of these, and we've already established Romaran tech isn't a match for our systems." Her brows scrunched together as she flicked and swiped. "Why can't I get through?"

Tony reached forward and tapped the little black device forgotten on the table. "N'Avon tech is better than Romaran." With a little smirk, he toggled the device off. "Now?"

Siti worked through her interface, her expression changing from puzzled to frustrated to triumphant. "Ha. I still can't get Zane. I wonder where Derek is?"

Joss fiddled with his own ring, and a map appeared above his palm. He pointed east. "That airstrip we saw from the roof."

"That's the Space Force base," Quinn said. "Tony and I were assigned there back in the day. In fact, that's where we met."

Siti nodded absently. "I could probably relay a call through the ship, but—"

"Your good friend Major Andrade would undoubtedly hear about it." Joss grabbed one of the bottles and opened it with a pop. "Maybe Nibs can relay for you."

"Maybe." Siti rose and moved to a corner, turning partially away from the group. "Derek, are you busy? No, I'm fine, but I need some help."

"Tell Nibs I said 'hi'!" Joss called.

Siti waved an impatient hand and turned farther away. Quinn didn't bother to suppress a grin as she pointed at Siti then at Joss. "Did you two grow up together?"

Joss snickered. "You'd think that, wouldn't you? But no, we didn't meet until a few years ago." He frowned. "Actually, it's been almost nine years. Wow. That's a long time. Siti's dad is the one who 'rediscovered' Earth, and she came with him. Then we went to the academy together. Derek was there, too. And our paths keep crossing." He looked out the window at the darkening sky and the buildings picked out in bright, colorful lights. "This is a pretty place."

Tony grimaced. "Too pretty. Everything here is carefully planned to look good. They even engineer things with minor imperfections so they look more real. It was the Federation's seat of power, and all designed to 'prove' everything was perfect and beautiful. The government is better now, but I still don't like the city. Plus it smells like fish."

"Only near the bay." Quinn chuckled. Tony had never liked Romara City. After having been imprisoned here for a few weeks, Quinn agreed with him. "But we keep a small apartment here because we end up coming and going a lot."

"Derek says he can't reach Zane, either." Siti walked back to the middle of the room. "It's possible he—Zane—turned off his comms. Seems like a bad idea, but—"

"I can see Dad doing that. If he wants to focus on discussions or whatever." Joss, who had slouched back in his chair, sat upright. "But that drone told us there were no meetings tonight. So, why would he—"

"You don't think he's being held against his will?" Siti clutched the back of the couch.

"No." Tony slashed a hand to cut off that line of thought. "The Federation might have done something like that, but those people are no longer in power. What would be the benefit of holding an ambassador hostage? Especially the ambassador from Earth? Wisnall I could see, but Torres makes no sense. Earth is our heritage, too."

"Maybe Fandagi thinks he can take control of Earth by holding Zane?" Quinn bit her lip as her gaze slid to Sashelle. "The Republic was supposed to return Hadriana to the caats, but the current administration keeps stringing Sashelle's people along. Maybe they think they can gain control over Earth, too. That would give them a much stronger position against the Colonial Commonwealth. We're the underdogs. And we all know how things go when two unmatched societies meet." She pointed at Sashelle. "The weaker one loses."

CHAPTER TWENTY-SIX
SITI

Back in our suite, Joss threw himself down on the couch. "The cat talks. That's bonkers."

"Is it?" I crossed my arms and leaned against the arm of the couch, tilting my head at Yasmi sitting on my shoulder. "We know aliens exist. Aliens wi—" I broke off. This suite was undoubtedly bugged, and Tony hadn't had a second jammer. I activated a private call to Joss. "One word: Darenti."

"Exactly. What are the odds we'd find two alien species—after all these years of only animals?"

I rolled my eyes. "*We* didn't find either of them. And it makes sense that any alien species would be different from us. Either way, she could be a helpful ally."

"You think she'll talk to my dad?"

I slid over the arm onto the couch cushion. "I think the more important question is will Zane hear her? Too bad Jake isn't here." I yawned widely, then winked and spoke aloud. "I'm off to bed. See you in the morning."

Shuffling a bit, I went into my bedroom and rustled around in the bathroom, brushing my teeth and combing out my hair. If Tony and Quinn were wrong and our rooms had cameras in them—the idea made me squirm—we were done. But Tony hadn't found any indication of video surveillance in his room. I went into the bedroom, changed from my semi-formal travel uniform into the comfortable duty blacks I'd kept in my bag, rumpled the bed, and turned out the light.

Tiptoeing to the parlor, I toggled my audio again. "Ready?"

"Ready." Joss ghosted to my side.

"I hope this gizmo works." I pulled out the doctored key card Quinn had rigged. It was supposed to let us exit the room without being tracked. Quinn had worked in communications in the Federation back in her younger days, and during their revolution had polished her hacking skills. Time to test how much.

I waved the card at the inside of the door. There was no lock here, just a handle to open the door. But the act of opening it would be recorded—unless Quinn's hack did the job.

Nothing obvious happened, as Quinn had warned us. I slowly pressed the lever down, easing the latch open.

Joss's hand fell on my arm, and his foot stopped the door from opening more than a crack. He flicked his holo-ring and turned on his uniform's camouflage setting. Our duty blacks were designed to make us difficult to see on most wavelengths—protection against predators on unexplored planets. The same technology was used by the Navy to fool the enemy in combat. With a smirk, I flicked mine on as well.

The hall looked the same as it had a few minutes before: well lit and empty. We eased down the corridor and used the card to open Quinn and Tony's suite. Tony pulled the door wide.

Excellent camouflage. Sashelle's comment came in loud and clear. Unlike with my audio implant, I couldn't distinguish individual words, but her meaning was unequivocal—and obviously sarcastic. *If we weren't expecting you, we'd think the artwork was going for a walk.*

Tony clamped a hand over his mouth, his eyes dancing. Quinn rolled her eyes and took the key card, heading down the hallway. The caat took off after her, like a wolf after a gazelle. Instead of pouncing on the woman, she loped past and sat down beside the stairwell door to lick a paw.

Bumping the huge caat out of the way with her hip, Quinn waved the card at the door lock. It clicked, but the light stayed red. She pressed the door slowly, avoiding the crashbar, and it swung open. With a smug grin over her shoulder, Quinn stepped inside.

Sashelle bounded past, taking the steps three or four at a time. I followed, staying close to the wall and moving slowly. If anyone happened to be looking through the narrow window in the door, an abrupt movement would disrupt my stealth tech. But easing up the wall should allow my shield to gradually conform to the colors and textures of the paint, rendering me mostly invisible.

I hoped. It seemed to work on most alien predators.

At the top of the steps, I crouched beside the door, poking my head up to peer through the narrow window. A man stood with his back to us—clearly intent on keeping people inside, not out. I waved Quinn's doctored card at the latch. It clicked, and the guy jerked in response to the sound.

I yanked the door open before he got completely turned around, and Sashelle landed against his chest, taking him to the ground. The man's eyes went wide, and he reached for his earpiece. Sashelle placed a huge paw on his hand, pinning it to the carpet.

Gun! I projected the thought as loudly as I could.

The caat batted the weapon out of the man's other hand as easily as I'd swat a fly. She bared her teeth at the man, big head shaking side to side. Her growl rumbled with menace. The guy's eyes went even wider, then rolled back in his head.

"Did he pass out?" I whispered to Joss.

"How do I know? I can't see past your butt."

With a silent groan, I stepped to the side.

"That was butts, plural. The caat is also blocking my way."

"Sashelle—"

I heard him. She moved off her victim, rolling him easily with one paw. *Yes, he passed out. My species is good at inducing terror. It's one of our defense mechanisms.*

"Inducing terror? Do you do… mind control?" One of the reasons the Commonwealth had interdicted Darenti was the inhabitants' ability to influence others through telepathy. Another species able to do that was terrifying.

Of a sort. It takes great concentration. Best used much like your magic— to make us blend in. But for short periods, I can... inflict fear. A sense of satisfaction rolled off the caat.

"Remind me to stay on your good side." I jerked my head at Joss. "Grab his arms."

"That modification Diz made to our implants should prevent her from scaring us, right?" Joss asked as he lifted the man's shoulders.

I shrugged and grabbed his feet, helping to drag him into the stairway. "Who knows. Can she hear us talking?"

Yes.

We both stared after the caat as she bounded away.

You think very loudly.

"Awesome." I tried to wonder quietly how to think less loudly. I couldn't tell if Sashelle's amusement was real or a figment of my imagination.

Tony slid past us into the hallway, Quinn on his heels. I dropped the guard's feet as they passed and grabbed Quinn's arm. "I thought we were leaving this up to the caat?" I whispered.

"We are. But we don't want to be here when he comes to." She nodded at the guard.

"Right." We'd decided to let Sashelle speak with Zane and relay to us as necessary. But that was before we knew she could scare someone unconscious. We'd thought she'd sneak into his room once we got her past the locked stairwell doors.

We hurried down to the corner where Sashelle waited. She stared at Quinn for a long moment, then turned to me and asked for the card key. Like the first time, the thought came in almost as a video rather than words, but her intention was clear. I held out the card.

The caat took it daintily in her sharp teeth, then eased away. Dropping to my belly, I slid forward and peered around the corner, trusting my camouflage and my location to hide me from anyone in the hall.

Two men stood in this section of the corridor, on the left side. They appeared to be watching the door across the hall. Sashelle crept along the floor near the left wall, somehow almost invisible against the beige paint. It shouldn't have been possible without tech like ours. She wasn't kidding about the ability to hide in plain sight.

Behind me, a door clicked, and Tony grunted in satisfaction. "This room is empty," he whispered. "We can wait here."

Sashelle reached the first man and paused, crouched unnoticed beside his feet. *This is the place.* After another long pause, the man walked toward his counterpart, asking something I didn't catch. Sashelle swarmed across the corridor, lifted the card to the access panel, then disappeared into the suite. Neither man appeared to notice.

"She's in." I squirmed away from the corner and stood. Quinn beckoned me from inside the room next to the corner.

I have made contact with the Earthman. Sashelle's report came in loud and clear. *He says he tried to leave the suite earlier and was asked to return. He attempted to make contact with others, including his son, through his magic ring, but was unsuccessful.*

"Now what?" I leaned against the wall beside the closed door. "Does he want to leave?"

Negative. He prefers to stay here and see how it plays out. I have delivered the device the Purveyor of Tuna gave me, and he will save it for emergencies.

"Purveyor of Tuna?" I repeated.

Quinn raised her hand, her expression blank. "That's my title. Quite the honor, I'm told."

"What's this device she mentioned?" Joss whispered.

"It's kind of like an emergency beacon." Quinn's hands went to her neck. "I tucked it into Sashelle's collar so she could deliver it. Activating it will alert us to his location, but it will also be obvious to anyone monitoring electronic emissions. They might not know what it is, but they'll know it's broadcasting."

Outside, a door slammed open. Someone yelled. Feet pounded down the hall toward Zane's room.

"I think our friend in the stairwell woke up." Quinn put her ear against the door. "Sashelle, you'd better hide."

Agreed. The Earthman has offered me a place.

Like a video, the scene appeared before my eyes. I could still see the room around me, but an image of Joss's dad superimposed over it. He sat in a chair in a room similar to my bedroom downstairs, except the furnishings looked more elaborate. As I watched, he rose and moved away from the desk.

"Can you see this, Siti?" Joss asked through my implant.

I turned my head, and the image of his dad superimposed over his face for a strange moment, reinforcing the familial similarities. "Yes."

As we watched, Zane pulled the chair away from the desk, and our point of view shifted as if the person holding the camera had crouched. Then we saw the opening beneath the desk and seemed to crawl into the space. Curling around, we faced the front again. Zane's face disappeared and his legs slid in beside us as he retook his seat.

Distant pounding echoed a knocking coming through the vision.

"Enter!" Zane called without moving.

"Sir."

The "camera" swung to the left, peering over Zane's legs through a gap between the spindles of the desk. The larger of the two men from the hall now stood in the doorway, one hand on his weapon, the other one holding the door open. "Are you alone?"

Zane's feet shifted as he sat up straighter. "I'm not sure how that's any of your business. I'm also quite sure you know the answer to that question. You've been stationed outside my door all evening. And no one has come in through the windows."

Joss smirked. "All one hundred percent true."

The guard grumbled. "Yes, sir. Still, do you mind if I check the bedroom?"

"Be my guest."

The man disappeared from view, and Zane's legs shifted again. After a long moment, the man returned.

"Would you like to look under the bed?" Zane suggested.

The guard flushed. "No, sir. It must have been a false alarm. I'm sorry to have disturbed you. Good evening."

"Good night."

THE ROMARA CONFRONTATION

After the guard left, Zane remained motionless for a long moment, then moved his chair back. As we emerged from under the desk, his brow went up in question. I got the impression Sashelle was talking to him, and he was responding, but the image faded.

Joss rubbed his eyes. "That was weird."

"It is. Every time." Tony massaged the back of his neck. "Gives me a little bit of a headache, too."

"Good thing she doesn't do it very often." Quinn's gaze pinned each of us in turn. "Now what? Will they search the whole floor?"

"Possibly. But would you believe someone who claimed a giant cat had attacked him and thrown him into the stairwell?" At their head shakes, I went on. "I think we'd better try to get out of here before they replace him with someone they think is more reliable."

At their agreement, I eased into the corridor. No one at the stairwell door. A quick check around the corner revealed the two guards had resumed their posts. I drifted down the hall and peered through the window. "Clear." The guy Sashelle had terrified was nowhere to be seen.

"We're moving." Joss's reply came as I used Quinn's card to open the door. We ghosted down the stairwell, then paused at the door to our floor.

Quinn took the card from me, then hesitated. "Anything else tonight?"

"I think we've done everything we can for now." I scratched my head. "Zane has a duress alarm. Do we need to get them to Harim and the general?"

Tony shook his head. "They already have 'em. Your folks don't, though."

"You mean Wisnall and Maroney? I'd bet anything they have their own emergency communications." I yawned. "They can take care of themselves. I'm ready for bed."

"You and me both." Joss yawned, too. "Is there a gym in this building? Tomorrow's supposed to be a leg day."

CHAPTER TWENTY-SEVEN
QUINN

AFTER THREE DAYS OF MEETINGS, Quinn was ready to call it quits. Auntie B had suggested Sashelle be invited to join the discussions—since a human representative of Hadriana had joined the republic council—but was rebuffed. Although Sashelle's contributions to the revolution were known and celebrated in the republic, the stories were treated more like folk tales than historical fact, and Hadriana caats were still viewed as mythical creatures.

The caats didn't help the matter by refusing to engage with the humans on their planet. And only Sashelle ever left Hadriana.

After his encounter with Sashelle, Zane Torres had thrown his weight behind Auntie B's proposal, but the other representatives balked at the idea. Wisnall even suggested, using extremely veiled language, that Torres was experiencing a mental breakdown.

"If they agree to you joining the summit, they have to recognize your species as sentient and sapient," Tony told the caat after they returned to their suite at the end of the third day. "Which would require them to entertain your claim to the planet. Hadriana might just be a potato farm, but those potatoes feed a lot of people. It would help if you'd speak directly to other humans."

Sashelle's eyes closed to slits, and disdain rolled off her.

Quinn got up from the couch in their suite's sitting room and crossed to the windows. Staring down at the city, she frowned. "Where's Francine? Liz said you were traveling with her."

She is visiting friends. She was not invited to the council. Of course, neither was I. The caat's growl increased in volume. *I believe it is time for the nuclear option.*

Tony choked, spewing his beverage across the coffee table. "Where did you hear that phrase?"

The Earthman taught me. Sashelle's growl turned to a purr. *I like him. He treats me like an equal.*

"Funny how we know exactly which Earthman she's referring to, isn't it?" Quinn asked Tony.

He frowned. "I see his face when she mentions him. Don't you?"

"That's what I mean." Quinn turned back to the caat. "What exactly is the nuclear option?"

We must bring the empress to Romara.

The two humans exchanged a look.

"The empress?" Tony asked.

"Is that the leader of all caats?" Quinn said at the same time. At Sashelle's affirmative, she went on. "If they won't include you, why would they include your empress?"

She has abilities beyond mine. Ways to ensure they listen.

"That's not terrifying," Quinn whispered.

It should be.

"I'm game for a visit to Hadriana." Tony picked up his soda. "Can Francine take us? Or should we call Liz?"

The Earthman has agreed to convey us. In his offspring's friend's ship.

"Offspring's friend—you mean Lieutenant Lee's shuttle?" Quinn looked out the window again, toward the airfield. "Does he have the authority to offer that? And does that little ship have the ability to make a hyperjump?"

He believes he can make it happen. And he will accompany us.

"Isn't he busy with meetings?" Quinn asked.

Tony shrugged, hands wide. "One would think. But if I understand the politics, Earth is a separate, neutral entity. He can come and go as he pleases."

"As long as Romara doesn't try to keep him here." Quinn's lips thinned.

"Maybe that's why he volunteered. To force their hand if they're trying to restrain him. If he makes a formal statement to the rest of the delegates but Romara won't let him leave, that sends a very clear message to everyone involved."

THE NEXT MORNING, Tony and Quinn, accompanied by Sashelle, arrived at the main auditorium early. They filed into a back row of the tiered seating, finding their usual places next to Siti and Joss. A long table on the stage provided seating for the official delegates, but none of them had arrived yet.

"When are these meetings going to end?" Joss groaned. "I've taken more naps this week than in the rest of my life combined."

"I doubt that." Siti smacked his arm and gave him a fierce glare. "And you aren't supposed to sleep. We're here representing the CEC and the Commonwealth."

"But it's so. Boring!" The last word burst out of him, so loud people in the next few rows turned to stare.

Siti flushed and motioned for him to lower his voice. "You knew when they attached us to State it wouldn't be exciting."

"Which is why I tried to say 'no thanks,' but you wouldn't let me."

"You never even suggested—"

"Kids." Quinn's single word cut them off mid-rant. "Do you know why we're here?"

"For the summit," they said in unison.

"No, today, specifically." Quinn waved a hand at the slowly filling seats. "Your dad didn't mention it?"

Joss shook his head in confusion. "No. I haven't talked to him since we—" He broke off to see who was within earshot. "Since the first night." He twitched his head toward Sashelle, as if they needed reminding.

Before Quinn could explain, the lights flickered. Music played and the front doors of the room opened. The delegates, including Auntie B and Harim, Ambassador Torres, Ambassador Wisnall, the N'Avonian representative, and a long line of others from Hadriana, Robinson's World, Daravoo, and every other planet in the Republic, strode in to take seats at the table. After an ostentatious fanfare, President Fandagi took the stage. Most of the audience rose and cheered, glaring at anyone who remained seated. The foreign delegates' support personnel—including Tony, Quinn, and their Colonial counterparts—ignored the glares and kept to their seats. Fandagi waved to the audience and moved to a glossy wood podium perched on a dais above the other representatives.

"Greetings, delegates and supporters. Welcome to day four of the summit. As you know, we've spent much of the last few days getting to know each other a little better. The visitors from the Colonial Commonwealth and from 'Earth' have told us much about their civilizations." Fandagi managed to say Earth with a tone of faint derision.

"Does he not believe we're from Earth?" Joss sat up a little straighter.

"If you'd been awake, you would have realized that three days ago." Siti crossed her arms defensively. "He's been implying we invented a shared home world that doesn't exist—it's a ploy to weight any agreements or consortiums unfairly. As if Earth will always side with the CC."

"We both know that ain't happening." Joss snorted and leaned back again.

"… and we have recently received communications from yet another planet requesting a seat at the table." Fandagi's words brought their attention back to the stage. He slapped his hands on the podium and turned to smile smugly at the ambassadors grouped around the table on the stage. "Representatives from planets named Gagarin and Lewei will join the summit. Until they arrive, we suggest all formal discussions be paused."

Wisnall cleared his throat. "That's two planets. Two of the original five colonies. And as we've told you several times, we also represent multiple planets. We need—"

"Thank you, Ambassador Wisnall. Once the delegate—or delegates!—from Gagarin and Lewei arrive, we can discuss representation." He grinned like someone had given him gold bars for his birthday. "In the meantime, this body is temporarily adjourned." He spun on his heel and marched through the hastily re-opened doors. Representatives from the Romara Republic planets followed him, leaving Zane, Auntie B, Harim, and Wisnall at the big table.

Audience members also rose to leave, their excited voices mingling into an indecipherable clamor. Quinn caught several jokes about an early weekend. When the room had cleared, she followed Tony and Sashelle down to the table at the front of the room, where the remaining ambassadors stood.

"—heading back to N'Avon for now." Ambassador Berdon from the N'Avonian Commonwealth shook hands with Wisnall and Zane. "It's been a pleasure meeting you both."

"You'll return when the others arrive?"

Berdon wagged a hand back and forth. "Probably, but I don't have high hopes for these talks. Clearly any decisions made here will be influenced heavily by the Romaran agenda. My government will send a formal invitation to both of yours to meet in separate discussion." The woman turned to face Sashelle as the sleek caat jumped onto the low platform. "And yours, as well, Ambassador Sashelle. I regret we haven't made an effort to reach out to your people previously."

At her words, Wisnall put a hand to his forehead and turned away, head shaking in disbelief or disgust.

Sashelle sat back on her haunches in surprise, then her velvety voice flowed through Quinn's mind, although it was clear—somehow—that she had deigned to project to everyone present. *We welcome this decision.*

Berdon's eyes went wide, then she blanked her expression so quickly Quinn wondered if she'd imagined the surprise. "We look forward to *mutually beneficial* discussion." With a deep bow to the other representatives, Berdon turned and swept out of the room.

"I like that woman," Auntie B said. "Smart lady."

Sashelle's wordless agreement wrapped around them and dissipated.

Zane rubbed his hands together. "Well, now, we have time to make a little excursion, don't we?"

Wisnall, who had dropped back into his chair, crossed his arms. "Excursion? Where are you going, Torres?"

Zane waved a graceful hand at Sashelle. "The esteemed representative from Hadriana has invited me to visit her planet."

"What is with you two?" Wisnall pointed at the caat. "That… animal is hardly a planetary representative."

"Didn't you hear her?"

"I heard something." He rubbed behind his ear. "I'm going to have my implant checked for hacking." He turned on his heel and stomped away.

Zane swept an arm toward the door. "I guess that rules out the *Intrepid*. Anyone got a ship?"

CHAPTER TWENTY-EIGHT
SITI

Tony, Quinn, Joss, and I arrived in the Hadriana system a couple of days later on the *Swan of the Night*—the ship we'd originally docked with when we arrived at Lunesco. It belonged to Liz Marconi, Tony's cousin, and her partner—and ex-husband—Maerk Whiting. The two of them ran a small transport company, along with other family members who were mentioned from time to time but not really discussed. I gathered they had been involved in some illicit activities and possibly had secret ties to the N'Avon government.

The *Swan* wasn't big enough to carry all of us, so Zane, Harim, the general, and Sashelle traveled with their friend Francine. They'd taken a shuttle to the transfer station in orbit around Romara, but the *Swan* had met us at the airfield on the planet. I'd caught a glimpse of Derek's shuttle when we departed but hadn't had a chance to say anything to him.

I wasn't sure what I would have said, anyway.

During the long transit, we'd gotten to know our hosts better, played a lot of card games, and napped. The *Swan* had a small workout room above the cargo hold, where Joss spent an inordinate amount of time. He'd been happy to run me through a series of body weight exercises when I asked, but an hour a day was as much as I was interested in doing.

As we finally approached Hadriana, I felt restless and ready to do something useful. "I'm not sure I like space travel as a vacation. I need to be on a planet."

"Have you ever taken a cruise?" Quinn asked as she dug the seat restraints out of one of the armchairs. "One of those giant ships with the buffets and shows and—" She frowned. "Or maybe you don't have those in your part of the galaxy?"

"No, we have them. But I've never—I've spent enough time on transport ships. The idea holds very little interest for me. If I'm going to vacation, I want to get there fast and put my feet on the ground." I dropped into the seat she indicated and fastened my restraints.

Joss took the armchair across from me. It looked like normal interior furniture but was bolted to the floor. He pulled the belt from inside and buckled it over his lap. "My parents did one of those cruises—Pleiades cruise lines, I think. They went to Sally Ride, Grissom, Kaku… Might have been one more place. They said it was super fancy."

I glanced at him in surprise. "When did they do that?"

"Our third year at the academy. Your dad suggested it for an anniversary present. Not sure which one." Joss turned to the others. "My parents were married five hundred years ago, then they went into deep sleep for a while. My sister and I were born while they were awake around two hundred, two-fifty years ago. When we were twelve, we went back into deep sleep until a few years ago. So things like 'age' and 'years married' are relative."

One hand still stuck in the couch cushions, Quinn gaped at him. "I still can't get used to the idea that you're two hundred and fifty years old. Why?"

As she and Tony buckled in, Joss explained about the Earth Exodus and the people left behind. "My father was lucky to find the Dome—he was diabetic and would have died without a source of insulin. And that's where he met my mom. But the air outside wasn't safe to breathe, so they put people in suspended animation—to fit more people inside. My parents were considered part of the staff, so they had to work some years in the middle—keeping the place running." He turned back to me. "My dad said he'd never do another cruise—it reminded him too much of being stuck in the Dome. He's like you—he wants to get outside and breathe."

"You grew up in there. Doesn't it bother you?" I asked.

He shrugged again. "As long as I've got a gym and my video games, I'm good."

The intercom pinged, and Liz's voice came through the speakers. "We've begun our descent to Hadriana. We're landing at New Ardennet field—it's nearest to Sashelle's home."

"Everybody buckle up," Maerk chimed in from the cockpit. "Our girl comes in hot!"

"I'm making a nice, easy descent, Maerk. Don't worry the—" The voice cut out.

"I wonder who Maerk is praying to this time?" Quinn leaned her shoulder against her husband's arm.

Tony chuckled and turned to us. "Maerk has a whole litany of saints he prays to. Different one for every situation. Seems to have kept him safe so far." He pulled out his comtab and pointed it at the big screen on the wall. "Let's see what kind of visual we can get."

He scrolled through a couple of channels, then found the forward cams from the cockpit. We watched as the ship slipped through the atmosphere and circled to land at a rough-looking airstrip tucked in a wide valley between tall, wooded mountains. A fence surrounded the strip, but there were no buildings in sight. A road meandered away up the valley toward a pass.

"The caats retreated from the plains when the humans moved in a hundred, hundred and fifty years ago." Quinn pointed a thumb over her shoulder. "I've never been to this part of the planet—it's much prettier than the area around Hadriana City."

"Quinn's ex-husband grew up on a potato farm outside H.C." Tony told them. "His mother was one of the big players in the industry."

Joss laughed. "Oh, yeah, the spud queen."

Quinn smirked at his comment. "She and her late husband kind of ran the planet. They were the big money behind the politics. The family owned the patents on a couple of root vegetables that had been specially engineered to grow well here, so they controlled crops all over. They certainly believed they were royalty."

"Here we go!" Maerk's voice carried through the intercom. "Saint Joseph of Cupertino, protect us!"

"You'd think he'd never landed a ship before," Tony said.

"Are you saying Maerk is driving?" Quinn feigned terror.

"Doubtful." Tony tightened his seat belt. "I hope not. I just meant you'd think he'd never landed *in* a ship before."

We touched down without incident, slowing as we rolled to the far end of the dirt strip. The ship rattled across the end of the field and slowed to a stop. "We're here," Liz said. "Running shut down. Have you thought about local transport?"

Quinn and Tony exchanged a flummoxed look. Joss and I had our grav belts, of course, but I wasn't certain the locals had anything similar.

Tony thumbed his comtab. "Do you have any ground transport aboard?"

The door to the cockpit opened, and Maerk strode in. "We've got the cycles, but there are only two. We don't usually carry a lot of passengers."

"That covers the four of us." I tapped my belt—we'd demonstrated their capabilities during the long flight here. "But I don't think Zane has one." I raised my brows at Joss.

He shook his head. "No, he does. But I'm not sure if he brought it. Why would he? Ambassadors don't usually do this." He waved his arm at the screen which still showed rolling hills backed by snow topped mountains.

Quinn rose. "Francine probably has something. Or maybe Sashelle's people will send a conveyance."

"You think they have that kind of tech?" Tony fumbled with his belt, then tossed the ends aside when it opened. "She's never shared much about her people, but I get the impression they live mostly… in the wild."

"I guess we'll find out soon." Quinn pointed at the screen again. In the distance, a point of light approached. "They must have waited for us to land first—Francine's ship has got to be faster than the *Swan*."

Maerk patted the kitchen counter. "She doesn't mean it. You're fast enough, baby."

"Is he talking to the ship?" Joss whispered to me as Tony and Quinn followed the tall man to the cargo hold.

I lifted both hands and shook my head. "Maybe?" Grabbing my backpack, I shrugged it on, whistled for Yasmi who flew to my shoulder, and followed the others.

As Quinn and Tony inspected the motorcycles parked in a tidy compartment near the front of the big cargo hold, Maerk opened the rear hatch. It folded down into a ramp, leaving an opening about three meters high. A cool breeze blew in, carrying scents of resin, wood smoke, and a spattering of rain.

I activated my shield. "It's a bit chilly here." Yasmi shook a few drops of water off her fur, splattering my face.

Tony glanced up from the cycle he'd wheeled out of the compartment. "Hadriana has very little tilt, so the seasons don't shift much. At our current latitude, it's generally cooler than most people enjoy, but above freezing, unless you go up into the mountains. Which we'll be doing. Do you have winter clothing?"

I tapped my sleeve. "Our uniforms are designed for all climates—at least all climates in the goldilocks zones. The personal shields protect us from elements and keep us warm, as long as we have the ability to recharge them. Most locations get enough sunlight to do that unless it's heavily overcast and very cold. A planet with a long night and cold climate can be problematic. Which is why we carry camping gear with high thermal conservation." I pulled on my backpack straps.

"If we were running a Phase 1 exploration, we'd drop living modules and generators," Joss said. "We can tap into wind, solar, hydro, geothermal, even magnetic. But our go bags have the equipment needed to survive any planet in the habitable zone for up to a week."

"And you brought those to a political meeting?" Maerk used a wrench to scratch his head. His wild, curly hair blew into his eyes, and he absently pushed it aside.

"We take our go bags everywhere." Joss tightened his shoulder straps. "Never know when you might need 'em."

"We didn't take them to the meetings." I chuckled. "But, yeah, we took 'em to the hotel. Everything is compact, so it's easy enough. And if power is plentiful, we can use our grav belts so we don't have to carry them."

A low rumble had been building as we chatted. It suddenly reached a volume that made conversation difficult. Somewhere outside our field of vision, the other shuttle landed with a rush, then the roar dropped to a low whine.

Maerk trotted down the ramp, peering around the side of the ship. "Looks like they're here."

Joss and I followed curiously while Tony and Quinn continued to unpack the second cycle. A sleek white shuttle rolled up beside the *Swan*, turning smoothly to park next to it. A personnel hatch popped open on one side, and a uniformed man waited for automated steps to fold down. Then he retreated into the airlock to allow the passengers to disembark.

Sashelle leapt over the steps, landing lightly on the dusty apron. Zane waved as he climbed down the stairs, stopping at the bottom to speak with the caat. Harim and La Gama followed him down. A stylish blonde woman stopped in the opening to speak with the uniform.

"Wow. She's—" Joss shook his head, wide eyes fixed on the blonde.

I waited for a second, but he didn't continue. "Joss Torres, did she render you speechless? I need to make a note of this for Zina."

He glared at me for a brief second, then went back to staring as the blonde descended the steps. She seemed to glide down them rather than walk. And how she managed to move at all in that tight skirt, I didn't know.

Tony came up beside us, casting a laughing glance at Joss. "That's Francine. She has that effect on some people." He clapped Joss on the shoulder, then strode across to bump fists with Zane and the others.

Francine got a hug, which surprised me—she didn't look like the hugging type. Beside me, Joss sucked in a breath, releasing it slowly when Tony stepped away.

I grabbed Joss's arm and tugged him toward the others. "Come on, let's go meet the future Mrs. Torres."

Joss choked. "I don't think so. I mean, yeah, let's meet her, but she's not—" He shook his head. "I think—I know I've seen her before."

CHAPTER TWENTY-NINE
QUINN

Leaving the prepped hovercycle inside the *Swan*, Quinn strode down the ramp to join the others just in time to hear Joss claim he'd seen Francine before. She stopped in surprise, turning to frown at the young Colonial.

"You couldn't have." Siti voiced what Quinn was thinking. The young woman waved at the dirt landing field. "She's from here. There's been no contact before us."

"She's originally from Rosiya," Quinn said in a low voice. "The Zielinsky family runs—or used to run—an organization that controlled a major portion of Federation space. The Russosken. They had covert agreements with the Federation, which meant they acted as the Federation's strong arm more often than not. In the revolution, we not only broke the Federation but also managed to break free of the Russosken. And Francine's siblings took control of the organization from their grandmother. They still participate in some questionable activities, but they've spent a lot more time and funds on making life better for people instead of breaking kneecaps and eliminating opposition."

"Your friend was part of the mob?" Joss's voice cracked on the last word.

Quinn shook her head. "Francine's family *was* the mob. Francine actually ran away years ago—Tony and I met her when she was working for my mother-in-law. Ex-mother-in-law. The potato czar."

"Wow." Siti rubbed her forehead. "I was not expecting any of this when we jumped to Berza."

"Where's Berza?" Quinn frowned.

"Here—well, no. Lunesco." Joss continued to stare at Francine as the small group moved toward them. "We designated it the Berza system. Probably named after some famous scientist or something."

"Stephan Berza was the man who—never mind." Siti took a step forward to knock knuckles with the new arrivals. "Good to see you all again. You must be Francine Zielinsky. I'm Siti Kassis."

Zane stepped up beside Joss and put an arm around him. "And this is the son I told you about, Francine." He muttered something to Joss.

The younger man nodded, never taking his gaze from Francine. "You look familiar."

The blonde smiled smugly. "I think the classic line is, 'haven't we met somewhere before?'" She paused for a long moment. "I'm sure I'd remember you." She turned to include the rest of the group. "Sashelle says—"

Another shuttle drowned out the end of her sentence. Every head whipped around in surprise. This ship landed vertically on the far side of the airstrip, rather than decelerating down the runway as the *Swan* had. They all flung up hands to protect their eyes from the debris, except Joss and Siti who wore those invisible shields. When the dust settled, the hatch of the Colonial Navy shuttle was already open.

"What the—" Siti broke off. "Andrade?"

A barrel-shaped man wearing a dark blue uniform lumbered down the steps, stopping at the bottom to look up and down the airfield. Another man in similar uniform followed him out of the ship—Lieutenant Lee. Without acknowledging Lee, Andrade pivoted and strode up to them. Lee stuck his head back in through the airlock hatch, then followed the older man.

Zane let his arm drop from his son's shoulders and waited for the Navy officers to approach. "Hello. Did Sashelle invite you as well?"

I did not.

"Yes, of course," the man lied in the same moment. He must have realized no one believed him because he backtracked. "Captain Wortman asked that I accompany you. I'm an expert intelligence officer. Major Vorlus Andrade, at your service."

Vorlus? Joss's wide eyes and comical mouthing of the name made a laugh bubble up in Quinn's belly. She shot the young man a mom-glare. Although his face went red, his smirk didn't disappear. She turned in time to catch Andrade's own scowl at the young lieutenant.

Zane extended a hand to the major's companion. "We've met before. You're a friend of my son's, right?"

"Derek Lee." Lee glanced at Joss. "Joss and I have a… a complicated history."

Joss reached out and punched Lee's arm. "That's one way to put it."

Lee rolled his eyes.

Siti snickered and whispered, "Bromance."

A sort of mental throat clearing brought every eye back to Sashelle. *Transport approaches.*

"You have transport?" Tony gestured at the *Swan*. "We were getting the cycles ready."

The caat's eyes closed to slits, and she transmitted a mental eye roll that said Tony was an idiot. *Yes. We have transport. Adopted from human transport but made our own.*

"What do you think that means?" Siti asked of no one in particular.

"I guess we'll find out in a moment." Quinn tipped her head toward the road that disappeared into the forest only a few yards from the flight line. A faint hum emanated from that direction, gradually increasing in volume. Then a large flat cylinder, about a meter thick and three meters in diameter, hove into view, seeming to float above the road. "Is that… It looks like my robot vacuum."

Air cushion disk. As the vehicle slowed, Sashelle leapt aboard.

"The caat is riding a vacuum." Tony covered his hand with his face, but the mirth in his tone made the action futile.

It's a meme because it's true. Riding the ACD is enjoyable. The disk eased to a stop beside the group.

"Your people developed this mode of transport?" Zane strode around the vehicle, observing it from all sides. He hunkered down to look underneath as it settled to the dust. "Remarkable."

It was based on technology observed in the early human incursions. We normally have little need for transport. My species is strong and fast. But this makes moving the elderly and infirm possible.

Quinn bit her lip to keep from laughing at the implied insult. Trust Sashelle to remind all the humans of their physical inferiority. Fair enough. Humans had been doing it to her for ages. "Do you mind if Tony and I follow on our hovercycles? I think your disk might be crowded with all of us aboard." And having an independent form of transport might be handy.

Andrade shouldered through the group to sneer at the disk. "We can use our grav belts."

Why is he here? the caat thought at Quinn. *He clearly doesn't think we're worthy of his notice.*

Quinn shrugged as she headed back to the ship for her cycle. "He's worried he'll miss out on something important? Or at least his superiors are."

Tony followed, steering his ex-cousin-in-law up the ramp. "Maerk, you and Liz stay here. We'll call if we need you." When the taller man tried to argue, Tony gave him a stern look. "You weren't invited. Don't be like that Andrade character. And you know we'll be safe enough. We trust Sashelle."

"It's not the caat I'm worried about." Maerk cast a dark look down the ramp even though he couldn't see the others from that vantage point. "Those Colonials make me nervous."

Quinn shook her head. "The only one who bothers me is Andrade. And obviously Siti and Joss don't like him either, so we're safe enough."

Waving farewell to Maerk, she and Tony rolled their cycles out of the ship and down the ramp. Once everyone else had climbed aboard the ACD—or in Andrade's case activated a grav belt—she turned on her cycle. The small wheels retracted as the bike rose above the dirt apron. Dust boiled up from the vehicle's downward push, and she eased it forward, hoping to outdistance the cloud.

"The ACD doesn't push out dirt," Tony said. His voice came through the helmets which linked to their comtabs. She wondered if this is what the Colonials' integrated comms felt like. It was completely different from hearing Sashelle, but she couldn't really define how.

"Maybe it really is a vacuum."

"That would be… I was going to say crazy, but we're way past crazy."

She glanced at Tony speeding beside her in the ACD's wake. "How so?"

He gestured at the people ahead of them, Andrade speeding along overhead. "Talking caat was a start."

"Sashelle has been talking to us for years."

His head waggled side-to-side in a yes-and-no action. "The last few years have been a plateau of the insanity, but now we've got flying people, long lost tribes of humans, and a vacuum vehicle."

Quinn looked away to hide her smile. "At least we're together for it."

They followed the ACD for several kilometers, then left the paved road for a narrower dirt track that wound deeper into the forest. After about an hour, the disk settled to the ground where the road ended in a clearing.

From here you must walk. Sashelle leapt from the disk and stalked to a path leading into the woods. Tony and Quinn pulled their bikes up beside the disk and shut them down, careful to leave space for it to exit the clearing.

"How does it know where to go?" Siti asked as she slid off the silent vehicle. "And what powers it?"

These things may be answered if our meeting goes well. With a flick of her tail, Sashelle sauntered away.

"Is the caat offering technology in exchange for our support?" Zane whispered to Auntie B.

The older woman shrugged and picked up a long, sturdy branch from beside the road. "Kinda sounds that way. I guess they've learned that withholding information and assistance is a better negotiation technique than helping people and expecting us to return the favor. Shame we had to teach them that by failing to honor our promises." She snapped a couple of twigs off the stick and tested its strength by leaning on it. "That'll do. Let's go."

Auntie B followed the caat into the woods, with Harim close behind. Zane swept an arm to allow Francine to precede him, then fell into line. Andrade dropped close to the ground but declined to turn off his grav belt. The three lieutenants went next with Quinn and Tony as the rear guard.

The path twisted through the woods, around huge pine-type trees. The thick bark gave off scents of lavender and vanilla whenever a patch of sunlight broke through the dense cover. It was cool, almost cold in the shade, but their exertion kept them warm. A heavy layer of fallen needles covered the path, and thick, prickly underbrush filled the area beneath the lowest boughs.

Joss looked over his shoulder at Quinn. "Do you know where we're going?"

She shook her head. "Not a clue. I never went beyond Hadriana City when we visited Reggie's family. I doubt any of them have been out here, either. Until we met Sashelle, we thought Hadriana caats were a myth. An excuse for poorly behaved housecats. You know, sorry Fluffy shredded your shoes—she's part caat."

Joss stumbled, caught himself, then activated his grav belt. He rose a few centimeters off the ground and turned to face Quinn, still moving along the path but in reverse.

"How do you know where to go?"

He jutted a thumb over his shoulder. "I tethered myself to Siti. Let's see if she notices."

"She noticed, Joss!" Siti called back. "You think I wouldn't feel your lazy bulk pulling against me?"

Joss made a face. "It doesn't work that way." He eased a little closer to Quinn. "My belt is providing forward—well, backward propulsion. She's just providing direction. Anyway, you're saying you don't know where Sashelle's people live? People? Is that what they call themselves?"

The pride, Sashelle answered, her mental voice strong although she was at least fifty meters ahead of them.

"How did you hear me?" Joss asked.

Your thoughts are concentrated and loud. How could I not *hear you?*

"Is that an insult?" Joss folded his arms.

The caat didn't answer.

"I think that means yes." Quinn didn't bother trying to hide her smirk.

"I like this caat." Joss turned around and dropped to the trail, smoothly transitioning from floating to walking. "I hope the rest are as sarcastic as she is."

We invented sarcasm.

Joss burst out laughing.

"And, no, we don't know where the pride lives." Quinn lengthened her stride to walk closer behind the lieutenant. "As I mentioned before, they retreated into the hills as humans took over the arable land in the valleys. I'm not sure what would have happened if humans had attempted to expand into the mountains."

They did, and we stopped them.

"Stopped them how?" Joss asked.

Humans are lazy. They want machines to do their dirty work. As the caat spoke, visions appeared in Quinn's head. She guessed by Joss's suddenly tense shoulders that he could see them, too. People dressed in historical attire used heavy equipment to pull down trees and plow the land. *When those machines stopped working, humans stopped trying.*

"What made them stop working?" The question floated back to them from farther up the trail, and Quinn realized Sashelle was transmitting to the entire group. Or most of it. Andrade seemed oblivious.

An impression of complacency accompanied the vision of huge caats ripping the logging equipment with massive claws.

"Yeesh." Joss shuddered. "Remind me not to get on her bad side."

"The terrain might have made using those machines more difficult, too," Tony muttered from behind her. "And the dropping price of potatoes."

"Economics. Cheaper to go somewhere else." Zane's reply was somehow amplified—probably Sashelle facilitating the conversation as they strode single file along the path. "So, that's your answer, Sashelle. If you want to get rid of people, you have to make it worth their while."

Heavy silence greeted that suggestion.

"I suspect there was a little mental pressure involved, too," Francine said. "As you can see, Sashelle is capable of implanting suggestions and impressions."

Siti looked back at Joss, her eyes narrowed. "Mind control."

"Not really," Francine replied. "Once you realize she's doing it, you can ignore it, much like ignoring a conversation. But I suspect those early loggers had no idea they were being influenced by the caats. Their machines were breaking, and they 'knew' fixing them wouldn't help. They 'knew' the terrain was getting more rugged and that going elsewhere would be easier. If you hear something enough times, you tend to believe it. And they were hearing this from inside their own heads."

CHAPTER THIRTY
SITI

Mind control, but not really. I activated my audio implant and called Joss. "Sound familiar?"

"I'm not sure this channel is secure," Joss replied. "That caat can hear what I'm thinking."

"She heard what you were saying." I bit my lip as I tried to work it out. "I'm hoping the inhibitor Diz put in our comm system is enough to keep her from reading our minds."

"It didn't stop us from seeing what she was sending. Or hearing her talk."

"Good point. Can you hear this, caat?" When I got no response, I cut the connection. Better to keep my thoughts to myself than to expose classified information in a compromised discussion with Joss.

The path grew steeper as we hiked up into the hills. Yasmi rode on my shoulder for a while, then launched herself into the trees. She soared from branch to branch, then returned to me, repeating the pattern many times. I started to think it might be time for a break when the trees ended, leaving us on a stony plateau overlooking the lush valley. We gathered in the sunshine, dropping to the large boulders to rest.

As she caught her breath, Quinn stared out over the trees, pointing at the airfield in the distance. "Why is that runway even here? Caats don't have spaceships, too, do they?"

"There's a small human town just beyond the river bend." Tony indicated the river's curving path. "Hidden behind that knoll."

"How much farther to your pride, Sashelle?" Zane asked.

The Lerrr Pride is here. The words clearly came from behind us, and we all turned to face the forest.

An enormous caat with brown and black coloring similar to Sashelle emerged from the path we'd walked. More caats, in all different colors, appeared from the underbrush like ghosts from the mist, closing in from all sides. Andrade and Harim both stumbled back a couple of steps, casting panicked looks at the sheer drop off now behind us. Yasmi ducked behind my braid, shivering a little.

Joss's fingers hovered over his grav belt controls. I cast a quick look at the gathered humans. Joss, Lee, Andrade, and I each had a grav belt. I hoped Zane had worn his, too. If each of us carried another member of the group, we could evacuate if necessary. We should have discussed this option before we arrived.

On a typical explorer mission, that planning would have been part of the process, but this was far from typical. I'd been letting the ambassadors take the lead, since we didn't have clearly defined roles. I should have insisted we lay out the scope and nature of our assignment before we left Romara.

Lee and Andrade threw another kink in the system. As the ranking officer, Andrade should be in command, but he'd arrived late and without invitation. And he'd made no effort to take charge. He seemed to have a separate agenda—probably reporting to someone back on Grissom. Technically, since he'd been selected for early promotion, Derek outranked me and Joss, but he had deferred to Andrade. I wasn't sure if he was there as Andrade's assistant or to keep an eye on him. I'd definitely gotten the impression no one on the *Intrepid* trusted him any more than we had on the *Observer*. But everyone seemed wary of him.

As these thoughts whirled through my head, the caats prowled forward then stopped a few steps beyond the trees, as if aware how nervous their appearance made us. I glanced at Joss, remembering his words. They probably knew exactly how nervous they made us.

After a long, pregnant moment, the largest caat sat back on her haunches, and her tail wrapped around her feet. Her brilliant green eyes seemed to glow as she looked us over. *Welcome, humans.* Sashelle crept across the stone to sit in the larger caat's shadow.

With a quick look at La Gama, Zane took one step forward, taking the lead. "Thank you for inviting us to meet with you. I am Zane Torres, representative of the human world known as Earth."

The tip of the caat's tail twitched. *I am Antinea, Queen of the Lerrr Pride and Empress of all the Prides. The kitten, Sashelle, tells me you can help us with the humans of this world. You may sit.*

Kitten? "How old is Sashelle?" I whispered to Quinn as Harim, Andrade, and the general took seats on a pile of boulders.

Quinn spread her hands, eyes still locked on the empress. "I've known her for years. And based on comments she's let drop, she wasn't young then."

"Maybe it's rank instead of age?" Joss suggested.

Stop talking! Sashelle's command came through loud and clear. *The empress doesn't speak your language. You're being rude.*

I bit my tongue, trying to stop the wash of red that blazed up my cheeks. Nothing like being reprimanded like a child in front of your superiors.

Zane cast a quick glare back at us as he slowly moved closer to the empress. "Perhaps we can speak in a more comfortable setting? Away from these... kittens?"

This location is quite comfortable. The empress unfurled her tail and curled it around her feet the other direction.

Zane bowed in acceptance and perched on the closest rock.

I called Joss on the internal comm. "How does she understand your dad?"

Joss's shoulders twitched in the tiniest of shrugs. "Maybe he's thinking loudly."

Sashelle glared at us again, so I disconnected.

For a long time, Zane and the empress conversed. Harim, Andrade, and the general appeared to be listening, but I heard only Zane's side of the discussion. He asked a lot of questions about their history and about the human incursion.

The rest of us stood nearby, silently waiting. As we waited, Yasmi gradually grew brave enough to leave the shelter of my braid and perch on my shoulder. Many of the caats curled up and appeared to snooze, but two enormous black ones prowled along the edge of the forest. When the larger of the two—its head topped out at my shoulder—made as if to go behind us, Derek and Joss both stepped into its path. The caat's eyes slitted, and its tail flicked back and forth over its back.

Derek's hand slid slowly toward his weapon.

The empress's head snapped in our direction and instantly every caat on the outcropping leapt to its feet, fur standing on end. Some of them even arched their backs and hissed.

Enough! The empress's voice thundered through the air, and she seemed to grow even larger than the bigger black as she rose. *Do not antagonize the humans. They are my guests.*

The larger black cat scurried away, dropping beside its smaller companion and rolling to its back. The little one put a paw on the big one's throat, popped his claws out with an audible snap, then retracted them and removed the paw. Unhurt, the larger one rolled to its feet and crouched in the little one's shadow.

As if in response, the human ambassadors rose and bowed slightly to the empress. The caats melted away into the trees, and Zane crossed the stony outcropping to us. "We're taking a break. Snack if you brought 'em." He pulled a water bottle from the bag he'd carried over his shoulder and downed it in a single drink. "And you don't have to stand all the time. Most of the caats are napping." With a clap to Joss's shoulder, he returned to the pile of boulders they'd been sitting on.

Joss and I found seats on another jumble of rocks near the cliff, far enough from the trees to not antagonize the caats. Quinn, Tony, and Francine had taken another pile near the point of the outcropping. They gazed at the view as they chatted and laughed together.

Derek wandered over. "Mind if I join you?"

I pulled off my backpack and set it on the ground between my feet. "Have a rock."

Derek chuckled a little as he pulled off his own bag. "You got any ChewyNuggets?"

"They aren't in the rotation anymore." I pulled a water pack from my bag and sucked it dry.

"What? When did that happen?" Derek opened a green packet and offered it to me.

I dumped a small pile of round, colorful candies into my hand and returned it to him. "I dunno, maybe six months ago?" I cast a questioning look at Joss as I held one of the candies out to Yasmi.

Joss accepted the packet from Derek and tipped a few of the sweets directly into his mouth. Handing the bag back, he chewed, then swallowed. "Closer to a year. Right after Darenti. The company bid too high, and they went with a new distributor. Almost caused a mutiny."

"These are good." I lifted one of the green balls between my thumb and forefinger. "Not quite chewy enough, but nice flavor. Listen." I leaned closer to the two men. "We need a contingency plan."

"In case these predators decide they don't like us?" Derek looked around the clearing, but the caats had all disappeared. "How far away can they hear us?"

I spread my hands wide and shook my head. "Let's say we need a plan in case of bad weather or natural disaster. If we each carry one other person—Joss, does your dad have his grav belt?"

"Yeah. He told me if there was a problem, you and I needed to grab Harim and the general. He figured Tony and Quinn could take their bikes. That was before we left all that gear behind." Joss leaned back on the rock and stared up at the sky, hands behind his head as if he hadn't a care in the world.

I tipped my head at our friends and the blonde woman. "Quinn, Tony, and Francine know Sashelle the best, so we'll have to hope she'll help them out. I'll take the general. You get Harim." I pointed at Derek.

"And Joss can make sure his dad gets away safely. The rest are on their own."

"Works for me." Derek offered me the candies again. When I refused, he dumped them into his palm and tucked the empty packet into his backpack. He popped one into his mouth and rolled it around.

I dragged my gaze away from his mouth, staring into the trees and hoping my cheeks weren't blazing again. The middle of a dicey mission was no time to be preoccupied with a handsome Navy lieutenant. I dug into my bag to find another water pack and hide my distraction.

Sashelle appeared beside me. *The empress wishes you to come with me.*

I poked a thumb at my chest. "Me? Now? Why?"

Yes, you. I do not know why. You may bring the glider. She turned and walked away.

"Do I just—" I flicked my hands at the caat as she strutted toward the trees.

"Not alone." Derek leapt up from the boulder.

"I've got her back." Joss popped to his feet.

Derek slung his bag over his shoulder. "You stay with your dad."

Sashelle waited by the edge of the forest. *You may bring the Flyer.* Somehow it was clear she meant Derek.

"I don't like this." Joss gripped my arm. "Wandering away from the group with a bunch of predators…"

She will be safe with me. And her mate will protect her. Sashelle's tail twitched. *Come. Now.*

"My mate?" The blush I'd banished earlier blazed up my face.

Joss burst out laughing, then slapped a hand over his mouth. "You two should see your faces!" Everyone turned to look.

The Son of Earthman must stop drawing attention to himself. Sashelle's disapproving tone matched her narrow-eyed glare. *I don't want the others to see us leave.*

"Yeah, Son of Earthman." I poked Joss's chest with a finger. "Go tell your dad what's going on."

THE ROMARA CONFRONTATION

"I suppose it's better than Caveman." Joss glared at Derek as he picked up his backpack, then sauntered across the plateau.

Derek and I leaned against the boulders, feigning boredom. The others went back to their conversations. Andrade, who had been sitting alone on the far side of the outcropping, rose to intercept Joss.

Now. He will not see us leave. Sashelle slid away down the path we'd taken to get here.

Keeping one eye on Andrade—who didn't even glance in our direction, I followed the caat out of the clearing, with Derek at my back.

CHAPTER THIRTY-ONE
QUINN

THE MEETING or summit or whatever they wanted to call it dragged on for hours. After the short break, some of the caats returned. One of the big black ones and the empress approached the ambassadors and they started again. Quinn sat with Tony and Francine on the pile of boulders near the tip of the stone outcropping, exchanging news about their friends and speculating on what the empress might be telling the ambassadors.

"Have you been here before?" Quinn asked Francine.

The younger woman shook her head with a little laugh. "Yes and no. I've been playing taxi driver for Sashelle since the revolution, but this is the first time she's come home. No, let me rephrase that. I dropped her here a few months ago. When you asked me to bring her to Romara, I had to come find her. But she met me at that airfield. I've never been invited up into the homeland." She stretched her legs out in the sun, scowling at her dusty boots. "I'm not really the outdoorsy type."

"You don't say." Quinn tried and failed to keep her lips from twitching. "How'd you contact her?"

"I didn't. When I dropped her, she told me if I came back, she'd know and meet me—or send a representative if she was unavailable. I think they have someone watching the airfield, and a relay system of some kind. I'm pretty sure their tech doesn't run to communications. They don't really need it."

"Speaking of Sashelle, where did she go?" Tony asked.

"I'm not sure. She said your young friends are honorable, by the way. She's not so thrilled with the major." Francine looked around the clearing as if ensuring they wouldn't be overheard. "I don't like him much, either."

"That seems to be the universal opinion. He tried to remove Siti from our little group—" Tony broke off and turned on his rock, his gaze roving over the outcropping. "Where is he? And Siti and Lieutenant Lee are missing, too."

Quinn turned in surprise. Joss sat atop the small pile of boulders near the edge of the forest, his head turning smoothly back and forth as he continuously scanned the tree line. The other two officers had disappeared. "Maybe they're sitting in the shade behind those rocks?" She rose and wandered over to Joss. Tony followed while Francine watched from her perch.

"Hey, Quinn." Joss's gaze seemed to snag on Quinn's face, then he went back to watching. "What's up?"

Quinn walked around the little pyre and stopped in front of Joss. "Where are Siti and Derek?"

Joss swallowed, his Adam's apple bobbing. He stared away from Quinn, then his gaze snapped back to her and his brows drew down. "They went with Sashelle. At the time, it seemed like a good idea. But now... How did she convince us?"

"Sashelle's ideas are usually sound," Tony said.

Joss scrambled up from the boulder. "She made it seem so reasonable."

"Don't panic." Quinn put a hand on the young man's arm. "Sashelle wouldn't put them in danger."

"Are you sure?" Joss asked. "How well do you know her? Aliens are... alien."

THE ROMARA CONFRONTATION

Tony's head tilted as he gave the younger man a questioning stare. "Have you met intelligent aliens before?"

"Yeah, I have." Joss paused, as if ordering his thoughts. "There's a planet—Siti's dad was the one who first encountered the locals. They seemed like nice enough guys—low tech like your caats, but smart. Friendly. Helpful. The Commonwealth put the planet under quarantine for a hundred years." Joss raised a hand to hold off their questions. "Yeah, Siti's dad is over a hundred years old. CEC used to use deep sleep too. It took decades to get to a planet that didn't have a jump beacon. That was before they created the unmanned probe beacons, like we sent to Lunesco."

He scrubbed a hand through his thick hair. "Anyway, about a year ago, we—Siti, Derek, and I—were part of a team that went back to Dar—to that planet. And it turns out the locals weren't all as… altruistic as we'd been led to believe. And I gotta tell you—this mind control thing… If Sashelle is covertly influencing our decision-making, that's not cool. I need to talk to my dad."

Tony grabbed Joss's arm. "It isn't mind control. Sashelle can project—you saw that when she first met your dad. But it isn't sustained. If she'd used it on you when Derek and Siti left, you would have realized as soon as she was out of range. You didn't think it was a questionable idea until we asked you where they'd gone. That makes me think you believed it was the right thing to do."

"I did. But they've been gone almost an hour now. And she wanted to make sure Andrade didn't know they'd gone."

"But your dad knows?" Tony darted his eyes toward the ambassadors.

"Yeah, I told him." Joss frowned down at Tony, then shook his head in confusion. "And he seemed okay with it, too."

"Have you tried calling her?" Quinn asked.

Joss swiveled to look at her, his jaw hanging open. Then his eyes closed. "I'm an idiot! We realized Sashelle could probably hear us on the internal audio—not intercepting the radio signal but hearing us thinking the words. So, we decided talking on the audio was probably not secure. And that got stuck in my head—not to use the system." He thumped a hand against his forehead, then went still as his gaze unfocused.

After a moment, his brows furrowed, and his gaze snapped back to Tony. "She says they're fine. That she'll meet us back at the airfield when the meeting is over. She was kind of giggling."

Quinn exchanged a look with Tony. She'd known Sashelle a long time, and while the caat's sarcasm often made her chuckle, she couldn't remember Sashelle ever doing or saying something that would inspire giggling. "Odd."

Joss blinked, and his intense glare snapped back to Quinn. "You don't think Sashelle is using her mind control to make Siti tell me she's okay?"

Quinn rubbed her forehead. "Let's stop calling it mind control. Caats can... influence what you see... or don't see. She can make herself appear larger or smaller. She can misdirect you so you don't notice her—as long as she's not doing something inherently noticeable. She can extend that 'field'—for lack of a better word—to others for very short periods of time, as long as they're staying still. But if you're paying attention—and realize she could be doing it, you can see the truth." Quinn pulled out her water bottle for a drink.

Tony went on. "She can definitely hear thoughts—but only clear surface thoughts. And she has to be nearby. We—especially Francine—can teach you tricks to keep her out of your head. But I think you're right about your comm system. If I understand it correctly, it requires you to speak inside your head—which is a clear surface thought. I've often wondered if there's some form of technology that could block her."

"We have something in our tech that blocks—but I don't think it works on Sashelle. In fact, I know it doesn't. Maybe if our friend Diz were here... He's the guy who developed the block, and I'll bet he could come up with a fix. He's brilliant." Joss bit his lip. "So, you don't think I should be worried about Siti?"

"I'm sure she and Derek are fine." Tony squinted across the outcropping toward the sun which sat low above the horizon. "Although it's getting late, so we should probably head back to the ship if we don't want to sleep out here." He headed across the rock toward the ambassadors.

He waited until Auntie B completed a statement, then leaned close to whisper in her ear. They spoke, then the humans all looked at their devices. After a couple more exchanges, everyone rose. At a wave from Tony, Quinn and Joss joined the group.

"We're going to adjourn for now." Auntie B slowly got to her feet. "The empress says there's a 'human shelter' nearby where we can sleep, but I think we'll return to the shuttles to rest." She leaned closer to Quinn. "I'm not sure it would be habitable, but we can check it out on the way back."

"Makes sense to me. Will Siti and Derek meet us back at the ship?" Quinn looked around the clearing, then frowned. "And is Andrade with them?"

Zane looked up in surprise, then focused on his son. "Did they take the major?"

"No, sir." Joss made a sour face. "No way they'd take him. But he might have followed them."

"Can you contact him?"

"I think I have his contact—hang on." Joss went still again. "Went to message, but I've never tried calling him before. Maybe that's his default. Or maybe he only responds to messages from up the chain. He seems like that type."

"Agreed. Send me his code." Zane made a gimme motion with his fingers and flicked his holo-ring. "I may not be in his chain of command, but I suspect he knows ignoring me would be the wrong answer." He pulled a small device from his pocket and stuck it into his ear.

They waited while Joss flicked the code to his father and the older man made the call. He muttered something, then swore. "He'd better be in trouble!"

"Not answering?" Joss's lips twitched as if he'd like to be a fly on the wall when his father next encountered Andrade.

Zane didn't reply but turned to the empress. "May we intrude on your land to find the missing members of our pride?"

Your kittens are fine, but the rodent does not belong on our lands. The Larrys will guide you. The empress turned her head as the two massive black caats materialized out of the forest.

Zane bowed and turned to the rest of the group. "Joss and I will look for Siti, Derek, and Andrade. The rest of you should return to the ships."

The empress lifted a paw. *I would prefer the Purveyor of Tuna and the Stealthy One go with the Son of Earthman.*

Everyone looked at Quinn. She raised both hands. "I don't know how they come up with these names, but that's me and Tony. I'd love to be known as something other than the woman who feeds the caat."

Service is honorable. We thank you for your care of the Eliminator of Vermin.

"Oh. You're welcome." Quinn made a little bow toward the empress. "We'll retrieve the human kittens and the, er, rodent. Francine can escort the rest of you back to the ACD."

Zane's lips pressed together, but he didn't argue. Instead, he offered an arm to Auntie B and followed Francine toward the narrow path. Just before moving into the trees, he stopped and turned back. "Do you want my grav belt?" He looked at Joss. "You can tether it to yours—"

"I know how to use a grav belt, Dad." Joss strode across the rocky plateau, hand outstretched. "And yes, thanks."

The older man removed his belt and handed it to his son, then wrapped an arm around Joss in a quick hug. "See you back at the ships."

Quinn waited for them to leave, then nudged Tony toward the black caats. The others had melted away while the humans focused on the belt transfer, but the Larrys remained. "You're both named Larry?"

The smaller caat's voice rumbled low, almost vibrating Quinn's teeth. *He is Large Larry. I am Little Larry.*

Tony chuckled and held a hand near his chest, measuring the smaller caat's height, then raised it to his forehead. "I guess that's accurate."

This way. Large Larry slunk down the path with Little Larry on his heels.

Joss handed the belt to Tony and turned to follow the caats. "One of you put that on. If we need it, you'll have to do a tandem ride."

"Like piggyback?" Tony slowed to strap the belt on.

"You wish." Quinn waited for him to click the buckle, then gave him a little push to keep up with the others.

CHAPTER THIRTY-TWO
SITI

When we'd been walking for about twenty minutes, we came to a wide river. Water crashed down the side of a cliff a few meters upstream, and mist dampened our clothing. I reactivated my personal shield.

Sashelle paused to drink, then looked upstream toward the cliff face. *You might need your magic belts. It gets difficult.*

I activated my grav belt and rose a few centimeters from the ground. Derek did the same. Sashelle loped toward the falls, veering to the drier stone on the right. She took a flying leap and scrambled up the rock face. Her movements appeared effortless, almost as if she were flying herself. We increased our altitude to the top where water flowed out of an opening half a meter below the lip of the cliff.

"Is this an artesian well?" Derek asked.

I don't know the source of the water. But it's clean. You may drink.

She waited while we filled our water packs. Although we had several liters in our bags, neither Derek nor I would pass up a chance to refill. I surreptitiously ran a scan on the water, and it came up clean. I got the impression the caat noticed and was amused by my tech.

At the top of the cliff, trees grew close to the rocky edge. Forest extended in every direction, and there didn't appear to be a path through the trees. I hovered near the edge. "How will we get through?"

We go west. Sashelle ran along the narrow rocky edge, balancing effortlessly as she traversed over the falls. Derek and I followed in the air. On the other side, the caat disappeared down a narrow path. Brush grew thick above it, low enough that we would have to crawl on our bellies to follow.

You may fly above.

"How will we know where to go?" I asked.

Follow my voice.

"How are we supposed to do that?" Derek asked. "It's not like we can hear it."

I held up a hand to silence him and closed my eyes to listen. "I almost hear... It's not a sound, but more like a feeling." Opening my eyes, I pointed up and into the trees. "This way."

We floated above the trees, following the impression of Sashelle. Rolling hills stretched for klicks in all directions, and the snow-topped mountains loomed large. Clouds scudded overhead, the brisk wind making me grateful for my personal shield. Sashelle changed directions several times, but we trailed far enough behind to smooth out some of her twists and turns. After we had traveled a couple of klicks, she stopped.

Come down.

With a shrug at Derek, I eased down beside a large fir-like tree. The strong vanilla and resin scent made me sneeze as my shield—set to semi-permeable—pushed the branches aside. As we neared the ground, we slowed to weave around the thicker branches, then broke through the lowest level.

A thick layer of needles covered the ground here, preventing the underbrush from growing. Or maybe the caats had cleared it. In the center of the small clearing, a jumble of fur in all different colors seemed to boil. On closer inspection, I realized it was a pile of kittens.

Derek cast a quick, questioning look at Sashelle, then crept closer to crouch beside the heap. He held out a hand and made a kissing sound. Several bright pairs of eyes opened and focused on him.

I gave Sashelle a side eye. "Why?"

Derek paused his noises. "Why what?"

I ignored him. "Why are you trusting us with your kittens?"

I trust you, she said. *And I want you to trust us. I know you're leaving soon, so I'm not worried you'll be back on your own. Plus, the nursery doesn't stay in one location.*

"Trust, but cautiously?"

Exactly.

One of the kittens—an orange one—extracted itself from its siblings and crept closer to Derek. He let it sniff his fingers, then slowly ran one over its head and down its back. It froze for a second, then leaned against his hand, purring.

I knelt beside Derek and touched a finger to the kitten's fur. "It's so soft." Yasmi crept down my arm to touch noses with the kitten. They seemed to make friends.

More eyes opened and tiny heads turned toward us. The orange kitten popped out delicate claws and scrambled up Derek's leg into his lap. He dropped to his butt, laughing. "You know what you want, don't you? Who's a good kitty?"

Another kitten—this one a mottled brown and white—ventured away from its peers, stopping beside my knees. I stroked it slowly, then carefully lifted it to my chest. "You are so cute!" Nearby, Yasmi wrestled playfully with a gray one.

Watch out. Sashelle's tone sounded more amused than cautionary.

I looked up just as the wave of kittens overwhelmed us.

Derek fell to his back, laughing. "There are so many!" Tiny bundles of black, white, brown, blue-gray, silver, orange, and brown fur surged over him. There were even some pale green and purple kittens. Some were solid colors, others were a mix of several shades. "Get her!" Derek laughed and pointed at me.

Dozens of the little creatures changed directions, swarming up my legs to my lap. I stayed upright, making it difficult for them to cover me completely, but they gave it their best shot. I could *feel* their desire to cuddle and petted as many of them as I could, squirming and giggling as they tickled my sides.

"I can't hear them, can you?" I asked as I came up for air.

Derek went still, frowning. "No, but I don't hear *her*, either." His gaze darted to Sashelle, watching us from the shadows.

"You don't?"

He shook his head sheepishly and shrugged. "I've been taking your word for it. I'm getting a feeling of… contentment? Maybe a little glee? But no words. And that could be me projecting."

I gently pushed a kitten away from my face as I *listened*. "Yeah, I see what you mean. It's definitely them. Someone is hungry." I sat up and looked around, trying to pinpoint the kitten projecting that impression, but there were too many tiny furry bodies jumping, rolling, play-fighting, and competing for my attention.

The young ones don't talk yet. Much like human babies. Sashelle prowled around the outer edge of the clearing, occasionally pushing one of the kittens back toward the center. Several different adult caats emerged from the tree line whenever a kitten strayed too far from its peers.

My audio implant pinged with Joss's code. Still chortling, I hit answer. "What's up Caveman?"

"Obviously Lee is still with you."

"He's a bad influence." I snickered as I carefully pulled a little tortoiseshell kitten from my chest and returned it to the ground. Its disappointment was clear.

"Where are you?"

"We're with Sashelle. Everything is fine. Is the meeting over? We can meet you at the ship." A little gray, transmitting distress and loneliness, caught my attention, and I reached over the others to lift her into my lap. She started purring as soon as I touched her, and the intensity of her satisfaction almost overwhelmed me. "See you then. Siti, out," I added as an afterthought as I toggled the audio off. My audio pinged again. "Did you forget something?"

"That's a weird greeting," Joss said.

"You just hung up."

"That was almost an hour ago." Joss's tone became concerned. "What's going on?"

I looked up in surprise. Deep in the forest, the thick trees blocked most of the sunlight, leaving us in a dim, cavern-like space where we couldn't see the sun. The kittens had consumed all of my attention to the point I hadn't noticed the passing of time. I checked my chrono and reached for Derek's arm. "Hey. We gotta go."

Half of the kittens had returned to their sleepy pile in the middle of the clearing, curled up next to a couple of adult caats who'd snuck in unnoticed. The rest still covered a good part of Derek and most of my lap. I pushed a few away from his arm and shook it. "Derek. Wake up!"

He sat up in surprise, the kittens tumbling harmlessly to the ground. Pulling one from inside his jacket, he looked around in surprise. "Did I fall asleep?"

"It looks that way. We've been here for an hour."

"No way." He carefully pushed the rest of the litter off his lap and stood. "I feel really good. Energized."

That's the kittens. Sashelle's tone oozed satisfaction. *They are life-giving.*

I set the gray kitten on the ground and gave it one last pat. "Where's Yasmi?"

Derek reached down a hand to help me up, his head swiveling to examine the clearing. "I haven't seen her in a while."

Your friend is sulking. Sashelle's head nudged my arm, turning me about ninety degrees.

I squinted into the dim forest and finally spotted my glider lying flat on a branch overhead. She definitely looked like she was put out. "Yasmi! We're just visiting. I'm not taking one home." I crossed the clearing to stand beneath her tree. "Come down."

The little glider sulked a few seconds longer, then launched herself at me, chittering complaints even as she landed and wrapped her tail around my neck. I stroked her body and nuzzled my cheek against her fur. "I'd never replace you. Not even with a caat."

Yasmi scolded some more, breaking off mid-squeak to hide behind my braid as a large black caat materialized from the dim forest. *The humans are coming. They look for their own kittens. And the Rat.*

Sashelle's head snapped up, and she sniffed the air. *I did not hear the Rat, but I smell him.*

"Rat?" I repeated.

"I don't think a rat would dare show up with this many caats around," Lee said.

"I doubt they're talking about an actual rat." I tried to calm Yasmi as the two caats stalked across the clearing. The other caats and the kittens scrambled away in the opposite direction, disappearing like water into sand. With a bunching of sleek muscles, Sashelle and the big black launched into the trees, almost silent as they leapt over the thick underbrush.

Someone yelled and thrashed against the underbrush. Then the caats returned with Andrade between them, each holding one of his arms in their mouth. When they reached the clearing, they spat him away as if he tasted bad.

"Major Andrade," Derek said. "What are you doing here?"

The major drew himself up, brushing at a damp spot on one sleeve. His shoulders shook, and fear rolled off him. "I was—that's none of your business, Lieutenant."

It is my business, the big black caat said. Sashelle, standing behind him, seemed to reinforce the intensity of the black, but said nothing.

I glanced at Derek and touched my ear. He shook his head. I turned to the major. "They say you aren't welcome here."

Voice shaking, Andrade went for belligerence. "They don't own this planet. I was exploring. It's what we came here to do."

Before I could contradict him, the black stalked to the major, seeming to grow as he approached. He put his face close to the major's, the force of his breath blowing the human's hair back. The caat's muscles bunched under the smooth fur as he leaned closer. *This is the Lerrr Pride's land. Would you permit a visitor to* explore *your home?*

Andrade closed his eyes and turned his face away, his Adam's apple bobbing as he swallowed convulsively. "I was sent here to get intel. It's my job. And no animal is going to stop me." Taking a shaking step backward, he reached toward his belt.

"He's going for a weapon!" Derek launched himself across the clearing.

At the same time, the black caat slashed a paw at the major. I don't know how Derek moved so fast, but the caat's paw caught him in the back as he tackled the intel officer, slamming both men to the ground with a resounding thud.

"Derek!" I scrambled forward, careful to avoid the big caat, and crouched beside the two men. Both lay still under the caat's paw. I looked up at the massive creature. "Please, will you lift your foot?"

The caat stared down at me, yellow eyes blazing, huge teeth poking out of a wide mouth. I tried to remember what Sashelle had said about the caats' mental abilities, but my animal hindbrain overrode logic with terror. I sucked in a terrified breath. "Please?"

After an endless pause during which the caat seemed to read every emotion coursing through my body, he lifted his paw and took one small step back.

"Thank you." I lunged forward to check Derek's pulse, which beat strong and steady. "Derek. Are you awake?"

"Yes." He cracked one eye open and stared up at me. "I was playing dead. That's what you do when predators attack."

I snorted a semi-hysterical laugh. "Are you hurt?"

"I might have a broken rib." He groaned as he rolled off the major.

"I'm alive, too. Thanks for asking." Andrade reached up to rub his head. "And I probably have a concussion. I'm taking this—" He broke off as the caat's head swung close to him. "I'm pressing charges."

An excellent idea. The big black turned away in disdain. *I'll notify the court.*

CHAPTER THIRTY-THREE
SITI

"The court?" I asked. "Caats have a justice system?"

Disdain fell on me like a weighted blanket. The huge black caat turned his golden eyes on me, narrowing them in censure. *Of course we have a justice system. We are not* animals. *No matter what that one says.*

I lifted both hands. "I wasn't implying you were. I dunno—I kind of figured you didn't need one. Like you all lived in harmony."

Derek snorted then winced and grabbed his side. "We assumed that on Darenti—obviously not true."

Andrade, who had been sidling closer to the trees as we talked, spun around to glare at Derek. "That's classified!"

My shoulders tightened, but I forced them down. I would not let Andrade make me defensive. "Not really. Sir. I read a paper in *Interstellar Affairs*—a study on Darenti justice. One of the scientists who lived there before—" I broke off. The incident that caused CEC withdrawal from the planet *was* classified.

Andrade's briefly gleeful expression changed to supercilious. "It doesn't matter. I'm not subject to an alien justice system."

Groaning, Derek slowly climbed to his feet. "We're on their planet. On their lands. I think you might be."

"I've done nothing wrong!" Andrade flung his arms wide. "It's not a crime to be here."

"You have no idea if that's true, sir." Derek gave a damp patch on his pants a swipe, then gave up. "Again—their land, their rules. Maybe the nursery is forbidden territory unless you're explicitly invited."

"Whatever." The major spun on his heel and stalked toward the tree line. Realizing he couldn't walk out, he reached for his grav belt. "Good luck enforcing that. The Navy won't leave me behind." He stabbed a finger at Derek. "And you'll be sorry you sided with these animals."

Cold fury wrapped around me, but I couldn't tell if it was my own anger or being projected onto me by the enormous black caat. I stalked closer to the major. "Don't call them animals! Sir."

"I'll definitely see *you* in court, Kassis. It will be my pleasure to take you down." Andrade tapped his grav controls.

With an ear-splitting shriek I'd never heard before, Yasmi launched herself from my shoulder straight into Andrade's face. He swiped at the glider, but she evaded his hand and scurried over his shoulder and down his back.

"Yasmi, what are you doing?" I lurched forward, but the black caat put a paw across my chest, stopping me cold.

"Get off me, you rodent!" Andrade spun and twisted, trying to grab the glider as she raced along his belt to one of his front belt pouches. She shrieked again, her tiny claws ripping ineffectively at the indestructible fabric.

"What has gotten into you?" I cried.

Sashelle leapt at Andrade, her front paws landing on his shoulders and pushing him to the ground. He landed hard then grabbed at the caat. Lying flat on his back, he tried to roll, but the caat held him pinned to the ground. The glider scrambled up Sashelle's arm and perched on the caat's back, chittering insistently.

Check his belt pouch. Sashelle's command came out cold and demanding. Neither of the men appeared to hear her, so I stepped around the big black caat and crouched beside the major. "What are you hiding?"

THE ROMARA CONFRONTATION

Andrade's eyes grew wide and horrified, then he clamped them shut. "Nothing! Get this thing off me! It attacked me—you saw it! Lieutenant Lee, I demand you act as witness."

"I'm recording, sir." Derek leaned against a tree, one arm wrapped around his waist, the other extended, with a holo-recording live in his palm.

I didn't know which side Derek had chosen, but I was going to do this by the book. Or at least what I thought the book would require. As far as I knew, no one had written an operating procedure for this kind of thing. I tried to unclench my jaw as I addressed the major. "Sir, as we are currently operating on another species' planet, and they have requested I search your belt pouch, I am complying." I reached for his obviously full pouch.

"You'll rot in Attica for this, Kassis!" Andrade's glee at my potential demise almost overcame his obvious fear of the caat holding him down.

Had he been gunning for me all along? It certainly felt like he'd targeted me, but I'd convinced myself that was ridiculous. Since my father had retired, I was no longer a useful target for his enemies. Besides, he'd managed to root most of them out of the Explorer Corps while he served. But Andrade's hatred of me felt personal.

Open the pouch, human. The big black's command almost physically pushed me forward.

Andrade twitched, as if trying to get away from Sashelle, but she held him tight. I leaned forward and peered at his belt where Yasmi had been scratching. It *wiggled*.

"What did you do?" I reached out and unfastened the cover.

A little orange kitten burst out of the pouch, spitting and hissing, its fur standing on end.

"You didn't." I stared at the man in dismay, then picked up the tiny caat, carefully avoiding its claws. A wash of terror-tinged anger splashed over me, the fear dissipating as the kitten realized it was not alone. Leaning as far away from the major as I could reach without getting up, I deposited the creature on the ground.

The miniature orange caat raced around me back toward Andrade, still hissing angrily. Before it could attack, the black caat put out a massive paw to block its path. The kitten hissed and fizzed a little more, then turned—obviously sulking—and slunk away.

"You tried to abduct one of their children, Major?" Derek stared at the older man, aghast. "Are you crazy? No one is going to—"

"Listen to yourself, Lee!" Andrade struggled to throw Sashelle off. The difference in their sizes made it seem like a trivial exercise, but he couldn't budge the caat still standing on his belly and shoulders. "They aren't children! They're pets! Taking a kitten away from—"

The big black caat moved so quickly it seemed to appear beside the major's head, its huge paw covering the man's face. *We don't negotiate with terrorists. By our laws, I could eviscerate you right now.*

"He can't hear you." I touched the caat's leg to get his attention.

The black's gaze swung to me, pinning me in place. *Then you will speak for me.*

The force of his anger held me immobile, and my jaw worked up and down for a few seconds, but I couldn't get anything out.

Little Larry, the human cannot speak. Release her from your anger. Sashelle's calm tone broke through the swirling in my mind.

Little Larry?

The big black caat blinked, and his anger flowed away from me. I got the impression it wasn't gone—after what the major had done, I didn't blame him—but I was no longer targeted by it.

"Major Andrade, the Lerrr Pride accuses you of attempted abduction." I listened to Larry, then paraphrased. "Due to the pride's desire to develop a relationship with Earth and the Colonial Commonwealth, you will be returned to your ship. They expect you to be prosecuted under the laws of your own government for this crime. Lieutenant Lee, you have been charged to take this message to your commanders."

Derek nodded jerkily and flicked his holo-ring. "Saved. I'm continuing to record."

"Understood." I rose and turned to Little Larry. "Lieutenant Lee will take the major back to their ship and ensure the evidence recorded today is sent to the proper authorities."

Larry removed his paw from Andrade's face, and the major sucked in a deep breath. Sashelle climbed off his torso, shaking each paw as if to remove something distasteful. Then she turned her back on him and kicked pine needles at his face like a cat finishing its business in a litter box.

As Derek coughed, clearly trying to cover a laugh, Andrade struggled to his feet, dusting his uniform ineffectively.

A branch snapped, and we all whirled to face the new intrusion.

CHAPTER THIRTY-FOUR
QUINN

FLYING WAS BOTH EASIER and more terrifying than Quinn expected. She'd used the Federation's version of a grav belt on rare occasions, but the Colonial model was faster. It also felt flimsy—as if it shouldn't really support the weight of two humans. Because they only had one extra belt, she had to trust Tony not to drop her.

Of course, she trusted Tony. But this belt, not so much. She kept her arms clamped around him, her feet resting on his. "This is not my preferred mode of transport."

Tony's arms tightened around her. "The belt's gravitational field includes you. You aren't going to fall."

She snorted in disbelief. "You're a grav belt expert now?"

"No, but that's what Joss said, and I trust his expertise."

They slid to a halt, hovering above the thick forest. Below, trees stretched away in every direction, rising and falling like waves over the darkening foothills. Quinn peered over Tony's shoulder, but the rocky outcropping where they'd spent the day had disappeared in the dusky distance.

"The caats stopped, so we're going down," Joss called. "We'll go slowly. The tethering program will make you follow my path, so you'll be right above me for a while as we go through the trees."

"Got it," Tony called back. "Ready?"

"As I'll ever be," Quinn muttered.

They descended through the thick trees, weaving between interlaced boughs. Their arms and legs brushed through the needles, releasing almost overpowering waves of resin and vanilla. Quinn sneezed.

"Are you allergic to pine trees?" Tony asked.

"No, but that's a lot." She sneezed again, eyes watering. She blinked quickly, unwilling to release her hold on her husband to wipe the tears away. "I definitely prefer the bikes. Or walking."

Tony's feet touched down, and he stumbled a little. Quinn's arms convulsed around him, and she blotted her face on his shoulder. "Are we there?"

"Yep. On the ground, safe and sound." He squeezed a little, then let go.

Quinn took a step away and wiped her eyes. With sunset, the forest was even darker than before, and the thick underbrush blocked their view. "Where are the others?"

Joss tapped her shoulder. "I'm right here. Siti and Derek are over that way." He frowned, a glimmer of light flashing off the whites of his eyes.

Light. Quinn turned to look the other way. A light flashed again, and voices rose. "What's going on?"

Joss pulled out a weapon and moved forward, ducking from tree to tree as he went.

"Are you armed?" she asked Tony.

He displayed a mini blaster. "Always."

Smothering a snort of laughter, she shook her head. "Of course. I'm not."

"You stay—"

"Here." She interrupted him. "I know. Don't want to be a liability." But she was speaking to the trees.

She waited in the dark, wondering which of Maerk's saints she should be entreating, as she listened intently. Voices rose, angry but controlled. Then a shout from Tony invited her to join them.

Pulling her comtab from a pocket, she activated the flashlight. A thick layer of pine needles covered the ground, muffling her footsteps. She wove through the trees, stopping behind Tony where he stood with his mini blaster pointed at the ground. Joss, Siti, and Derek stood on one side of a clearing, staring at Andrade on the other. Siti and Joss each held a small, bright lamp that cast shadows on the caats prowling around the edges of the clearing. The two Larrys and Sashelle had been joined by three more caats. Quinn wasn't sure if they were part of the empress's entourage or not—the shadows and the caats' constant movements made recognition difficult.

"What's happening?" she whispered.

"I'm not sure." Tony reached back to take her hand, then stepped forward to join the other humans. "What's up?"

The Rat tried to abduct a kitten. Sashelle's mental tone clearly identified Andrade as the subject of her anger and conveyed disgust as well as a desire for vengeance.

"Kitten?" Tony looked around the space.

Siti darted a look at them, then turned to continue watching Andrade. "There were a bunch here. Sashelle brought me and Derek to meet them. It was a show of trust. And that… rat took advantage of it."

"Watch your language, Lieutenant!" Andrade took a half-step forward, then seemed to think better of it as the caats all turned to focus on him. "I am still your superior officer!"

"You may outrank me, but you're hardly superior. Sir. I don't work for you." Siti moved closer, glaring at the older man. "Sir. And I won't stand by while you endanger our relationship with the caats and threaten their young. Sir."

Joss moved forward, clearly offering support.

Derek stood nearby, his gaze trained on the trees. Quinn felt bad for the young Navy officer. He clearly wanted to back his friends, but standing up to your boss was a hard thing for any military officer, as she well knew.

"Sashelle?" Quinn whispered. "We're on your land. What do your people do to kidnappers?"

Sashelle's tail whipped violently, uprooting a swathe of the prickly underbrush. *Humans don't want to know. I have counseled the empress to banish him. We need a good relationship with his people.* Frustration and anger came through loud and clear.

Tony moved closer to the center of the clearing, pulling Quinn along with him. "If the caats are willing to send him home, we need to get him out of here. Caat justice is swift and violent."

Andrade sneered. "Animals don't have a sense of justice."

"You are digging your own grave." Siti threw up her hands in disgust. "Sir." She cast a disappointed look at Derek. "Maybe we should walk away. Let him deal with this on his own."

In unnerving synchronicity, the caats around the perimeter moved inward, shrinking the space around the humans to a two-meter circle. A little shiver went up Quinn's back. She didn't fear Sashelle, but the rest of the Pride were unknown. *If the caats were Russosken soldaty, we'd all be dead.*

True. Why do you think I spend so much time with the Ambassador? She's very caat-like. Dark humor underlaid Sashelle's thought about Francine.

Derek lifted a hand. "I've spoken with Captain Wortman. I am to return the major to the ship at once. With your permission." He bowed to Large Larry. "I have forwarded the video and will give a full report on his activities tonight. He will be held accountable. Major, your weapon." He put out a hand and stepped closer to the older man who stared him down.

The major ignored him, still glaring at Little Larry.

Derek made a gimme motion. "Sir? Your weapon."

Growling under his breath, Andrade cast a quick look around the circle of predators, then pulled his blaster from its holster. "I won't forget this, Lee."

"I could have walked away and left you here with the caats, sir. I doubt you would have had the opportunity to register a complaint." Derek took the weapon and removed a piece which he tucked in his pocket. He shucked his backpack and slid the blaster into the top, then shrugged it back on. "Your grav belt."

"I'm not giving you my belt!" The major's belligerence lasted only until one of the caats moved closer. "I need it to get out of here."

"Your belt, sir. I will tether it to mine." Derek waited, hand outstretched.

"Of all the—!" Andrade seethed as he unbuckled his belt, muttering threats at all three younger officers. "You will regret siding with animals."

The caats moved inward again, pushing past Tony, Quinn, and the Explorer Corps officers. Their hot breath ruffled Lee's hair and blew Andrade's jacket tight against his barrel-shaped frame. The younger man focused on the control panel of the major's belt, seemingly unconcerned by the ring of predators around him. Sweat appeared on the major's brow, and a drop rolled down his cheek. His breathing sped up, and his face went pasty white.

After a long moment, Lee returned the belt to its owner. "Put that on, and we'll go." He turned to face the smaller black caat and bowed again. "On behalf of the Colonial Commonwealth Navy, I deeply apologize to the pride and the empress. This man will not be allowed on Hadriana again. I will do everything in my power to ensure justice is served."

Little Larry looked the young lieutenant over from head to toes. After a long moment, he took a half step back. *We trust you, Derek Lee, to hold this man accountable. The future of our relationship with your people hangs in the balance.*

Siti repeated the caat's words.

Derek sucked in a deep breath. He bowed one more time. "I will strive to live up to your trust."

"You coward. Snake. Traitor!" Andrade grew increasingly abusive as Lee lifted off the ground. With a jerk, Andrade's belt kicked in, and he rose in the lieutenant's wake. He brandished a fist at the ground. "You'll all regret this. I won't forget your part, Kassis! You and Torres and your stupid pets."

With a snarl, Sashelle launched upward. Her claws popped out, and she raked them down the side of Andrade's leg, shredding his pants. The other caats howled in rage, sending chills up Quinn's back. Sashelle dropped to the ground beside her, growling.

Tony peered at Sashelle's claws as they popped back in. "No blood? You missed?"

Sashelle's denial came through in a wave of anger. *The empress decreed he should leave unmolested. She said nothing about his clothing.*

Quinn pressed her lips together to hide a smirk. *He actually tried to kidnap a kitten?*

He did. Like the Dirt People, he thinks we're sub-human. We think he was intending to use the kitten as a hostage. Only the pride's desire to collaborate with the Earthman and the other Colonials spared his life.

"Did you hear that?" she asked Tony as Sashelle followed the other caats into the trees.

He nodded. "That man is—" He broke off as if he couldn't come up with a word bad enough. "I hope Derek's report is taken seriously."

"We'll back him up." Siti rubbed a hand over her face. "Hopefully three lieutenants against a major…"

"He has that recording. Plus, my dad will vouch for us. And speak for the caats." Joss flicked his grav belt. "We should get back to the airfield, too. It's late, and everyone is tired." He met the others' gazes. "And I'm not sure I want to spend a night in the caats' lands. Not that I don't trust them, but all it would take is one rogue."

"As we've seen." Quinn gestured at the sky. "I don't know if a rogue caat is likely, but I concur."

CHAPTER THIRTY-FIVE
SITI

WHEN WE RETURNED to the airfield, the Navy shuttle was gone. Joss and I trudged to the sleek *Rossiya Attaché* while Tony and Quinn returned to the *Swan* with a promise to have dinner waiting for us.

"They're good people." I rubbed my shoulder as we waited outside the ship's hatch. "They could have thrown all of us to the caats, and I wouldn't have blamed them a bit. I can't believe he tried to take one of those kittens."

The hatch popped, and Joss climbed the steps slowly with me on his heels. We waited again for the outer hatch to close and the lock to cycle. Joss glanced up at the obvious camera above the interior hatch. "I wonder why they don't pop both ends."

I lifted a shoulder. "Maybe they're worried about Andrade trying something."

"But he's gone." The door popped open, and Joss went in.

"We *think* he's gone. Maybe he got the drop on Derek, landed at a nearby location, and came back here to do who knows what." Francine lounged against the wall by the door. "That guy was bad news from the get-go. Sashelle warned us. Not that I couldn't tell on my own."

I tried to hide a stab of worry. "I don't think he could get the drop on Derek. At least, I hope not. And you're not telling me anything new about Andrade. I'm still not sure why he's here. Phase 1 teams don't usually have an intel guy—especially not a Navy one."

She jerked her head away from the airlock. "Come down to the lounge. Your dad's waiting."

"I'm betting Ministry of State visits always have an intel guy. Probably, they're usually dressed up as an assistant or something." Joss yawned as he followed Francine through an interior hatch, then stopped in surprise. "Wow, this is... ritzy."

Inside, the ship bore little resemblance to the *Swan* or the Navy's VIP shuttle. Where the former was designed for family-style living and the latter was an efficient—if comfortable—transport, this ship looked like a high-end restaurant. Two large, round tables stood in the center of the room, with padded chairs, white tablecloths, and elegant china. On one side of the room, a bar held rows of expensive liquors, complete with tall stools and a bartender in formal attire. Thick carpet covered the floor, and subdued lighting gave the compartment an intimate aura.

Zane rose as we entered and gestured to the empty places. "Kids, grab a seat."

As Joss dropped into a chair, Francine went to speak with the bartender in a low voice. I took another empty spot, setting my backpack on the floor beside my seat. "Where are Harim and the general?"

Zane's lips twitched. "Apparently the exertions of the day were too much for our esteemed colleagues, and they chose to retire. Or so they claimed. I suspect the general is compiling a report for her superiors."

"I'm not sure I believe the general has superiors." I touched the corner of the heavy white napkin folded into a crown. "I mean, technically, Harim is her boss, but we've seen how that relationship works."

"True. Maybe she's actually tired, but I find that hard to believe. The woman is a force." Zane sipped the brown liquid in his short, squat glass, then lifted it toward Francine as she returned to the table.

"You certainly know how to travel in style. I wonder if I can get a ship like this."

Francine let out her charming, musical laugh. "No one but Dusica could afford to travel like this. Although as the 'Earthman' I'm sure there are plenty of folks who'd be happy to accommodate you."

He lifted a hand and shook his head. "I'm not for sale. But I'm not above accepting help when it's offered freely." His eyes narrowed. "It is being offered freely, is it not?"

"There is no free lunch." Francine waited for Zane to pull out her chair, then sat gracefully. "But in this case, your part of the deal was to meet with the empress. Thank you for that." She raised a perfectly manicured finger as her gaze traveled to the bulkhead. "One moment." Clearly the Russosken had audio implants like ours.

The bartender approached with a list of beverages ranging from sparkling water to Alteirien Zinglfed, which turned out to be eighty percent alcohol with a natural hallucinogenic. Joss opted for a soft drink while I took a non-alcoholic cider. Time enough to imbibe after we reported to his father.

We took turns explaining what had happened with Major Andrade. At some point, Francine concluded her call and asked a few questions. Then she folded her hands on the table and waited.

Zane shoved a hand through his hair, clearly lost in thought. With a deep breath, he picked up his glass and drained it, then returned it to the table with a clunk. "We saw Derek and the major return to their shuttle, of course. But they weren't in any mood to stop and chat. I'll include a summary of your report in my communique to Earth. And my observations to the Colonial Commonwealth." At Francine's raised brows, Zane explained, "Earth is considered neutral ground. As such, the other governments are often interested in my take on political situations. I'll forward the same report to Gagarin and Lewei, of course, but I doubt it receives the same level of consideration."

"I suspect it gets more," I said. "They like to keep up on what we're doing, and your reports give them a—theoretically—unbiased window." I tipped my head at Joss on the word "theoretically."

"Yes, they'd be fools to believe I'm completely independent when I rely on the Commonwealth for transportation and my son is in their employ." He turned to Francine. "Another reason I was grateful to accept your offer. This gives my efforts a little more authentic independence."

Francine leaned forward and made eye contact with Zane. "What did you think of the caats?"

He sat back in his chair, letting the bartender refill his glass as he considered Francine. When the server left, he held his drink up to the light as if admiring the color. He set the glass down without tasting it. "I think they've been treated poorly. If my understanding of Hadriana history is correct—" He glanced at me. "I read several books on the trip out—" Another deep breath came out in a heavy sigh. "Those were written by and for humans, of course. And the empress filled me in on their side. She was actually here when humans arrived over a hundred years ago!"

"Caats live a very long time," Francine said softly.

"And they were here first. But if everything I've read and understood is correct, the humans had no idea the caats were sentient and sapient. They dropped in—as we humans are wont to do—and started building. But to be fair, no one stood up and said, 'Hey! This is our planet!'"

Francine's blue eyes narrowed, and she slapped a hand on the table. "They didn't know they had to say anything. By the time they realized what was happening, it was too late. And you've seen how most humans react to a talking caat!"

Zane raised both hands in surrender. "I'm trying to paint an impartial picture, Francine, not saying I agree with what happened. But having seen firsthand how difficult it is to convince a technologically superior force that your sovereignty should be respected—" He cast an apologetic glance at me and shrugged. "It was hard enough for us, and we spoke the same language. And looked like the invaders."

He sipped his drink. "I one hundred percent agree the caats deserve a place at the table. But I don't think they're going to be able to send the 'Dirt People' packing. We flew over Hadriana City on the way in—there are hundreds of thousands of people there. Relocating all of them—or even a portion of them—is going to be too much to ask."

"Unless the empress has something to offer in return," I said.

Every pair of eyes—including the bartender who I suspected was listening in remotely—snapped to me.

"What do you mean?" Zane asked.

I shrugged. "The Commonwealth didn't swallow Earth—we couldn't because Gagarin and Lewei wouldn't let us. It's the shared birthplace of humanity. All of us, right?" At Francine's nod, I went on. "Not that we knew about you back then. But my point is Earth had that status to trade on. Right now, Hadriana's main export is potatoes, grown by the Dirt People." I grinned as I used Sashelle's derisive nickname for the local human population.

"Potatoes?" Joss spoke for the first time, his tone disbelieving. "That's their primary export?"

"A very valuable one," Francine said. "Believe it or not. This has always been the problem. The caats have nothing to trade. They don't grow anything. They don't build or manufacture. For the most part, caats are happy to exist, to hunt, to sing, to enjoy their lives."

"Sing? The arts have value." Zane sat up straighter. "Would humans enjoy caat singing?"

Francine snorted delicately. "Definitely not."

"The caats also have communication skills we don't." I tapped the audio device implanted behind my left ear. "That might be of use. And someone—Doug, maybe? Back on Lunesco?" I cocked my head at Joss, but he lifted both hands in denial. "Someone said something about Sashelle 'vetting us'… What was that about?"

Francine's eyes widened. "Yes. Caats are able to read humans. You know they can hear—for lack of a better word—surface thoughts. They can also read intentions. Doug has had Sashelle vet every person who works in his command center—he won't bring someone new on until she's had a chance to check them."

"Why didn't they notice Andrade's intentions, then?" Joss asked.

We all stared at him. I'm pretty sure my jaw hit the table.

"I—" Francine bit her lip. "I don't know."

When Francine invited us to stay for dinner, I regretfully declined since we were expected on the *Swan*. Francine immediately called and invited Tony, Quinn, Liz, and Maerk to join us, too. By the time they arrived, another staff member had set the second table, and the bartender poured wine. The general and Harim emerged from their suites, and we left the politics behind to enjoy the meal. The food on the *Rossiya Attaché* was as fabulous as the décor, and we returned to the *Swan* stuffed and tired.

The next morning, we woke early. I rolled out of the top bunk, making sure to kick Joss lightly as I climbed down to use the facilities.

"Go away, Siti. I'm sleeping."

When I returned, he let out a loud and extremely fake snore. Tossing a pillow at him, I made my bed quickly and grabbed the slippers we wore inside the ship. "Don't sleep too late. You'll miss breakfast. I heard we're having potatoes."

"We had potatoes yesterday." He rolled over to face the wall.

"You've never objected to them before."

"I'm not really objecting. Maerk makes them tasty enough." He sat up and rubbed his eyes. "And they're definitely better than a steady diet of meal pacs."

I gasped and clutched my chest. "Who are you? No real explorer would utter such blasphemy." I slid the door shut before he could respond.

Down in the main compartment, Maerk stood beside the stove frying potatoes, onions, and peppers. "I'm doing them with spicy sausage today, Siti." He pointed at the pile of dishes on the counter. "Set the table, will you?"

"Sure." I took the pile of plates and laid them on the big table. "Any idea what the plan is for today? Are we meeting with the caats again or—"

The caats are meeting with you. Sashelle lifted her head to look over the back of the sofa.

I jumped. "I—I didn't see you there."

A sense of satisfaction oozed from the caat. *I didn't want you to see me.*

I frowned. "Is this part of that misdirection thing you mentioned before?"

A simple demonstration.

"It works." I finished setting the table, then perched on the edge of the armchair across from the caat. "I understand you can read intentions, too."

The caat's eyes closed to slits. *You're wondering about the Rat.* An image of Andrade accompanied the statement.

"Yes. Why didn't you know what he was planning?"

Sashelle licked a paw, her gaze avoiding me. I waited, sensing she'd answer when she felt like it. With a heavy mental sigh, she turned back to me. *I'm not sure. From the beginning, he was murky. Difficult to read. I didn't like him but couldn't read him well enough to know why. The others agreed, but rather than banishing him, we agreed to watch him. Unfortunately, we didn't watch him closely enough.*

"But he didn't get away with it."

We don't like the possibility he represents. A human who cannot be read is a danger to us. We will have to assume anyone else who is murky is an enemy.

"You've never run into another person you couldn't read?" I pulled a decorative pillow from behind me and settled back into the chair. "What about Derek? He doesn't hear you—can you hear him?"

The caat blinked in surprise. *I didn't hear his thoughts. Some humans are quieter than others. But I could still read his intentions. I would not have taken him to the kittens else.*

"Why are you here now? Are we going back to the empress?"

No. We return to Romara. And the empress comes with us.

CHAPTER THIRTY-SIX
QUINN

If she never had to return to Romara City again, Quinn would be happy. She thought that every time she came back. Since the revolution, the nightmares induced by her stay on death row had receded, but they still haunted her sleep each time she had to come back. Maybe it was time to retire from public service for good.

Not that she held an official position of any kind. But her relationships with Tony, Doug, and Auntie B kept her tied into the politics. And now that Sashelle had convinced the Earthman to speak on behalf of the caats, well, it was a strange new world.

They'd refused the quarters the government had offered this time, instead staying in their small apartment in a nearby residential area. Ambassador Torres had opted to stay in the hotel, even though the Romarans had tried to restrict his movements the first time, and the young CEC officers had been forced to lodge with their contingent.

Sashelle and her empress—who had traveled with Francine on the *Rossiya Attaché*—had also taken quarters in the government building, mainly to remind the humans that they, too, were ambassadors. The representative from Hadriana had not been amused, but with Torres's support of the caats, the humans gave in. Despite the economic significance of Hadriana's potato exports, the planet was considered a backwater by the rest of the republic.

"The Leweians and Gagarians have arrived." Tony looked up from his comtab as he approached the breakfast table. "Siti says the talks will resume this morning."

"I'm glad we don't have to attend them." Quinn pushed a plate of toast toward her husband.

"Apparently Siti doesn't, either." He turned the device so she could read the screen. "She's asking if we can meet her later today. And she wants Sashelle, too."

"Not sure if we can make that happen." She put some jam on the toast and took a bite. Despite her disdain for Romara, she enjoyed the piffleberry jam. It didn't keep well, and piffleberries grew only on Romara, so one had to come to the planet to get it. One small point in the planet's favor.

"I called Francine. She's staying with the caats." He scooped some jam onto his own toast. "I wonder how Sashelle convinced Francine to become their human mouthpiece."

"She's always called Francine *the Ambassador*. Probably some agreement with the Russosken none of us will be happy with." The revolution might have broken the Russosken, but Francine's sister was doing her best to return the organization to its former glory—minus the underworld threats, killing, and extortion. Mostly.

After breakfast, they walked to the park near the republic buildings. Siti, Joss, and another young man in CEC uniform waited beside the fountain. As they approached, Sashelle materialized from the trees nearby.

"You got out," Tony said to the group.

"I think they gave up on trying to lock us down. Probably when we willingly walked back in." Siti looked around, her gaze stopping on a man sitting on a bench, then on a couple snoozing in the sun. "But I'm sure they're watching."

"Doesn't really matter. They won't see anything." The third officer stepped forward to bump fists. "I'm Chymm Leonardi di Zorytevsky. Everyone calls me Diz. We're doing a little experiment."

"Diz is one of the CEC's tech geniuses." Siti tapped behind her ear. "He's made some modifications to our comm systems in the past to—well, the reason is classified. But it turns out there's been a recent update to the systems. Most of us haven't got it, but I was wondering if that was why Andrade wasn't readable for Sashelle. So, we're going to see what happens when he upgrades mine."

Tony's eyes widened. "Is that dangerous?"

"No." Diz shook his head, hard, and pulled a couple of devices from his bag. "I wouldn't test anything dangerous on Siti! As she said, it's an official upgrade, but it's in a beta rollout. Only a few people get them until they're sure how it interacts with different comm systems. I checked the logs—Andrade is part of the beta group."

Quinn kept an eye on the man on the bench Siti had identified earlier. He seemed to be reading a newspaper, but didn't even flinch when the breeze shook the pages. It was a poor disguise, since very few people read actual paper anymore. By the time Diz started plugging things together, the spy wasn't even trying to hide his interest. Keeping her back to him, Quinn casually stepped into his line of sight. Tony caught her smirk and grinned back.

"Who do you think he belongs to?" Quinn whispered to her husband.

He shrugged. "Could be just about anyone. If the Colonials didn't want observers, they should have picked a different location."

Diz looked around the park. "Is the—what did you call them? Cay-uht?"

"Caat." Tony jutted his chin at Sashelle who stood beside Diz. "She's right there."

The young man nearly jumped out of his skin. "When did you get here?"

I cannot speak to the Wire Wielder.

"Hmm. That kind of makes sense." Quinn lifted a hand to catch Diz's attention. "Lieutenant, do you have this new upgrade installed?"

"Call me Diz. And yes, of course." He tapped the spot behind his ear. "I'm usually at the top of the beta list."

"Then perhaps that *is* why you can't hear Sashelle." Quinn frowned at the caat. "But she was still able to misdirect you. Interesting."

"Misdirect?" Diz beckoned to Siti.

Quinn pointed at Sashelle. "You didn't see her walk right up and sit next to you."

Siti laughed. "That probably had nothing to do with Sashelle. Diz is kind of oblivious when he's in his tech zone."

Diz laughed self-consciously and bowed to the caat. "That is so true. My apologies."

Accepted. The caat nodded back.

"Did you hear that?" Quinn asked.

"Hear what?" Diz fiddled with his devices some more.

"Again, hardly conclusive with Diz." Siti closed her eyes and gripped Joss's arm as she swayed a little. "Okay, got it."

"I've just upgraded Siti's implant." Diz made some more adjustments to his device. "If Sashelle would please attempt to communicate with her?"

Sashelle nodded at the young man and turned to look at Siti. *Can you hear me, Explorer of Lunesco?*

"Wait. I can't tell if I can't hear or—" Siti turned her back on the group. "Try again."

Your brother is a hamster, and your father smelt of elderberries.

Quinn burst out laughing. "Did she get that from you, Tony?"

"Of course." Her husband grinned at the caat. "But it's 'your *mother* is a hamster…' Humans prefer to insult parents, not siblings."

Siti glared over her shoulder at them in mock anger. "What in the world—did she insult my mother?"

"Did you hear it?" Diz asked excitedly.

"No." A shadow crossed Siti's face. "Can you reverse the upgrade? I like being able to hear her."

Diz raised a hand. "Of course I can, but first we need to finish testing." He turned to look at the caat. "Can you hear Siti?"

Sashelle's head cocked to the side and her eyes half-closed. *Tell her to think something.*

Quinn repeated the caat's words.

"I'm trying." Siti closed her eyes again. "Oh—hang on. I'll call someone. Joss and I speculated the subvocal communications were easy for Sashelle to pick up on." She went quiet for a few seconds, then her eyes went wide in surprise. "I didn't know you were here!"

Who is where? Sashelle asked.

Quinn touched Siti's shoulder. "Don't talk out loud."

The younger woman raised a finger. "Sorry, I'm talking to my dad. I'll do it silently." She moved away, her gaze on the horizon, ignoring the others.

"What's her dad doing on Romara?" Joss asked.

"The admiral is here?" Diz looked up from his devices. "Didn't he retire?"

"I think you're missing the important factor," Tony said. "Can Sashelle hear whatever Siti is saying to him?" He raised a brow at the caat.

No. Sashelle's single word sounded unhappy. *I can still read her, though. She's not murky like the Rat. More like Derek Lee.*

Quinn blinked in surprise. Sashelle rarely used names. "And you said you could read Derek but not communicate directly."

The caat's head dipped in agreement.

"Have you ever met someone murky, like Andrade?"

Many people are murky. I come across them often when traveling with the Ambassador. I haven't previously spent enough time with a murky one to realize they were inherently untrustworthy.

"To be fair, maybe they aren't all." Quinn tried to deflect Sashelle's obvious disagreement with that statement. "On the other hand, trust has to be earned, so…"

Exactly. Sashelle's head snapped around as the young couple dozing on the grass rose. *Who are they? I can't hear them at all!* Her tone sounded alarmed.

"This is Tiah Ross. She's from Earth." Joss beckoned for the couple to join them. "And you know Derek. Don't you recognize him?"

Sashelle's eyes widened in an expression of surprise Quinn had rarely seen on the caat's face. *She's deadening my—* The caat bolted away, coming to a stop across the park from the group.

"It's probably a good thing you're the only one who likes to travel," Joss told the slender young woman. Brown hair curled around an olive brown face, lighter than Joss's but darker than Siti's. She limped slightly as she walked.

"What's going on?" Quinn watched Sashelle with concern.

"Tiah's from a group of people who—it's too hard to explain without covering the last five hundred years of Earth history." Joss frowned. "Tiah's people lived in the Dome with us, but they didn't do the deep sleep thing. Her great, great, great, I dunno how many great grandparents were some of the original Dome residents. Because the Dome's capacity was limited, the gene pool kind of—" He interlaced his fingers. "We think the homogenous genetic patterns created some—"

"I have a weird effect on some people." Tiah sighed. "Apparently, I cancel out some... psychic capabilities. Some. Not all."

"You say it like psychic abilities are the norm on Earth." Quinn squinted at the young woman. "You aren't saying that, are you?"

Joss raised a brow, but neither of them answered.

"I think that means she *is* saying it," Tony said.

"Not the *norm*," Joss said. "There's a whole range of capabilities. And Tiah's dampening effect helped Diz develop his adaptations. She even provides a blanket effect—which is why Sashelle didn't notice Derek." Joss grinned. "We've used that in the past."

"That sounds like a story I need to hear." Tony held out an elbow to Tiah. "Why don't we walk over that way while you tell me, so Sashelle stops freaking out. Although I've never seen her like that, so it's kind of amusing."

Quinn gave Tony a little push. "Good plan. I'd like to hear more, too, when Sashelle's... elsewhere."

The slender woman took Tony's arm and the two of them strolled away. Sashelle watched from a distance, then cautiously approached.

Diz clapped his hands together once, drawing Siti's attention. She lifted her finger again, then nodded, and her eyes focused on the young man. "That was my dad. Did it work?"

"Tiah cancels Sashelle's abilities." Joss ticked things off on his fingers. "You can't hear the caat with your implant upgrade, and she can't hear you. But she can still sense your intentions?" He raised a brow at the caat.

Sashelle moved into the circle. *I concur with the Son of Earthman.*

"Ooh, getting formal now, aren't we?" Joss snickered.

"What did she say?" Siti asked, clearly aggrieved to have missed the byplay. "Diz, turn this thing off."

"On it." Diz fiddled with his devices and nodded. "I think I've isolated the correct frequencies. Try talking to her."

Siti stared at the caat.

I heard that.

"Yes!" Siti pumped a fist in the air. "You should fix Derek's too."

Derek blinked in surprise. "You can do that?"

"Why not?" Diz flipped through his screens. "It's my design."

"But I didn't get the upgrade from you—whoa!" Derek stared at the caat. "Your voice is amazing."

Pleasure rolled off the caat.

"I'm sending a control app to your holo-rings." Diz swiped and flicked as he spoke, pausing often mid-word to concentrate on the task at hand. "This will al— You can use it to— Hang on. Okay. The green icon means comm— wait."

Siti crossed her arms and rolled her eyes. "Diz, finish what you're doing, then explain."

"Roger."

They stood in the sun while Diz did his thing. Some of the group wandered a few paces away to sit in the shade as it took longer than anyone seemed to expect. Finally, the young man looked up in triumph. "Got it! The green icon means 'communicate.' If you activate it, you can talk to Sashelle. If you flip it to red, she can't hear you. Kind of like initiating a call."

"What about other caats?" Siti flicked her holo-ring and played with her settings.

Diz gulped. "I assumed they were all using the same—ah, crap. Do we have anyone else to test on?"

Quinn pointed at the government building on the edge of the park. "The empress and her entourage are right in there."

CHAPTER THIRTY-SEVEN
SITI

We returned to the auditorium as the meeting broke for lunch. While the others filtered out of the room, Zane and Antinea—the caat empress—lingered in their seats on the stage. They'd provided Antinea with a large, low table—since she was too big to sit in a human chair—and a bowl of water.

Leaving Quinn, Tony, Joss, Tiah, Diz, and Derek near the entrance at the top of the auditorium, I jogged down the stairs toward the stage. When Zane paused to look up, I approached. "How's the meeting going?"

Zane glanced at the caat and spread his hands wide. "Hard to say. The locals aren't thrilled with having the empress here. As expected. The Lunesco contingent has been supportive, of course, and strangely, the Leweians have too. Wisnall thinks they see it as a bargaining chip."

While we appreciate their support, we will not be blackmailed by it in the future. Antinea smugly flicked her tail from side to side, then rose and stretched. *If we are taking a break, I will hunt.*

"I think they've provided a buffet." Zane rose, too, and gestured toward the door.

Hunting is more fun. She leapt off the little table then up into the pipes and conduits that filled the shadowy area over the dais.

Zane hopped down the two steps to the main floor and headed up the shallow stairs toward the rest of our group. "How'd the testing go?"

I explained what we'd discovered as we climbed. "And Tiah, as expected, creates a dead zone."

"Interesting." He shook hands and bumped fists with the others. "Tiah, will you join us for the afternoon session?"

The thin woman ducked her head. "Do they want me there?"

"I don't really care." Zane put a hand on her shoulder. "As part of the triune, you deserve to be there. I only wish we'd managed to get Ortiz to join us. He wasn't keen on leaving Earth."

"If he's part of the triune, isn't travel from the planet part of the job description?" I asked. Earth was represented by a three-person committee: Tiah represented those who had grown up in the Dome, Zane spoke for the thousands who had spent hundreds of years in suspended animation, and Ortiz's ancestors had survived outside the Dome. The little committee wasn't strictly representative—the third group was much larger than the other two—but more about considering all points of view. Zane often spoke on behalf of the entire triune.

"It is, but he just got home from Grissom and his wife is due any minute. I suggested he send a substitute, but he left it to us." Zane squeezed Tiah's shoulder again and let go. "But let's grab some grub before the meetings start again. And I'll introduce Diz to Caitlin Maroney—the Colonial ambassador's assistant. She can help you set up more testing."

"Do you want to eat in the cafeteria?" Tony asked doubtfully. "Or the buffet?"

"You got something better in mind?" Zane's eyes sparkled with interest.

Tony jutted a thumb over his shoulder. "Tocco van down in the courtyard. They cater to employees of the senate, so it's fast, inexpensive, and delicious."

"And the weather's perfect." Quinn turned to lead us to the elevator. "If they'll let you out."

"I think we're good. They gave up on the sequestration after I complained." Zane moved to the back of the little car and turned to face the front, tapping the decorative railing running around the walls at waist level. "This reminds me of the old days."

"Really?" I frowned at the mirrored surface as the doors slid closed. "You rode in an elevator before?"

"We had one at the Dome, but it was dead before I was born." Joss poked the button marked with a swirly, illegible symbol.

"That's the parking garage." Tony tapped a different button. "This one is the ground floor."

"When I was a teen, I lived near Washington DC. It was the capital city. Not of Earth, but of my country." Zane rolled his shoulders as if the memory had caused them to tighten. "Lots of tall buildings there. Most elevators had music, though."

"Interesting idea." Quinn's brows drew down as she stared at a small grate above the buttons. "There's a speaker here. No reason they couldn't pipe in music."

"But what to choose?" As the door opened, Tony put out a hand to hold it. "Classical? Indie Flet? DerpPunk?"

"No, please!" Quinn cried in mock horror.

We crossed a vast lobby with high ceilings and a wall of glass looking out on a green space. A low barrier blocked our exit. We scanned our room cards on a panel, and our faces and text appeared in response. Then the barrier slid open for us to exit one at a time. Tony led us out the automated glass doors into a large courtyard. Trees grew in a neat border around the outside edge of the paved area, partially obscuring the wall enclosing the space. Tables sat in tidy rows, and a line of boxy vehicles stood between the trees on two sides.

While we waited in line at the vehicle Tony indicated, Quinn explained the differences between Indie Flet and DerpPunk to a fascinated Tiah and Joss. As the line moved, Zane hesitated, letting a little space grow between them and himself, Derek, and me.

"I spoke with Captain Wortman," Zane said in a low voice. "Major Andrade has been restricted to the ship. Wortman didn't want to do that."

"What?" I propped my fists on my hips. "You saw the vid—he tried to abduct a baby! That's not—"

Zane lifted a hand. "I got the impression there are forces beyond Wortman's control at play."

"My captain would love to take him down." Derek glanced around to make sure we weren't being overheard. "He's been a complete pain in the backside this entire mission—this gave Wortman the excuse to do something about him." He raised both hands to ward off my angry reaction. "I'm not trying to trivialize what he did. It was heinous. But Wortman is a by-the-book kind of guy, and when you're dealing with people with connections, you have to be…"

"Above reproach. With rock-solid evidence." I nodded in agreement. "Hopefully your video provided that."

"He didn't say it on the record, but that's why Wortman assigned me to ferry Andrade around. He wanted me to watch and report. And I think he knew my previous connection to you and Joss might allow me to tag along where another pilot would have stayed with the shuttle."

Zane grunted absently and took a couple steps to close the gap between us and the food van. "Order at will, officers. It's on me. Or rather, on the Romaran charge account."

Joss, standing a few feet away, turned to frown at his father. "You couldn't'a said that a few minutes earlier, Dad? I had to borrow money from Tony."

Zane laughed and asked the proprietor which menu item was his most popular. After ordering, we took our beverages and joined the others in a shaded corner of the courtyard.

"I want to thank all of you for your help in this endeavor." Zane lifted his glass of sparkling fruit drink. "And Empress Antinea asked me to extend her thanks to you as well. Without us, she would not have a seat at the table."

"She doesn't really have a seat," Joss said under his breath. "More like a stool."

I rolled my eyes and nudged him with an elbow.

"Based on my experience with Sashelle, I'm surprised the caats admit we helped." Quinn's lips twitched as she cast a pointed glance at her husband.

Tony nodded in agreement then frowned. "We probably shouldn't judge the entire species based on our interactions with one member."

"Good point, but do you really think the empress is less... *superior* than Sashelle?" Quinn turned to the rest of us. "She has never made a secret of her belief that humans are less intelligent and less capable. Luckily, she has other characteristics that make her less annoying."

I heard that. Sashelle seemed to appear out of thin air beside the table.

"I intended you to." Quinn chuckled. "I saw you jump over the wall."

"You saw her?" I frowned at the two security guards patrolling the edges of the courtyard. "No one else seems to have noticed."

"She was using her 'don't notice me' field." Quinn raised a brow and looked at each of us in turn. "It only works if you aren't expecting to see her. And she has to be unobtrusive. I was looking at the wall, wondering if it's intended to keep us in or intruders out, when she poked her head over the top. Since we were talking about her, I think that made it easier for me to notice. I suspect the guards *didn't* see her —or didn't pay attention to her because a normal cat wanders through on a regular basis."

That is correct. Sashelle sat beside the end of the table. *I smelled it.*

I gestured at the caat, whose head was clearly visible above the table. "No one is going to confuse Sashelle with a house cat."

Not correct. I successfully impersonated a house cat for months.

Joss held a hand at the height of Sashelle's head. "How? House cats are small." He dropped his hand close to the ground.

I was somewhat smaller then. Sashelle's eyes closed halfway, and she projected an impression of satisfied mystery.

"She's never successfully answered that question for me." Quinn laughed. "But when we first met, I thought she was a really big house cat. Actually, I thought she was a stuffed animal until I picked her up.

But when you see a furry animal snuggled on the couch next to your eight-year-old, you don't assume it's an alien."

You're the aliens.

"Fair enough."

The vendor called out our names, and Tony and Joss got up to retrieve the food. While we ate, we chatted about the similarities and differences between the "toccos," our tacos, and the Earth food with the same name. Two used a flat bread made of corn flour, but each of the three had a different spice palate.

"Sashelle, did you come to see us for a reason?" Zane asked after we'd demolished the food. "Or just to share the toccos?"

I came to report to the empress. And to eat something I didn't have to catch myself. Her pink tongue swiped around her mouth.

"Traveling with Francine has made you soft," Quinn said.

"Speaking of Francine, why does she look so familiar?" Joss asked. "I've seen her before we met on Hadriana. Even her voice sounds familiar."

Quinn frowned. "How is that possible?" She raised her brows and tilted her head. "I suppose you might have seen her on some kind of broadcast while we were traveling? She's not unknown in the social media spheres."

"I don't think so." Joss stuck his finger in one of the spicy sauces and licked it. "We didn't—" His eyes went wide. "Water!"

While the rest of us scrambled for water, Zane handed over the last of his fruit juice. "Try this first."

Joss downed it and sat back, coughing. "That was… intense."

"Too much for the Caveman?" Derek had been uncharacteristically quiet but obviously couldn't let a chance to needle Joss slide.

Joss shoved the plate toward Derek. "Let's see you try, Nibs."

I stood. "If this is going to devolve into a display of manly spice level one-upmanship, I'm out."

The others rose, too. "I need to get back in there," Zane said. "Sashelle, are you coming?"

I have already been inside. This building stinks of SwifKlens. It is my least favorite scent. She flicked her tail in agitation. *Even worse than potatoes.*

"Do potatoes have a smell?" Joss stacked the last of the debris into a bin Tony had retrieved from the tocco van. "Other than dirt?"

The caat's tail swished more violently, but she didn't answer.

CHAPTER THIRTY-EIGHT
QUINN

As the others cleared the table and headed back into the large building, Quinn put a hand on Sashelle's head. "We need to talk."

That's never good.

Quinn laughed as she dropped back onto the bench. "You've been watching too much human entertainment with Francine. Which is what I wanted to talk to you about."

My favorite is the one with the witch. She listens *to her cat.*

"That's not what I want to talk about." She waved to Tony, waiting by the big glass doors, and he went inside. "Has Francine been to the Commonwealth?"

Many times. Sashelle sank gracefully to her belly on the warm stone beside Quinn's feet. *She lived there when we did.* Her tone clearly chided Quinn for her poor memory. *She has visited friends there in the intervening years.*

"I don't mean the Krimson Empire. I mean the Colonial Commonwealth. The one our new friends came from."

The caat lifted her head to stare at Quinn, then looked away. *That commonwealth was unknown to your people.*

"You aren't answering my question—which I find suspicious. But not unusual." Quinn drummed her fingers on the table. "That commonwealth was unknown to *my* people." She gestured at the humans around them, some of whom gave her strange looks—no doubt wondering about the crazy woman talking to a cat. "Was it unknown to her people?"

How would her people know about it?

"Ugh!" Quinn rolled her eyes. "I guess I need to talk to Francine. Is she still on Romara?"

I certainly hope so. She's my ride.

WITH A QUICK MESSAGE TO apprise Tony of her plans, Quinn took the subway out to the airfield where the *Swan of the Night* had dropped them after their visit to Hadriana. The *Swan* had departed—Liz had reminded her passengers multiple times that she had a business to run and cargo to shift. Francine's sleek ship occupied the parking spot nearest the building, as if its owner couldn't be allowed to walk farther than necessary.

Quinn snorted. She might be projecting her long-time distaste for the ultra-wealthy—and the Russosken in particular—on a parking situation. But Francine always managed to get the best of most options. As she crossed the tarmac, Quinn looked for Sashelle, but the caat had deserted her somewhere on the subway. She wasn't worried —Sashelle had proven her ability to independently navigate human worlds many times over the years. But it was fun to play Spot the Caat.

Before she could pound on the ship's hatch—which would be satisfying but futile—it popped open, beckoning her inside. Quinn glared up at the camera she knew was hidden in the corner and strode through the open internal hatch to the corridor. "Francine, where are you?"

The other woman's voice came through the speakers. "You may join me in the library."

Muttering under her breath about the size of Francine's ship—it had a library?—Quinn followed the lights guiding her through the dining room and up a set of stairs. This part of the ship boasted a less ornate décor with flat white walls and serviceable gray carpet. The lights stopped halfway up the corridor outside two doors. The one on the right said "captain" in bold letters, while the one on the right slid aside at her approach.

The compartment was small, with two low bookshelves below a curved window offering a view of the airfield and Romara city. Francine sat curled up in a large armchair with an open book on her lap. Her blonde hair cascaded down her shoulders, and her blue dress set off her brilliant eyes. Beside her, a small table held an elegant tea service and a plate of cookies. She waved a graceful arm at the matching chair on the other side of the table. "Please, Quinn, join me."

Quinn plopped down in the big red chair and refused the tea Francine offered. "Just had lunch. With Tony and the Colonials. And Sashelle."

"She told me she was going to the Senate. Did she speak with the empress?" Francine lifted a fine porcelain saucer and raised the cup to her lips, pinky finger extended.

"I don't know and don't care. I want to know when you discovered the Colonials."

Francine jerked, her tea sloshing over the edge of the cup into the saucer in an uncharacteristic display of surprise. Quinn tried to hide a smile—it wasn't often she got one over on Francine. She should have waited until Francine took a sip—although that might have resulted in a spray of tea across her own face.

The younger woman returned the cup to the table, untasted. "What are you talking about? They came to you first. You discovered them."

"They came to Lunesco. But you've been to their worlds, haven't you?"

She fiddled with the cookies, straightening them on the plate. "What in the 'verse makes you say that? No one here knew anything about them until they suddenly showed up—maybe you invited them to Lunesco? Why else would they go there?"

"Right. I invited people I knew nothing about to come to a backwater planet on the fringe of Romaran space." Quinn resisted the urge to slap Francine's fingers away from the cookies. That chocolate one looked tasty.

"Likewise, how would I go to their world, since no one knew they existed?" Francine extended the cookie plate toward her guest.

Quinn snatched the chocolate cookie. "You knew they existed."

"Why would you think that?" The blonde returned the plate to the table and took one of the shortbreads.

"Because that boy—Joss—has seen you before." Quinn nibbled at the chocolate. Smooth and creamy as one would expect from a cookie at Francine's table.

"Please. People say that all the time." Francine patted her hair in satisfaction. "It's a classic pickup line."

"I doubt he was trying to pick you up. He's at least ten years younger than you."

"Are you calling me old?" Francine clutched her cookie to her chest in mock horror.

"No, I'm saying you're close to forty, and he's less than thirty. Or two-hundred and fifty, depending on how you count. And to be fair, you don't look that old." She glared at Francine's smooth completion and lustrous hair. "But he didn't say it in a 'hey baby' kind of way. The first time he said it, I thought maybe you have a doppelgänger on one of their worlds. But today he mentioned it again, and he said he recognized your voice. Doppelgängers don't have the same voice or accent. So, I'm guessing you've been to the Colonial Commonwealth."

Francine put her uneaten cookie on her saucer and stood. She paced across the room, her movements bearing an uncanny resemblance to Sashelle's prowling. At the far wall—which was only a few meters away—she turned. "This is classified."

Quinn crossed her arms. "You aren't part of the government."

"The Russosken have their own classification system." Francine waved that away. "And Dusica will—I don't want her to know about this."

Quinn reared back in her chair in surprise. "Dusica doesn't know?

I thought she—well, I'm still not sure what 'this' is, but I figured she'd be in the thick of it."

"No. She doesn't know." Francine took a deep breath and let it out slowly. "Last year—about seven months ago—Sashelle and I were near Daravoo. We were—to be honest, we were kind of bumming around. Dusica had sent me to Robinson's World, to meet with some… constituents."

"Is that what you're calling your mafia cells now?"

"We aren't a mafia. You know Dusica has worked hard to root out the violent strains in the family. She's really trying to build a legitimate business, and she's actually doing a great job. But I get tired of all of the meetings and schmoozing—I'm more of a free spirit. When we were done on Robinson's, I faked a communications error, and we went to Daravoo. It's as ugly and barren as they say, by the way."

"I know. Tony and I were there on the *Swan* a while back." She rolled her hand, indicating Francine should continue her story.

"You know End is working for us?"

Quinn nodded. Liz and Maerk's son, End Whiting, had taken a few years away from the family business to fly with the bigger organization.

"Okay. We left Daravoo, headed for jump, but we picked up a signal from an unexpected beacon. It was on a different frequency, but End was sure it was a jump beacon. Very similar technology to ours. In fact, we suspect—well, I'll get to that in a minute. End's gotten enough training in navigation systems to decipher everything. Long story short, we decided to jump to its point of origin."

Quinn gasped. "That's so dangerous!"

Francine lifted a hand in denial. "It isn't. Like I said, the tech was *very* similar to ours. Almost as if it evolved from a common ancestor."

"Are you saying our jump tech—which originally came from N'Avon, by the way…" Quinn frowned as she worked it out. "The Colonials have jump beacons based on N'Avon tech?"

"Or N'Avon has tech based on the Colonials'." Francine shrugged. "I doubt we'll ever know for sure. The Russosken have always had myths about mysterious strangers with fabulous technology. I suspect someone jumped out here—way back in the day when jump tech was first being tested. And somehow that connection got broken. You hear stories about the brave lives lost in the early days of jump—maybe they weren't lost, like dead, but *lost* lost. Like in a star system too far away with no way to get home."

She waved both hands. "That part doesn't really matter. What does matter is we jumped. And we ended up at Grissom—the planet from which your Colonial Explorer friends originate. We got picked up by their military immediately. Whisked away to their secret government headquarters. We were treated nicely—far better than I expected, but —" She waved a hand down her body. "I look like someone who should be treated nicely. The language is still close enough, as you know, for us to communicate. And I explained what happened. Sashelle helped me… depart when I decided I'd had enough questioning. I really didn't want to give our coordinates to a militarily superior nation. Then we flew home."

Crossing the room, she sank gracefully back into her chair. "I'm not sure why they let their explorer corps 'discover' Lunesco without warning them." She made air quotes around *discover*. "They knew our approximate direction, so when they got probes back from this side of the galaxy with obvious digital traffic, they should have assumed it was us and sent the Navy. But who knows how their politics work." She picked up the shortbread, making a face when it crumbled in her hand from having soaked up the spilled tea. "Maybe they sent the *Loyal Observer* before news of my visit had reached the CEC. Or maybe their Navy was up to something—they assigned that major to the mission, which I gather isn't normal."

"Did you share this information with anyone else?" Quinn asked.

Francine gazed at her for a long moment, then shook her head. "I'm not affiliated with any government entity. Or even with the Russosken."

"This is a Russosken ship."

"Whatever. I work for Dusica, but that doesn't mean I have to tell her everything."

"You didn't tell her about a brand new star system and millions—

probably billions—of potential new customers?" Quinn's eyes narrowed.

"She's got her hands full. And does she really need to be *more* wealthy? When is enough credits enough? When I left the Colonials, it was pretty clear to me they were going to come looking for us. And it was obvious they are militarily superior to us. You've seen what happened to the technologically inferior race on Hadriana. I didn't want that happening here. At least not any sooner than it needed to."

"You could have warned us—so we were ready for that technologically superior force!" Quinn jumped up from her chair, flinging out her hands. "We could have—"

"What? Magically accelerated our tech development to match theirs? That's pretty unrealistic. I figured if anyone knew, some idiot would decide to seek them out and they'd swoop in and take over. We'd be relegated to the wilds of our planets like the caats. I thought we'd be safer to just hunker down and try to stay below their notice. Sashelle agreed."

Francine flicked some imaginary cookie crumbs from her skirt. "Maybe you're right. It's too late now. They know where we are. And fortunately, thanks to Zane, they're treating us fairly, for now."

"Does Ambassador Torres know your story?" Quinn gestured at the ship around her. "You two traveled together for almost a week."

Francine nodded. "He does know. And he agreed to keep it quiet. What I can't figure out is how that son of his recognized me."

"I guess you'll have to ask."

CHAPTER THIRTY-NINE
SITI

When I joined Joss in the hotel gym a few days later, he sat up from the weight bench in surprise. "Don't you prefer to run?"

"I already did that." I patted my stomach. "Gotta work off all the toccos and sovapitas. But I'm bored. I'm glad we're headed home tomorrow. I need a real mission. Besides, I wanted to ask you a question."

Joss rolled down to his back and put his hands on the bar. "Shoot."

"You said you recognized Francine. From where?" That wasn't really what I wanted to know, but I didn't feel like I could just blurt out my question about Derek's whereabouts without a warmup.

He let the weight drop back into the holder and activated his audio implant. When I accepted the call, he reached for the weights again. "She's been to Grissom. My dad confirmed it. She's wacko. About seven months ago, she intercepted a CEC jump probe, figured out how to reverse the course and jumped to Grissom, sight unseen. Even I'm not crazy enough to do that! Who knows where they could have ended up?"

"But if you took your own beacon already programmed to your home destination—isn't that what the early explorers did?" I grimaced because my first mission had been one of those 'early explorer' style ventures.

"Yeah, but they flew direct. So, they knew how far away they'd gone. If you're jumping based on unfamiliar coordinates using an alien device—actually, that does sound kind of fun. But I'd want an idea of how far I was going, so I could calibrate the return beacon."

I shrugged and sat in front of another weight machine. "Maybe they were able to pull that data from the drone. But more importantly, she went to Grissom? How did we not know?"

"That's probably why Andrade was assigned to our mission. They knew we might encounter people." Joss sat up and glowered at me.

"Then why send us? Why not send a diplomatic delegation on Derek's ship?" My cheeks grew warm as I said his name, but I pushed down my emotions. Sending us in blind to a potentially hostile planet was criminal. The CEC wasn't a full military organization. Sure, we carried weapons—as did our ships—but they were to protect against threatening animals, not other humans.

Of course, the line between "threatening animal" and "angry intelligent local" was sometimes hard to find. But so far, the CEC had done a decent job of threading that needle. The Navy had a more checkered past. Which might be the reason they'd sent us instead.

"And why wouldn't they warn us?" I added some weight and rolled back to pull the bar from its slot.

"Are you sure they didn't?" Joss moved to a mat to do some sit-ups. "I'll bet Captain Salu knew. She probably left everyone else in the dark —to see how we'd handle it."

"That's not—" I broke off and did a set. Why was I defending her? We'd spent a few weeks working together on pre-mission planning, then a couple of days in transit. I didn't really know her. And if she'd been ordered to keep it secret, then she had no choice. I mentally ran through our discussions—had she tried to tip me off? In retrospect, some of her comments might have hinted we'd discovered humans.

"I guess the why is above our paygrade. Why not follow Francine home and establish relations that way?" I reconfigured the machine for a different exercise.

"Do you know who she works for? Who her family is? The Colonial Commonwealth wants to interact with legitimate governments, not the mob."

"Good point. So now what?" I took a deep breath and lifted the bar off the rack. Simulated weights were supposed to feel the same as real ones, but they always felt wobbly to me. We used them on missions—carrying a bunch of weights on a ship in transport or to a planetary mission made zero sense when you could achieve the same effect with grav tech. But on a civilized planet, I preferred the real thing. Plus, big heavy plates were way cheaper than the devices used in the simulator. But this was a high-end hotel for foreign dignitaries, so maybe Romara wanted to project opulence and prosperity. I grunted as I lifted, closing my eyes so I could imagine real plates on the ends of the bar.

"Now we leave it up to the government wonks and go back to doing our real jobs." Joss paused to grab a small rectangular device. It lit up when he pressed a button, and he tapped in a number. Or at least I thought it was a number. I'd been using my visual translator—newly updated with Romaran text and numerals—to set the weights. While their spoken language was understandable, their script deviated substantially from ours. Which seemed odd in a digital age. The shapes should be set in stone—or in pixels. Maybe someday I'd care enough to dig into their history to see what changed and why.

"But you still haven't told me why you recognized Francine. Where'd you see her?"

"At a bar, of course. I was out with Stillz and Hangdog—a couple guys from my last squadron—and we went to this swanky place in Virgilton near the embassies. I noticed her because, well, you've seen her—" He grinned and winked. "But there was something… off. Of course I went over to try my luck, because Stillz and Hangdog were egging me on. Tried to get her contact deets. Her accent was weird, and she didn't have a holo-ring." He shrugged. "I struck out, so I forgot about her. Until I saw her here."

I barked out a laugh. "That's got to be a hit to your ego."

He waved that off. "I *am* hard to forget. But she probably gets hit on all the time. I mean, look at her." He held the little box against his chest and did some more sit-ups, grunting against the extra weight.

"Yeah, I know. She's hot." I did another set. "Maybe now that she knows you better, she'll reconsider and want to have all your babies."

"No thanks. I'm not ready to settle down. Besides, she has a girlfriend. And honestly, she's way older than I realized back then. So, no time for lots of babies."

"How many do you think you're going to have?" I dusted my hands with the high-grade chalk they provided in cheerful blue bags and rolled down to do a third set while I needled him. "Even in her late thirties, she could carry a couple. And with the right med pod treatments, probably half a dozen, easy. Or you could use an artificial—"

"No matter how hot she is, I'm not gonna marry a mafia princess." Joss adjusted the weight device to zero and jumped to his feet. A little bot skittered out of a hidden door to clean the mat. "Not now, not ever. But speaking of settling down, what's up with you and Nibs?"

His question drove my instinctive defense of women out of my mind. "Nothing."

"Why not?" Joss headed for the door. "He wants you. You want him. It's so obvious. You're both here. What are you waiting for?"

"He's here? I've been looking for him—" I blushed hard under Joss's knowing gloat. "Fine, I admit I'm interested. But where is he?"

"Last I heard, he was in the sauna." Joss sauntered out the door.

I stared at the blank panel as it closed behind him. Derek was here? Not just still on the planet, but in the building? In the week since we tested Diz's upgrades to our audio devices, I hadn't seen him at all. As a shuttle pilot, he'd probably made numerous trips to the *Intrepid,* and I figured he must be bunking up there. My one attempt to make contact had resulted in a stumbling, apologetic, garbled message that he didn't return.

Which now that I thought about it—okay, I'd been obsessing over it, but now that I knew he was actually in the building, I was not happy. Was he avoiding me?

I finished my workout, determined not to modify my schedule for someone who couldn't be bothered to call me back. After a shower, I dressed in the new Romaran dress I'd been unable to resist. Thankfully, our governments had worked out an exchange system, and I was able to convert enough credits to buy it. The fabric draped beautifully, and the style flattered my figure. After a quick pep talk to my reflection in the mirror, I headed to the bar to meet Quinn, Francine, and Tiah for a multi-cultural girls' night.

As I stepped into the elevator, Sashelle appeared beside me.

"Don't do that!"

Do what? The caat sat down and licked a paw.

Yasmi jumped out of my trendy new handbag to snuggle with her new best friend. The caat pretended to ignore her.

"Sneak up on me. I need to find out how Quinn spotted you in the courtyard last week."

She got lucky. I sneak up on her all the time. Sashelle switched paws. *Why are you dressed in mating attire?*

I choked. "This isn't—I'm wearing a pretty dress and going out with some friends. Are you joining us?"

In a human mating ritual? I think not.

"I told you—"

I've been around humans a long time. This is what unattached females do to attract a mate. But you already have one, so why are you doing it? She dropped her paw to the floor and looked up at me. *For some males, playing hard to get works. I don't think that's the case with yours.*

"Why do you keep saying I have a mate? I am one hundred percent single."

If you keep saying it, maybe you'll believe it. The caat sounded exactly like Joss. The door opened, and the caat sauntered out with Yasmi riding on her shoulders. She paused to look back. *Your mate thinks the same. But you're both lying to yourselves. I'll bring your mouse home later.* And she darted across the lobby and out the door.

Shaking off the comment, I strode across the lobby to the hotel lounge. Francine, Quinn, and Tiah sat at the bar with brightly colored drinks in front of them, laughing over something. I slapped my now-empty purse on the counter and slid onto a stool. "Am I supposed to take dating advice from an alien?"

Tiah spit her slushy orange beverage across the bar. "Alien matchmakers?"

Quinn called the bartender over to mop up. "Sorry about this."

"No problem, ma'am. I've dealt with worse." He wiped the counter, took my order, and hurried away to make my drink.

"I assume you're talking about Sashelle?" Francine gave me a sympathetic look. "If she offered advice, it means she likes you."

"She asked me why I'm participating in a human mating ritual when I already have one." I gestured at my dress and the bar.

Tiah frowned. "But Quinn and Francine have significant others. And I'm not really looking right now…"

"Neither am I!" I took my drink from the bartender with a grateful nod and slurped down a sweet, fruity gulp. Brain freeze hit hard. "Ow!"

The others commiserated while I fought the headache. The pain disappeared as quickly as it arrived, and I sagged in my seat. "That always gets me."

"That's one reason I drink those on the rocks." Francine lifted her glass. "But for what it's worth, Sashelle is pretty accurate at matchmaking. Or rather, at knowing when two people belong together."

Quinn lifted a brow. "She never said anything to me about Tony. That was you."

"Where do you think I got the idea?" Francine smirked. "Not really, but Sashelle definitely approves of you two as a couple. And she nudged me toward Marielle." She turned back to me. "You know she's good at 'vetting' people, as Quinn likes to call it. Her ability to read intentions extends to those of the romantic variety. I'd definitely consider her suggestion. Even if the form of her observation is off-putting. That's just how caats are."

Tiah laughed. "Zane said the caats were looking for skills to use as leverage in trade talks. Maybe they should add matchmaking to their list."

"You ladies want some company?" a smarmy voice said.

I spun on my stool to decline, then recognized Tony. "It depends. Are you buying?" I fluttered my eyelashes at him.

Joss, standing behind Tony, laughed and pointed. "Siti, you are terrible at flirting."

I rolled my eyes. "Some of us don't practice as much as you do."

"We've got a table over there, if you all want to join us." Tony pointed toward the back of the dimly lit room. "But we don't want to intrude on girls' night." He and Joss wandered away.

"What do we think?" Quinn looked at Francine, Tiah, then at me. "Join the boys, or do our own thing?"

"I think we should definitely join the boys. At least for a few minutes. If they're buying." Francine took her glass and headed across the room.

Quinn watched her walk away. "You'd never know her family owns several star systems. Cheapskate."

I frowned at Quinn as I picked up my frozen drink. "What's that all about?" I frowned at the drink as the room seemed to sway under me. "How strong is this thing?"

Quinn put an arm around me and guided me in Francine's wake. "Have you eaten anything today? These hit hard if you're running on empty."

As we approached, the men rearranged chairs to make room for us. Somehow I ended up next to an empty seat. "Is someone sitting here?"

Joss jerked his chin toward me. "Nibs is right there."

Derek appeared behind the empty spot like Sashelle, but carefully avoiding my gaze. "I thought it was just us guys tonight."

"Not for you." Joss chugged the last of his drink and popped up from his chair. "We gotta go." With impressive skill, he herded the rest of the group out the door, leaving me and Derek alone.

"That was not subtle at all." I carefully sipped my very cold, very strong drink.

Derek gazed after the others. Was he wishing they'd stayed? Or that he'd gone with them? "Are you going to sit down?" I pointed at the empty chairs around me. "Or leave me feeling like a loser with no friends?" I bit my lip. Tipsy Siti had no filter.

He pulled out the chair and sat. "I, uh, talked to the caat today."

My ears burned, but I tried to pull off nonchalant. "Sashelle or Antinea?"

His lips twitched as he glanced at me. "Sashelle. I'm not important enough to be noticed by the empress."

"Me, neither." I played with my glass, waiting.

"She said something that made me realize I've been stupid."

I stared at my drink so I wouldn't have to look at him. The icy green crystals sloshed in the glass as I made careful wet rings on the tablecloth.

He leaned back in his chair. "What, no comeback? I was expecting a 'what's new?' or 'tell me something I didn't know.' What's the problem, caat got your tongue?"

I darted a look at him. "That was terrible."

He spread both hands. "Never claimed to be a comedian. That's Caveman's schtick." His gaze captured mine and bored into me as he leaned closer. "Listen. I like you. A lot. More than like. And Sashelle made me realize there's no reason not to just say it. You make me crazy, and I love that. I think I might even love you."

Heart pounding, I sucked in a deep breath. "You do?"

He gave me an enigmatic look. "I don't risk my career, repeatedly, for anyone else."

I blinked owlishly. "Good point. Thanks."

"That's it? Thanks?" He pushed the chair back, muttering something under his breath that sounded like, "Stupid caat."

"Wait." I grabbed his hand before he could rise. It was warm and solid. He turned his, so our palms met, and squeezed gently.

"You have something to say, Kassis?"

I took in a deep breath. "I talked to the caat today, too. And I think she's right."

"Right about what?" The corners of his lips twitched, and his gaze softened. But he was still going to make me say it.

"I think I might love you, too. Or at least be willing to find out."

He rolled his eyes and pulled me to my feet. "Good enough for now."

We sealed it with a kiss.

Or almost did. Because that's when I spotted Marika. And my dad.

CHAPTER FORTY
SITI

Leaving Derek staring after me, I stormed across the room. "Dad, what are you doing here? And with her?"

Marika LaGrange and I had met on that first mission to Earth. I thought she was my friend, until she stabbed me in the back. And turned out to be a Gagarian spy. Then Joss, Derek, and I encountered her again on our last mission before we graduated from the academy. We'd captured her, and last I heard she'd been sent to prison.

The redhead—a more polished and elegant version of the Marika I remembered—smiled and extended a fist to bump as if we were still friends. "So good to see you, Siti. Nate was just telling me you've had quite the career since our encounter on Saha."

I ground my teeth and ignored her fist. How dare she call my dad "Nate" like they were old friends? Last time she'd seen him, she'd been in handcuffs. And the time before, she'd been a second term explorer on his team—so far down the chain of command he'd only known her name because she'd befriended me. "Why isn't she in prison?"

"A government exchange sent her back to Gagarin years ago. She wasn't in Attica for more than a few weeks." Dad raised a brow at Marika.

"Days, really. They were quite happy to get me back." Her smile faltered as if that weren't quite true, then brightened when she spotted Derek coming across the room. "Ooh, you're still with the sexy Navy guy?"

"We aren't talking about him. We're talking about you." I glared at her, then turned to my dad. "Why. Is. She. Here?"

"Marika is part of the Gagarian delegation." Dad smiled apologetically. "And I've been added to the Colonial team. Ah, Derek, good to see you again." He put out a fist as Derek came to a stop behind me.

"Likewise, sir." Derek darted a look at me. "Everything okay?"

"Yes," Dad said.

"No," I said at the same time. "It's not. That woman is a convicted Gagarian spy, and now she's part of the Gagarian ambassador's team."

"Yeah, I remember." Derek frowned. "Not much we can do about that. They get to pick whoever they want. And I'm sure we've got some spies on our side, too. It's kind of how this whole thing works."

"Another reason I don't work for the Ministry of State." I pressed my lips together then turned to my dad. "I'm supposed to head home tomorrow. Do you want to ditch this turncoat and spend some time catching up, or—"

Dad put a hand on my arm. "Siti, be polite. Marika is just doing her job."

Marika smiled slyly and fluttered her lashes at Derek.

My fingers curled into fists. Derek put his arm around me and gave me a little shake.

Dad's gaze snapped to Derek and back to me. He smiled. "I'm happy to see you two have finally figured things out."

I ground my teeth. Why did everyone think they knew better than me? It was my love life, not theirs. Although my father had tried to set us up in the past.

Derek's hand tightened on my shoulder as if he could hear my thoughts. "Thank you, sir. It's very new."

"Aw, that's sweet! We should celebrate!" Marika raised a hand to call the bartender over. He hurried to her side with stomach-turning speed.

While she spoke with the server, Dad turned to me. "The good news is you aren't leaving tomorrow."

Derek and I exchanged a look. "I'm not?" I asked.

"Neither of you are. You've both been attached to the diplomatic delegation permanently. And we're all going to Earth."

If you enjoyed this story, you might like to read Sashelle's origin. You can get it if you sign up for my newsletter—check out the QR code on the last page of this book. You can unsubscribe at any time, of course. And stay tuned for book 6 in the *Colonial Explorer Corps* series.

AUTHOR NOTES

April 2025

Thanks for reading *The Romara Confrontation*! I hope you enjoyed it as much as I did. Siti and Joss have such a great friendship—writing them is always fun.

If you want more CEC action, I have a short story about Siti's dad, the Hero of Darenti Four. *The Darenti Incongruity* was originally published in the anthology *The Expanding Universe 8* but is now available only to my newsletter readers. (In digital format. You can still buy the paperback of TEU8.) You can sign up for my newsletter here. If you do that, you can also download a prequel about Zane—get his story of living on Earth 500 years in the past in *Abandoned World*.

I don't like to talk current politics in my books, so let's just say the last few months have been… tumultuous. Take care of yourself and your community. And keep reading!

As always, I have a list of people to thank.

First, thanks to my alpha reader, science fiction author AM Scott. She directs me back to the straight and narrow when my story veers too far off track. She's my in-real-life, born-of-the-same-parents sister, so she's been doing that essentially my whole life. Most of the time I appreciate it.

Thanks to Paula Lester, my editor. She still has to wrangle all the commas I miss and does an outstanding job. She probably despairs of me ever learning lay-lie-laid (and honestly, she should probably give up trying.) I value her patience, dependability, and quick turn-around!

Thank you to my beta team who catch the mistakes I put back into the book when fixing the ones Paula finds. Barb, Anne, Jenny, Paul, Larry, and Steve, you make these books so much better!

Thanks to my amazing sprint team. Marcus, AM, Hilary, Paula and Lou keep me showing up every day to write a bit more. They also offer commiseration, humor, and the occasional whip cracking when needed.

My deep appreciation to Jenny at JL Wilson designs for Siti's fabulous cover!

Thanks to the Support Husband, Dave. We celebrated our 30th anniversary last month, and I am thankful every day that he's still on this ride with me. I love you.

And, as always, thanks to the Big Guy who makes all things possible.

ALSO BY JULIA HUNI

Space Janitor Series:
The Vacuum of Space
The Dust of Kaku
The Trouble with Tinsel
Orbital Operations
Glitter in the Stars
Sweeping S'Ride
Triana Moore, Space Janitor (the complete series)

Tales of a Former Space Janitor
The Rings of Grissom
Planetary Spin Cycle
Waxing the Moon of Lewei
Tales of a Former Space Janitor (books 1-3)
Changing the Speed of Light Bulbs
Sun Spot Remover
Warp, Rinse, Repeat (coming fall 2025)

Friends of a Former Space Janitor
Dark Quasar Rising
Dark Quasar Ignites

The Phoenix and Katie Li
Luna City Limited

Colonial Explorer Corps Series:
The Earth Concurrence

The Grissom Contention

The Saha Declination

CEC: The Academy Years (books 1-3)

The Darenti Paradox

The Romara Confrontation

The Gagarin Reiteration (coming 2026)

Recycled World Series:

Recycled World

Reduced World

Krimson Empire:

Krimson Run

Krimson Spark

Krimson Surge

Krimson Flare

Julia also writes earth-bound romantic comedy that won't steam your glasses under the not-so-secret pen name Lia Huni

FOR MORE INFORMATION

Use this QR code to stay up-to-date on all my publishing, and get access to my free bonus stories:

Printed in Great Britain
by Amazon